by

Autumn Jordon

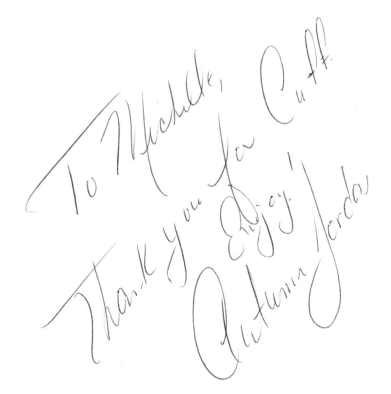

To Michelle,
Thank you for Cuff.
Enjoy!
Autumn Jordon

This is a work of fiction. Names, characters, places and incidents are either the product of the author's imagination or are used fictitiously, and any resemblance to actual persons living or dead, business establishments, events or locales, is entire coincidental.

A Noble Oak Publications/ published by arrangement with the author.

Contact Information: www.autumnjordon@yahoo.com

Publisher: Noble Oak Publications
Front cover design by Rae Monet

Published in the United States of America

Kudos for Author Autumn Jordon

"Jordon delivers a smart suspense with heart-warming romance". 2009 Golden Heart Finalist & Carina Press Author of 'Under Fire', Rita Henuber.

"Autumn Jordon writes with such a breathtaking ease, you forget you're reading a book and not living every delicious and heart-stopping moment yourself." Darynda Jones, NY Times Best Selling Author of 'Third Grave Dead Ahead'.

Other Titles By Autumn Jordon

His Witness To Evil
In The Presence Of Evil
Obsessed By Wildfire

Dedication

To Jim, as always, without your support and love,
I would not be who I am. You are my hero.

Thank you to my Ruby Sisters, Rita and Bev,
and dear friend Mary Ellen.
Without your encouragement and advice, I'd probably have no book.

And a special thank you to my parents, children, and Aunt Fannie for always supporting my dream. I love you all.

And finally, to Michelle for giving me the team name C.U.F.F. You Rock!

Chapter One

Nicole filled her lungs and steeled herself against the fear threatening to erode away her courage. Courage she'd worked so long to nurture. An escape attempt could cost her her life.

Unbroken by the round-topped Appalachian Mountains to the west, a summer storm steam-rolled across the flat meadowlands of New Jersey. Heat lightning lit her son's room for a split-second. Luka's dog whimpered and snuggled closer to him.

Nicole pushed away from the door's frame, padded across the carpet and stood at the foot of Luka's bed. She traced his tiny form through weary eyes. Not only did her life depend on her remaining strong, but so did Luka's.

Katrina was the name Gorgon Novokoff called her. She'd learned to respond to the Russian name quickly or suffer the consequences.

Nicole Carson was the name she repeated to herself every single day for the past eight years so she wouldn't forget who she'd been.

Remembering her mother's smile, tears welled in Nicole's eyes, blurring her son's face into a fuzzy profile. She brushed her fingers across the raised seal on the birth certificate clutched in her hand. "Becca Smith," she said on the tail of a sigh. The name passed her lips again and again. Becca was the name of the girl who had become her comrade.

Becca was dead.

A tear fell to her cheek and Nicole swiped the drop away, fearing her son might wake and see her sorrow. She doubted Becca's parents knew of her passing. There hadn't been a death certificate issued in her name, which meant Becca's body had never been found.

Staring at Luka, love pushed against the boundaries of Nicole's heart. She had no doubt Becca's parents still prayed for her return. One day, she would fulfill her promise to her friend and find Becca's parents. She'd tell them how much their daughter had loved them. Maybe knowing that Becca was with God would give them peace.

She folded the priceless document she'd retrieved today from the post office. She'd rented a box several months ago under the assumed name Becca Smith. With everything to help her and Luka disappear now in her possession, Nicole had only to choose the best time for their escape. But when? Gorgon had no business trips planned.

And then there was the matter of the guards he always left behind, 'to protect her and Luka'. How would she get by them?

Behind her, the window blinds chattered in response to a cool gust, and Max growled at the odd clamor.

Nicole slipped the certificate into her dressing gown's pocket, crossed to the window and slid the pane closed, locking the frame in place. The Labrador mixed mutt closed his eyes and nuzzled his dark nose against the blanket covering Luka until he found the perfect position.

Becca Smith was a good name. They'd be lost in a sea of Smiths.

Becca Smith. She repeated her new name like a mantra. Her and Luka's life would depend on neither of them slipping up, ever.

The light from the hallway fell across her son's

angelic features, and Nicole smoothed Luka's bangs back from his forehead. His ruddy color resembled her complexion. His hair was straight and auburn like hers. As was his button nose and full lips. But his eyes, they were the color of a raven's wing, like Gorgon's. However, they didn't hold the spirit of death in them.

Yet.

They glistened with hope and innocence.

She intended to raise her child as a compassionate man, not a killer.

She kissed the sleeping four year-old's forehead. Had her mother sung her to sleep and read endless piles of books to her like she did for Luka?

Trapping one hand over her heart, she thought about the memory tucked into the black recesses of her mind. Her mother had done the same, and more. One day, she would like to see her parents and her twin siblings again. Ashley and Justin would be nearing their twenty-first birthday soon.

Nicole Carson.

Would her family still love and welcome her into their home, knowing she'd become the mistress of a Russian businessman? A businessman no one dared cross.

Or would they turn their eyes away from her in disgust? Or in fear? And what about their grandson? Would they look upon Luka as the son of a monster?

Nicole tucked the thin blanket around her son. She would never forget her little boy. With her last breath, she'd cry Luka's name and she hoped her parents had never forgotten her. She had to believe they hadn't, otherwise, she'd lose her courage. Her hope.

She pulled her thoughts back from the brink of depression. Time was running out. She had to leave before Luka would remember his father, and Luka's soul became part of the arch-angel's plans.

Luka was Gorgon's only child. Gorgon's pride. The one who would follow him as head of the Novokoff family. If the mafia prince knew of her plans to escape, he'd kill her and take Luka to be raised by his barren wife.

She ignored the panic constricting her chest, and gave her son a final kiss. Then she tucked his precious over-sized, stuffed rabbit, which carried a portion of their escape funds, under the covers next to him and backed out of the bedroom.

In her room, the king-sized bed she shared with Gorgon loomed in front of her.

She touched the tender area below her eye. Two nights ago, one of his business acquaintances had engaged her in a discussion and after the dinner gathering Gorgon reminded her she was his property.

She hadn't done anything but listen to the man.

As if God was prompting her to rush, thunder cracked overhead. She had to hide the birth certificate. If Gorgon found the document, she'd be dead.

Rushing to the walk-in closet, she flung the double doors wide. The few possessions they would take with them were crammed into her gym bag under her work-out clothes and towel. Soon, no one would own her or Luka.

She and Luka were healthy, thank God. Whatever they needed after their escape, she'd buy.

Nicole snagged the bag from the back corner of the closet. As she crossed to the bed and opened the bag, the zipper whined, breaking the omnipresent silence which reigned throughout the house. Peeling back the padding inside her right running shoe, she stashed the onion-skinned paper toward the toe and pressed the lining back into place. The other running shoe held a key for the car she was never allowed to drive without Gorgon's permission. The key had presumably been lost by Luka months ago.

Inside the lining of the canvas bag, she'd sewn in hundreds of dollars she'd stolen from Gorgon's sister-in-law, Gali, over the past four years. At last count, the stack of tens and twenties in her bag and Luka's stuffed toy rabbit totaled nine-hundred and eighty dollars.

The money had never been missed by Gali or her husband. Gali was a shopaholic and Donnie gave her free reins to his share of the family fortune.

Gorgon was not like his brother in that aspect. He dished out only the obligatory funds when she needed them.

Gali liked Nicole, despite the fact she was Gorgon's mistress. They were the same age—not old like Gorgon's wife, Eva. Gali adored Luka and visited them often which had proven fortunate for Nicole.

Nine hundred and eighty dollars was not a lot of money to start a new life, especially with a child, but she had the diamond earrings and bracelet and a few other pieces Gorgon had given her as Christmas gifts. She'd pawn them when she could.

If she wanted more upfront, however, there was the cash Gorgon kept locked in the wall safe. She turned toward the picture hiding the safe. She'd have to grow balls in order to take his money.

What if Gorgon went into the safe before she and Luka could disappear?

The memory of a previous insurrection surfaced and she felt the pressure of his fingers biting into her windpipe and recalled the burning of her lungs struggling for air.

The security system buzzed and Nicole jumped a foot off the hardwood floor, knocking her gym bag off the bed. Looking at the keypad, she saw that the front door entry alarm blinked. Who had entered?

Gorgon was not to come here tonight and his men would not dare enter the house without him.

"Katrina, where are you? Come here, now."

She gasped at Gorgon's bellow. He was home.

"Coming," she answered, pushing fear from her tone. Her fingers fumbled as she struggled to zip the zipper. She haphazardly tossed the bag to the back of the closet as was her custom to do and with a soft click closed the double doors.

She scanned the bedroom, looking for anything that might give away her plans to escape. The bedding was still untouched. On the dresser a candle flickered, a soft lilac scent wafting the air. The book she'd been reading earlier in the day laid on the divan. Everything appeared as if she'd been enjoying a quiet night reading.

Satisfied her secret was safe she hurried from the room and stopped at the hall mirror. She touched the makeup covering the purple skin under her eye while willing her pounding heart to stop its clamor.

"Katrina."

"I'm here." She smoothed her palms along her nightgown and headed down the spiral staircase, wearing the smile Gorgon loved.

The octagon foyer, dimly lit by the chandelier above, cast faint, multi-colored leaf patterns on the marble floor.

"I'm sorry. I was reading. I was not expecting you."

Before she reached the bottom step, Gorgon stepped out of the shadows and she stopped. Her smile faded. On his six-four frame he carried a motionless young girl. Her head rested against his broad shoulder and her long blonde hair cascaded over his black Armani suit.

"What has happened?" He frowned at her stupid question. Her stomach twisted with the knowledge of what had happened to the girl.

"Take my briefcase," Gorgon ordered, while shifting the girl up against his chest.

"Who is she?"

"That is no concern of yours."

Feeling the strength leaving her legs, Nicole steadied herself with the banister as she climbed down the remaining steps. By the careless way Gorgon jostled the young girl, Nicole knew the teenager was not just asleep. She'd been drugged.

Gorgon handed off his briefcase. "Open the door to the guest room."

His dark eyes, made narrow by his pulled brow, made her heart pound a wild rhythm as she scurried by him. She knew the family business, particularly this part. She had been a stolen jewel plucked by Gorgon off the child prostitution train. He reminded her time and again that he had saved her and she should be grateful.

Placing the briefcase next to the staircase, she wanted to ask, "Why have you brought her here?" But, questioning Gorgon would bring his wrath.

"Turn down the comforter," he ordered, after following her into the guestroom.

The girl moaned behind her and Nicole peeked over her shoulder.

"Shhh, my treasure." Gorgon laid his cheek against the girl's forehead and smoothed her hair while he held Nicole's gaze.

Bile rose in her throat. My treasure. Gorgon had used the pet name he'd given her eight years ago.

Chapter Two

Nicole fought the urge to run from the bedroom. Her blood thundered through her veins. She jumped when Gorgon snapped his fingers, gaining her attention, from the other side of the bed.

"I'm going to take a shower. Undress her. Wash her," he commanded.

The girl lay motionless on the bed between them.

His hands remained at his sides, but her windpipe closed as his lust-filled gaze held her in place. He notched up his chin trying to hide the truth from her, but she knew. He intended to take another mistress.

"I was told she is a virgin. Make sure I was not lied to. I will be back." Without waiting for an answer, Gorgon stalked from the room, leaving Nicole alone with the girl.

Disgust coated her tongue and caused her bile-laden stomach to roll.

The door clicked closed. Nicole turned and stared down at the child. She smelled of cigarettes, urine and semen soaked blankets. And, filthy handlers.

Nicole knew from experience that the girl had already been inspected. Being a virgin had saved her from a life of prostitution, for the time being.

The girl's blonde lashes rested against her sun-kissed skin. Freckles bridged the child's nose and danced across her cheeks in a light sprinkle. A small blemish below the right lobe of her button nose off-set the symmetry of her pink, plump lips. Lips that had never been kissed by anyone other than a parent, grandparent, or a young boy after a football game.

The girl couldn't be more than thirteen years old, two years younger than she had been when Gorgon had bought her here.

"Susie." The denim jacket had the name blinged across the collar on one side and a multi-colored butterfly on the other.

The child's skin was warm to the touch, and even though Nicole used the best creams to moisturize her body, this child's skin was much softer than her own.

Tears moistened Nicole's eye as she struggled to remove the jacket under the girl's dead weight. Butterflies were free. Susie would never be again.

Susie dropped back against the plush satin pillows like a rag doll. Her long blonde locks held a hint of red and sprawled across the white pillowcases, resembling shoots of a searing fire.

Luka's presence had stopped Gorgon from bringing others home before this girl. What had changed?

Was it her disgust for him? Her dreams of freedom? Her need to feel love the way a woman should? All had driven her to refuse his wants on several occasions over the past few months, only to provoke Gorgon's anger for doing so.

Had she cursed him in her sleep? Had she spoken of her plans?

No. He would not have let her live until morning if she had done so.

Did Gorgon plan to replace her?

Fear captured the breath from her lungs at the thought. If so, he would have her killed. Then he'd take Luka to his wife to be raised as her own. Eva would not refuse him.

Nicole's muscles twitched as adrenalin flowed into

her system. She fought the urge to race up the stairs, gather Luka from his bed and escape while Gorgon showered. There wasn't enough time.

They had to escape tonight. Gorgon had chosen the time. Her mind whirled as scenarios played out in her thoughts and were dismissed. Her stomach twisted while she studied the girl. Maybe while Gorgon was busy with his new treasure she and Luka could slip out of the house unnoticed. By morning they would be several states away from their New Jersey prison.

Hope threaded through Nicole as she worked the details out in her mind. *Yes. Her plan could work.*

"Mom," Susie called.

Nicole folded and laid the girl's coat on the cushioned chair in the corner.

Empathy held Nicole spellbound. How could she leave this child here? Would the teenager be strong enough to withstand the horror she'd endured, or would Susie die under Gorgon's hand?

Tears blurred Nicole's vision while she removed the girl's right sneaker. What choice did she have? There was no way she could escape with both Luka and Susie in tow. And even if there was a slim chance she could, she didn't have the money to transport them beyond Gorgon's reach for long.

Nicole removed Susie's left shoe. She could leave the girl somewhere safe and place a call to the authorities as to her whereabouts.

"Mommy," Susie whimpered again and then moaned while thrashing her head from one side to the other. The child's upper lip beaded with perspiration.

Brushing Susie's hair from her face, Nicole laid her hand on the child's forehead. The girl was burning up.

"God's watching over you. Gorgon will not take you tonight if you're sick," Nicole whispered as she soothed the child by stroking her hair. "Your poor mother. She must be sick with worry."

The door opened behind her.

Nicole spun around.

Barefooted, his dark hairy legs planted wide on the plush carpet, Gorgon blocked the doorway. His robe hung open and Nicole saw that droplets of water still clung to his black chest hair. His sandalwood cologne wafted toward her like long fingers.

"What have you been doing, Katrina? She is not washed."

Backing up to the head of the bed out of Gorgon's immediate reach, Nicole said, "The girl has a fever. She's been tossing about. I was about to get a cold towel to wash her and give her some fever reducer."

The Russian's dark gaze dropped to Susie and his fingers stretched and then clenched around his robe's tie. "I was told she was in good health."

If Gorgon thought Susie was diseased, he'd dispose of her. He might even hand her off to his loyal men outside to do what they wanted with her. Afterwards, her lifeless body would be dumped in a landfill and covered with tons of plastic bottles and garbage. No one would find her bones for hundreds of years, if ever.

Nicole fought to keep the trepidation she felt from entering her voice. "I'm sure it's nothing. She has been through much. I know."

Seeing the mixture of anger and lust in Gorgon's eyes, Nicole knew she couldn't let anything more happen to the girl. Somehow she had to save at least one child from Gorgon's family business. "Her body needs rest and nourishment. I'm sure that in a few days she will be just fine."

He released his disappointment in a huff. "Take care of her. I will wait for you upstairs in our bed."

Knowing what his words meant, Nicole shuddered inside.

When Gorgon disappeared from view, she turned to the child. As her fingertips brushed across Susie's cheek, the child turned into them. How was she going to save them all?

Nicole hurried and finished undressing Susie down to her training bra and matching panties. Then she sponged the girl with cool towels and forced medicine and tiny bits of fruit flavored Popsicle into her mouth. After thirty minutes, the child slept. Now she had to face Gorgon.

Outside, wild gusts of wind and rain slapped the window panes.

In the foyer, Nicole stood motionless, clutching the banister, while a battle raged within her. She closed her mind to the fear at disobeying Gorgon. She focused on the dream of Luka having a normal life. She wanted Luka to grow onto a good man. She wanted him to graduate from college, get married and hold his newborn children without fear of the family's enemies.

She took a deep breath and stared at the floor above. She had no choice, if she wanted all those things for her son, she had to act. She was out of time. Either she killed Gorgon or he would kill her.

Backtracking, she hurried to the kitchen. Her trembling fingers hovered above the knife's handle. Gorgon had made it very clear that any defiance on her part and not only would she suffer, but so would her family.

She loved her parents and siblings. Her one hope to save them and Luka and herself, was to kill the bastard upstairs.

The paring knife sang as she slid its blade from the butcher block caddy. A larger butcher knife would give her the confidence of doing serious damage in one strike, but would be hard to conceal from Gorgon. The smaller knife would be better for her planned surprise attack.

On shaky legs, Nicole made her way up the stairs. Her moist palm cradled the paring knife hidden in the folds of her gown. She would need to cut Gorgon's carotid artery for him to die within minutes. Would she be able to do kill him? She'd never hurt anyone in her entire life. And she'd been trained by Gorgon to cower at the cast of his anger.

"Remember his ruthlessness," she whispered and recalled the moment Gorgon had killed a man for disobeying an order. He had done so without a wasted movement.

Could she steel herself against his will and stand up to him? Do the same to him as he had done to that man?

She bit her lip and tasted the saltiness of her own blood. She had no choice. If she missed her mark, her last breath would not be far off, and Luka and Susie would be lost forever.

The lights in the bedroom were off. The candle she'd placed on the high bureau earlier still flickered. Its rays danced across the ceiling and Gorgon, who lay sprawled on the bed in all his glory.

She held her breath. He did not move. Was he asleep?

Her fingers curled around the knife's handle. Could she cross the room and plunge the knife into his neck without waking him?

Determined, she took a step inside the room.

"Why are you tip-toeing?"

Nicole jumped, almost dropping the knife. "I— I thought you slept."

He stretched his arms above his head, exposing his chest to her. "Nah. Did you take care of the girl?"

She tightened her grip on the knife, anticipating the way Gorgon's body would give way when she drove the blade into his neck. "I gave her some medicine. She's sleeping now."

"Is she a virgin?"

His member stirred and it took every ounce of control in her not to rush toward him and strike the cold bastard. The son-of-a-bitch didn't care if Susie's pain had subsided. All the monster cared about was whether he'd have the pleasure of tearing away her virginity.

"Yes," she said only the one syllable, afraid if she'd say more he'd hear her detestation for him in her tone.

Beyond the French doors that led to a balcony, lightning flashed across the sky.

"Excellent. I would hate to cut Ralph off at the knees."

Nicole faltered in step. Gorgon did not speak literally, she was sure.

"He has the knack to find many good girls." Gorgon yawned.

Good meant virgins. She wondered how many he had deflowered himself instead of selling them to the highest bidder.

She went on guard when Gorgon sat and shifted up onto the pile of pillows behind him. "It is getting late, and I have an early meeting."

"You are not going home to your wife tonight?"

"Nah."

"It is her night."

"I make the decision where I sleep. Come here." He patted the mattress.

"I must use the bathroom first," she said, feeling the knife slip in her sweaty palm. She needed to dry her hands, calm her nerves and regain her strength before approaching him.

"Be quick, my treasure."

Nicole turned and closed the bedroom door so Luka would not be awakened. Then with her head lowered she hurried to the bathroom, feeling Gorgon's eyes following her. Standing before the mirror, she ripped a hand towel from the bar and covered the knife before twisting the knob, turning on the cold water. She scooped and splashed her face. While patting her face dry, she reviewed one more time the steps she would take to end Gorgon's life.

Inhaling a quick breath, she dropped the hand towel and picked up the knife. "I am ready." She snapped off the lights and entered the bedroom. She would wait until he was at the cusp of his release when he'd be at his weakest. Then she would make her move.

He slid from the bed, stopping her from approaching her bedside. His swollen member bobbed toward her. "On your knees."

Nicole's heart sank. Pleasuring him this way would not allow her to cut his neck.

"I said come here." Impatience rumbled in Gorgon's voice.

Nicole couldn't move. Her feet had become one with the floor. She didn't want to be degraded again.

The candle sputtered and its glow shadowed the angry angles of Gorgon's jaw.

"Are you dumb, woman?" Gorgon crossed the hardwood floor and slapped her.

Pain ripped through her skull and Nicole shook her head to ward off the stars developing behind her closed eyes. All the feelings she'd held in check for years flooded to her bloody lips. "I hate you, you son-of-a-bitch."

His fist shot out.

She tried to dodge him but he grabbed her upper arm

and yanked, exposing the knife.

Realization of her plan narrowed Gorgon's eyes, but before he could tighten his hold on her, she thrust forward with all her might. His lower abdomen gave way as she pushed the blade into its hilt. A gush of warm blood soaked the metal handle, making the knife slick, and her hand slid free.

"Argh... You bitch," Gorgon screamed in pain. "I will kill you."

He backhanded her and Nicole crashed back against the bureau. The candle on top toppled and crashed to the floor, sending broken chunks of glass and hot wax across their feet.

Nicole's blood thundered through her veins. If she was going to survive, she had to kill Gorgon, now.

A dark line streamed from his abdomen, through his pubic hair to his limp penis. Grabbing the bed, he turned toward the nightstand. Toward his gun.

Max barked once in Luka's room and Nicole sent up a silent prayer that he'd remain quiet. She had to finish Gorgon, before Luka woke and came to investigate the noise. Glass crunched under her slippers as Nicole shoved him onto the mattress.

Again, he wailed with anguish.

Her fingertips grazed the cold steel before he grabbed her by her long hair, tearing strands by the roots from her scalp. He yanked her away from her only hope.

"You will not defeat me," he growled into her ear.

She was no match for his strength. "You want to bet." Nicole went limp, reached back, snared the knife and gave the blade a final twist. Gorgon's muscles and organs crackled as they ripped apart inside of him. His cry left her eardrum ringing.

He released her and she grabbed the gun. Turning, she found Gorgon on his knees. His head lulled to his chest, before he crashed to the floor. A crimson pool spread around his hips while his twitching fingers stilled.

Chapter Three

Reasoning had kept her from putting a bullet through Gorgon's head. His men would've heard the shot. She would have no means of escaping two armed men. She'd been lucky once tonight.

Max whimpered behind the garage door which separated the hallway leading to the kitchen from the garage. Her heart broke. She didn't want to leave the dog behind. He was family but she had no choice.

Nicole strained lifting Susie's dead weight into the trunk. The combination of medicine, high fever and days of malnutrition had left the teenager drained. Under the circumstances, that was a good thing. Wrapped in a blanket and tucked into the car's trunk, she prayed Susie would remain quiet.

She closed the lid, hurried around the car and peeked into the back window. Luka, on the other hand, was healthy as a baby ox. She hated that she had drugged her son, giving him a tiny sip of antihistamine, but she had to make sure he remained asleep. He slept peacefully in his car seat, despite her movements and the clap of thunder overhead.

She slid into the car and took a moment to settle her nerves. There was no turning back the hands of the clock. She was Gorgon's murderer. Now, she had to escape his family.

The garage door rumbled overhead.

Nicole ignored the pain in her shoulder and neck as she shoved her gym bag onto the front floor board. With the taste of blood still on her tongue, she started the car and backed out from the double bay garage, and headed down the short driveway leading to the main road. Mid-July and still she shivered.

Two of Gorgon's men always manned the gate at the bottom of the hill. Wrapping her fingers around the steering wheel, she prayed both Susie and Luka would remain asleep. Her fingers fumbled to touch the cold steel of Gorgon's gun tucked along the seat. Would she be able to use the weapon if she had to? What if they told her to get out of the car as they'd done on several occasions and saw the gun? What if they wanted to check the entire car and found Gorgon's new treasure? What if hearing their voices, the child cried out for her mother?

No. She pushed the gun down between the seat's cushion and the console. Their escape would not play out like that. She'd killed once tonight. She would again, to save them all.

Ahead, a woman stood with Marco. His girlfriend Tiffany.

Marco was the one bodyguard who had special privileges because he'd been with the family eons.

As the headlights crept up on the couple, the petite mousey brunette stepped out of Marco's embrace and disappeared into the shadows along the brick wall which surrounded the estate. Marco held up his hand, and Nicole slowed the car to a stop and shifted into park.

Marco's flashlight blinded her through the glass.

Nicole lowered the window with one hand and raised the other to shield her eyes. "Put that down, before you wake Luka."

A gust bellowed through the opening and made the moisture at the nape of her neck feel cool.

"Gorgon did not say he was sending you out, Katrina. Where are you going?"

Peter, the other guard, walked around the far side of

the car, checking the rear seat.

Heat lightning seared the sky.

Nicole lifted her chin so that Marco would see the bruise left on her cheek from Gorgon's slap and the split of her lip. "I didn't like him bringing that girl into our home," she spat. "He told me to go to his brother's for the night. I imagine he wants to be alone with his new prize."

The smirk that grew on Marco's face sickened her. He knew what she implied.

"Gila waits for us." She put the car into gear.

"Wait." Marco grabbed the steering wheel. "We will need to check with Gorgon." His smile made her pulse kick up a notch. "You understand."

She was betting their lives on the fear Gorgon caused his men. Keeping her cool, she shrugged as if his intentions made no difference to her and shifted the car into park again. "Of course. I'm sure he won't mind if you disturb him. Our fight was small." She held up her hand and displayed the tiny distance between her thumb and index finger. "But know, I will not accept the responsibility of your blood."

Marco's smile faded. His hand fell away from the steering wheel and he nodded to Peter, who met him at the car's grill.

Nicole leaned towards her window and tried hard to hear their muffled conversation. Apparently, Peter didn't think disturbing Gorgon was in their best interest. Marco agreed.

Peter headed toward the gate and Marco returned to her window. "Okay. You go right to Donnie's. I will call Gila and let her know you are on your way."

Again, she shrugged, holding back the sigh of relief waiting to escape her lungs. "Do what you must."

When she was away from these people, she had to watch her speech. Over the years her speech patterns had picked up the parlance of the Russian tongue.

Peter's stare prickled the hair at her neck's nape as she drove through the gate. In her rearview mirror, she saw Marco pull his cell from his pocket. Tiffany came out of the shadows and stood next to Peter.

She had to hurry. "Be patient," she said gripping the steering wheel.

Under the haze of the street lights, Ash Avenue had never looked so wonderful. Nicole tapped the gas and drove away from hell.

Rounding the corner as if she was going to Gila's, Nicole fought to keep from panicking. She had to think straight. Gorgon had kept her in line for years, first threatening her family and then telling her how disgusted they would be to find out she was a whore. Then he used her son as a weapon against her. Well, Gorgon didn't rule over her any longer.

Once out of the sight of Gorgon's men, she stomped on the accelerator. In a minute, Marco and Peter would wake Donnie from a sound sleep and know that neither Gorgon's brother nor his sister-in-law were aware of her late night visit.

One of the men would come after her. The other would go to the house and find Gorgon dead. She had maybe fifteen minutes, at the most, before the whole Novokoff family would be alerted and any and every man and woman under their power would search for her.

A crack of thunder shook the car and rain drops smashed against the windshield. Nicole turned on the wipers and curled her fingers tighter around the steering wheel. Where could she go that they'd be safe? She'd heard more than once while eavesdropping on Gorgon's conversations that he had friends on the police force. Friends who'd turned their heads or gave up information for a sizeable dollar. If captured by the cops, they'd make sure Susie was returned to her family, stating they found her in a drug induced state, walking along the highway. They'd take Luka away from her and hand him back to Gorgon's family and charge her with his murder.

She had to get as far away as she could first.

Through the glistening windshield, thirty miles ahead, the New York skyline reminded her of a snow globe she'd once purchased while on a middle-grade school trip to the Museum of National History. The glow from the city's many lights sparkled around the building rooftops in a huge arch.

The Novokoffs would assume she'd head north on RT 278 and then into New York because she was somewhat familiar with that route, having accompanied Gorgon into the city on occasions. Instead, she turned onto RT 202 and raced south. Within miles, she headed west on the smaller RT 23.

Each town the road cut in half had fewer stop lights. The fast-food chain restaurants diminished, replaced by family owned businesses. Not familiar with the two-lane road, Nicole drove the speed limit and remained alert to every traffic sign. She couldn't be stopped by a local cop and have her plan foiled.

A Medivac helicopter crossed the sky in front of her. Its red lights were a sign of hope in a sea of darkness.

Leaving the next town, Nicole checked her rearview mirror, again. She hadn't noticed anyone following her, but that didn't mean she couldn't pick up a tail at any corner. She wasn't sure how far west the Novokoff family's connections reached.

The next hour seemed like thirty while Nicole traveled along the rain washed RT 94 to RT 80 West and made her way into Pennsylvania by crossing the Delaware Water Gap Bridge. The car's dash clock now said the time was one AM. The rain had stopped. Luka still slept. She had to get Susie out of the trunk. She hadn't dared stop before this to check on the girl.

Nicole picked an interstate exit that had no signs for a rest area, restaurants or gas stations and drove up the ramp. Parked at the stop sign, she noted darkness surrounded her. Under her headlights, large trees covered the swells of the mountains surrounding them. She chewed her bottom lip, wondering which way she should take. There wasn't a building in sight in either direction. Turning the wheel, she headed south.

The roads became unmarked as she followed her sense of direction and continued to take road after road, south and west. Spying a pull-off into a wooded area ahead, she maneuvered the car off the road.

In front of the car, beady eyes glowed and shifted toward her. She hadn't seen a possum in years. The long-nosed creature scurried into the underbrush before she opened the car's door. Cool air and sweet freedom cradled her in their arms.

The wind swirling through the tree tops reminded her of the sound of the ocean off Cape May. She took a moment to breathe in the fresh air before she hurried to the rear of the car and opened the trunk. The storage light clicked on and flooded over Susie's deadpan face.

Nicole's heart caught. She prayed the child hadn't died, caused by inhaling the car's fumes.

"Hey." She poked the girl's shoulder.

Susie stirred and Nicole exhaled the breath she'd held. "Come on. Let's get you out of here."

She laced her arm under the child and helped her into a sitting position. Behind her, the purr of a car's engine grew louder, and then a beam of pure white light searched the area before finding them.

Chapter Four

Lightning ripped across the restless, murky sky in front of the descending helicopter.

US Marshall William Haus grabbed the panic bar. "Damn it to hell." Air escaped his lungs in one gush at the craft teetering to the side a mere fifty yards above the marked landing site next to the PA State Police barracks.

"Bitchin' wind." The pilot's curse, grimace and the fact he fought to control the bird didn't bolster Will's belief that the jockey trip from New Jersey was going to end well. He knew without turning around and confirming his hunch that Chase Hunter and Aden Nash, two members of his C.U.F.F. force, smirked at his angst. Instead, he squeezed his eyes closed and braced for an impact to write home about. Maybe.

Damn. He hated to fly in choppers. God knew his fear and was screwing with him again.

The copter jarred true and Will jerked right in his seat. Between a slit of eye, he peeked out the window and saw the building below steadily grow larger.

The moment the landing rails kissed the wet tarmac, he ripped off his seat belt, shouldered the door open, and jumped out of the whirly bird. With his worn boot heels planted on the ground, he drew a breath. He'd survived the flight. Now he could again concentrate on his job, 'catching the bad guys'.

From the corner of his eye, he saw the chopper's rear door slide open. Chase jumped from the craft while Aden hesitated, catching his scowl.

The frustration over tonight's bust going sour curled

Will's fingers into fists. He glanced over his shoulder. His men wore solemn faces, which was a good thing. If they cracked even one joke over his helo phobia, he might lose restraint and sucker punch one of them. He wanted to hit something or someone real bad.

"We had Novokoff," he yelled, venting his anger over the sound of the chopper's blades whacking the air above him.

"We'll get them, boss." Aden jumped to the ground and Will kept a watchful eye that the man didn't stand to his full height.

"If we had arrived ten minutes earlier, we would've caught the bastard with his pants down and maybe cracked this ring apart," Chase hollered around Aden's chest while they stalked as a trio toward the State Police Barracks.

"Try to raise Kyle again," Will ordered Aden who had already fished his cell out of his pocket and checked for a signal in this rural setting. "I want to know what the fuck happened? A freakin' year's worth of work down the drain." Will pressed a hand to his burning gut. How many more young lives would be lost until he had the opportunity to nail Novokoff's ass to the wall again?

The last words he heard from Kyle, aka Peter, one of his people who had infiltrated the mafia's ring, was an urgent cry to back off. Since then Kyle had dug in and had gone silent. What the fuck had happened? Hell had to have broken loose in the Novokoff's world for Kyle to cry 'WOLF' in the last moments before they'd infiltrated Gorgon's home.

"We dropped into a freakin' dead zone," Aden stated. "There's no goddamn service."

"Keep trying." The cell Aden carried was one of two they had that Kyle would respond to. Gary had the other. Their cells displayed on Kyle's phone as the Russian owned whore house, in case Novokoff's men checked Kyle's calls. Technology was wonderful until the bad guys caught up.

A state trooper, bearing the ID tag of M. Balliet, greeted them a few yards beyond the chopper's blades. "Captain just went into the interrogation room with the suspect," the officer shouted over the chopper's whine down. "And your partner is also inside."

Balliet fell into step next to Will. The kid didn't look old enough to shave much less be a cop.

"Why is the captain talking to her?" Will worked with Ebberts before. He knew the captain was thorough, but taking down the Novokoffs was his case and Will wanted his Ts crossed too. One misstep could mess up a conviction.

"The suspect didn't want to give up her fingerprints," Balliet answered.

"Why didn't Ebberts order them taken? She was found with the girl," Chase asked over Will's shoulder.

Balliet shrugged. "The woman looks like she's been roughed up a bit. Cap thought he could calm her down. Get her to offer them instead of forcing her."

"She drugged up?" Aden who also walked behind the cop leaned into them.

The cop's neck arched back as he stared up over his shoulder at Aden. He stumbled and Will caught his arm. "I know. He's tall. Comes in handy at times."

Balliet's Adam's apple dipped before he responded, "Nuh. I don't think so. No alcohol on her breath either, but she sure seems real nervous."

Will caught his gaze. "You find her?"

"Yes, sir. I caught a glimpse of her car's tail lights as she turned into the road leading to the water authority. No one goes back there at this time night. At least no one with business there. With all the shit we've heard about terrorists and bio-warfare, I thought I should check it out."

Will dipped his head in a quick nod. "Good job."

"Thank you, sir."

The prior day's blistering sun and the recent cool rain caused steam to rise in swirling waves from the tarmac.

The officer matched Will's slightly longer stride for stride while they stalked up the path from the landing pad to the building's entrance. At the last second, Balliet rushed ahead of Will, by a step, and yanked open the glass door in time for him and his men to pass through without breaking their gaits. Then they followed Balliet down the hall illuminated by bright fluorescent bulbs and into a room where Will found Gary, his right hand man, waiting.

"It's about time." Gary turned from the two-sided mirror. "You guys stop in AC without me again?"

"Hell yeah," Chase chirped, flashing Gary his dimple. "We didn't want any old married fart slowin' us down."

"Tell him, boss." Aden chuckled, blowing on his cell. "The slots were hot."

"Don't get him started, guys." Will headed for the two-way glass while Gary, Chase and Aden continued their never-ending debate over the advantages and disadvantages of being married. Balliet was right. Someone had roughed the woman up. Her rushed make-up job did little to hide the damage. Under the bright lights, he could see the tint of black and blue markings on her cheek bone and the purple rimming her eye. Her red lower lip was way too puffy to be considered just plump. She was a looker nevertheless.

"Aden, you get that signal yet?" Will broke into the friendly squabble behind him without taking his eyes off the auburn beauty.

"Workin' on it."

"Work harder. Let me know the minute you hear from either Kyle or Jolene. Chase."

"Yes, boss?"

"Talk to Balliet. Go over everything that he saw and his conversation with the suspect. Find out word for word, if anything, that Susie Lakes said to him." He hooked a thumb toward the woman on the other side of the glass. "And then find her car. If it's here, take a look around. Don't touch anything though. Make sure no one else does either. I want our forensics team to go over the vehicle ASAP."

"Got it."

Before the door closed behind his men, Will said to Gary, "How's Susie Lakes?"

"Alive," Gary answered, stepping up to the glass. "She's at a near-by hospital. Mercy Hospital. I have two agents standing guard over her. Her parents have been notified and they're no doubt already in the sky, courtesy of the FBI."

"Good. I love happy endings. Just wish there were more of them."

"I hear you."

"What about the other kid?"

"This one says he's her son. He does call her mama. We took his prints and are running them through Lotus. Lucy is on trail. She'll text as soon as she has the info. If he's in the system, we'll know soon."

"Lucy is the tech-guru. If any information can be found on the kid, she'd find it." Turning to Gary, Will pointed to the two-way mirror. "Did the captain get any answers from her of why Kyle called off the operation?"

"Nothing yet. He just went in a few minutes ago. He's keeping her on edge for us."

"Is she who I think she is?"

"Yeah. I pulled Gorgon's folder the moment I got Ebberts's call. Thumbing through the pages I found a couple of pictures. We have Gorgon's mistress." Gary held up a picture of the woman and Novokoff together. Gorgon Novokoff's one arm was around her slim waist and he was pointing at something off in the distance with his other, covering her face from her button nose down. "She's partially hidden in the photos but I'm pretty sure it's her."

Will had seen the photos before. The woman's head was always lowered and her entire face or profile hidden by body guards or the Russian mafia prince.

"You think Gorgon found the radio chip Jolene planted in Susie's jacket?"

"No. If he did, he would've cleaned up real quick by killing the kid and having his men dump her body. I'm sure he wouldn't have sent her away with his mistress." Will shook his head. "No. Something else went down. Have you been able to get a hold of Kyle on the other line?"

"Negative. He's not answering his cell."

"Damn." Will had hoped Kyle had checked in with Gary while he was in flight. "How about Jolene?"

"Nothing from her either."

Will trapped his hands in his back jean pockets and studied the woman, who according to his informants, was Gorgon Novokoff's mistress, Katrina. He'd seen the pictures of her sent via Kyle's cell phone, but the bits of snapshots hadn't done her justice. She stood about five-foot six. Her short skirt and form fitting tank top did little to hide her curves and legs that went on forever. Her toes, peeking out from the crisscross leather bands of her sandals, were painted a pale red, as were her nails. Katrina's auburn hair curled about her shoulders in shiny waves and when Gorgon's woman looked into the mirror opposite him, her misty-coated eyes reminded him of seasoned acorns against ice.

Her pale skin was a tale tell sign that she didn't spend a lot of time gardening. Novokoff had kept her under wrap. Her complexion was flawless except for the bruises on her cheek and under her eye. A tiny mole sat on her upper lip. Susie Lakes and Katrina had that feature in common.

Will twisted the intercom knob on the wall next to the glass and sat back on his heels, watching her body language as he listened in on the conversation between the captain and the Russian woman.

Ebberts sat at the square table filling the room's center.

"Damn it. I want to see my son."

Katrina was trying to pack her tone with strength but her voice had a slight hiccup. She dropped her gaze from Ebberts time and again. She was afraid to make direct eye contact.

"We don't know if the boy is your son."

Katrina lurched forward like a lioness and slapped the table, surprising Will.

"He's my son. He has told your men he is."

He had to give Ebberts credit. The older man hadn't flinched at her show of fury.

"It is not right you do this— to hold us."

Ebberts held her hot glare, relaxed back onto the hardback chair and hit her with a smirk.

Katrina blinked. Tears laced her lashes as she eased back from the table. She snagged her sweater from the chair's back and stuffed her arms into the sleeves as if she was done with Ebberts and had the option to leave the room in a huff.

"You were found with a kidnapped girl. I think we

have plenty to hold you," Ebberts said.

With her arms folded across her chest, she kept the table between her and the senior officer, and side-stepped to the back wall of the tiny cubicle. Shivering, she pulled her light sweater close over her breasts.

"I told your comrade. I found her."

"And you put her into your car's trunk. Why would you do that?"

"She is sick. With a fever. I didn't want my boy to get sick."

Ebberts chuckled deep in his throat and sat forward in his chair.

"Nice try, but I'm not buying that story. You know what I think?"

Katrina's spine straightened. Will saw fear surface in her brown eyes. She knew Ebberts could charge her with kidnapping and take her son away.

"I don't think you had anything to do with Susie's abduction, but I think you know who did."

"You're a crazy man. I know nothing of this kidnapping."

The door behind Ebberts cracked open and another officer stuck his nose into the room. "They're here, sir."

"Good. I'm done with her anyway," the chief answered without taking his eyes off the Russian.

Katrina's eyes widened. "Who is here?"

"Who do you think?"

Katrina kept her gaze latched on Ebberts while she backed up against the wall. "I— I don't know."

Her strong façade slipped away and she withdrew into herself.

"What do you make of her?" Gary laid down the file he'd read and came to stand next to him.

"Not sure. Her dialect… She's not Russian like I thought."

"Maybe American born Russian?"

Will shrugged. "Maybe."

"The kid looks like her. I think she's telling the truth about him being her son. We can order DNA just to be sure, but that is going to take weeks. She acts scared shitless at being separated from him."

Will chortled. "Maybe she is scared to death at being caught dumping a kidnap victim."

"True." Gary nodded and a moment later shook his finger at him. "What I don't get, if Gorgon didn't find the chip, why would he pull Susie off the market, take her home and then send her off with his mistress to be discarded in the woods? You think he's that quick?"

Will shook his head. "Gorgon takes his time with his victims. He likes to control them. You know that." He looked back to Katrina, zeroing in on the bruise on her cheek that had become more visible by her wiping away tears. "Maybe he didn't send them away."

"Are you thinking she took Susie on her own? Why would she do that?"

"Maybe she didn't like that Novokoff brought the girl home. He hasn't before, at least not while under our surveillance."

"So you're thinking Katrina was getting rid of the girl to protect her turf. Okay, I'll buy that, but Gorgon wouldn't just let her walk."

Will's instincts made him jiggery. Some huge development was storming and he needed to know what the fuck it was. "Maybe he didn't. We need to know what happened at Gorgon's tonight."

"Let me try Jolene again. Maybe she contacted Kyle." Gary pulled his cell from the front pocket of his Dockers. The guy always dressed like he was heading out to a golf match. Will preferred the cowboy look minus a Stetson. Worn jeans, worn boots and a tee shirt so thin he could use it to strain coffee grounds.

While Gary tried to reach the agency's undercover woman, Will's cell vibrated on his hip. He snagged the phone from his belt and read the text message from his office, his boss. "Damn."

"What's wrong?" Gary said at the same time he'd said damn.

"Linkson wants a report now."

"Bad news travels fast."

"You get Jolene?"

"Nah. She went silent too."

Will's cell phone buzzed again and he frowned at his boss's insistence.

"He knows you're not in Jersey anymore."

Will shut his phone down and shoved it into his belt pouch. "Yeah, well until I find out what happened, I can't give him the answers he wants. I'm going in there. With Kyle and Jolene both silent, Katrina is the only one who can tell me why Kyle screamed code wolf."

Inside the interrogation room, the captain stood up from his chair.

Will wasted no time heading for the door. Gary grabbed his files and followed on his heels.

A second later, Ebberts met them in the hall. "Will. Gary. Let's talk in here."

"I need to talk to her ASAP." Will pressed past Ebberts. A vice grip slapped his shoulder.

"Whoa. Give me one minute, guys. She agreed to fingerprints as long as I let her see the boy. My guy is going to take her down the hall to processing. While he's doing that, let's talk."

"We already identified her. The fingerprints will confirm who she is."

Ebberts's hand fell from his shoulder. "You did?"

"She's Novokoff's mistress." Will turned to Gary

and snagged the file from under his partner's arm.

At that moment, the door behind Ebberts swung open and an officer led Katrina by the elbow out of the room. The handcuffs she wore hung loose around her thin wrists.

Something inside Will stirred as her wary eyes latched onto his. Her thick black lashes batted, concealing her thoughts and she turned away.

"Come with me." Ebberts led the way into his office where he rounded his desk and took a seat.

Gary nodded to him to follow and Will's teeth ground at the delay, but he had no choice. The officer led Katrina down the hall. Will watched the easy sway of her hips for a moment before he turned and headed into the captain's office.

Ebberts moved aside his mug containing cold coffee, clearing his desk pad. "Novokoff's woman, uh? The only ID, a birth certificate she had on her, was for a Becca Smith. Ring any bells?"

The captain gained his interest fast and Will shook his head. "No."

"I'll have Lucy run the name." Gary pulled his phone again and moved to the back corner of the office, already texting a message.

"Take a seat." Ebberts indicated the chair in front of Will.

He shook his head and kept his stance behind the hardback chair. He didn't have time for a chit-chat. His people could be in danger. He needed to know what was going on with them.

Will flipped a picture of Novokoff with his arm around Katrina onto the captain's desk. "We know her as Katrina. She has been sighted with him numerous times over the past five years. The boy is most likely hers and Novokoff's."

Ebberts studied the picture and then looked up at him. "The pictures are not very clear. You can't see her whole face. How can you be sure?"

"We're sure. And there's more. We were seconds away from a sting op when the operation was called off. My undercover agents have gone silent. Then Katrina shows up here with Susie Lakes. The only way we're going to know what happened is from Katrina."

Ebberts handed the picture back to him.

Gary flipped his phone closed and looked at Will. "Becca Smith disappeared from her home in Wyoming eight years ago. Lucy is sending the info over to your desk officer, captain."

"You think she's Becca?" Ebberts asked pointing to the door.

"Fingerprints will tell," Gary responded.

Will saw hope in the captain's eyes. Unfortunately, his gut told him Becca Smith was gone. "Get Katrina back to the interrogation room as soon as your man is finished with her."

"I promised her she could see the boy." Ebberts stood and hiked his belt as if to say, 'my word will stand'.

"Sorry. I didn't." Will ignored Ebberts's huff and turned to his partner. "As soon as you get any additional details on her, on Kyle and Jolene, on any fuckin' thing that has to do with this operation, bring them to me ASAP. I'm going to talk to Gorgon's woman."

Chapter Five

Seeing they were headed to the interrogation room again, Nicole skidded to a stop, yanking her arm from the officer's grip. "Wait a minute. Where's Luka? Your boss said I could see my son."

"I have my orders." The state trooper's fingers bit into the sensitive underside of Nicole's upper arm again, causing her to wince. He flung open the door with his free hand and forced her inside the tiny room. He treated her like the Russian whore he thought she was and for the sake of the safety of her family, she bit back the urge to set him straight.

"And I know my rights—" Her protest cut off in mid-sentence. One of the strangers she'd seen standing in the hallway with the captain a few minutes earlier, the one whose intense glare made her feel lower than the underside of a leech's belly leaned against the back wall, apparently waiting for her return.

A silver badge hung from the belt circling his trim waist. He tucked his cell phone into his jean's pocket and pushed off the wall.

Like many men, his blue eyes trailed over her, except his scrutiny held not a hint of lust. Loathing laid in their coolness.

Nicole dropped her gaze to the murky gray pattern of the floor and folded her fingers in prayer like fashion even though she didn't believe in prayers. God had abandoned her a long time ago.

She had to remain strong and use her head. These cops believed she had a part in Susie's kidnapping. She had to make them believe her when she said she did not. She had to get away from the Novokoffs, and she had a feeling this man who stood as tall as Gorgon's six-foot-two frame was her best hope to do so.

"Leave us." The marshal's deep tone revealed his authority.

Nicole peeked between her dark bangs and noted his attention passed over her shoulder.

The cop's grasp fell from her arm leaving coolness where his heat had scorched her. He obeyed the man's order without so much as a stumbled objection.

This officer could only know part of her story, she thought. She had been fingerprinted as a first grader at her elementary school twenty some years ago, so the likelihood of the officers finding out her true identity anytime soon was not good.

Her parents couldn't be told she'd been found. Not yet. Maybe never. If the Novokoffs thought they had any contact with her, Gorgon's family would wipe hers away. Killing Gorgon had signed her death warrant. Vanishing from the Earth's crust was her only hope, and her family's.

This man was strong. His chest and arms stretched his navy tee shirt to the point that every slight movement of his pecs and biceps showed. A shadow of whiskers lined his strong jaw and his upper lip was set with determination.

Nicole's hands curled into fists. She had to be strong too, damn it. She couldn't let this cop see the quake that made her knees knock. This man was just like Gorgon. He wanted something from her. Well, she wanted something too. She wanted to disappear to a place where the Novokoff's would never find her or Luka.

The door clicked closed behind Nicole.

She steeled her nerves and met the marshal's somber

eyes. "Who are you?"

"U.S. Marshal William Haus." He flipped the round badge clipped to his belt with a hook of his thumb before walking toward her. "And you are?"

"Becca Smith."

An amused twinkle flashed in his eyes. "Really? Is that the story you want to stick with?"

William Haus toyed with her. By the way his gaze traveled over her, she'd say he knew who she'd been the last eight years. Katrina. "Are you in charge?"

His brow cocked. "Of?"

"This. The captain and his men."

"No." He shook his head and pointed to the chair. "Sit."

"I think I would like to stand."

"Suit yourself." He pulled out a chair and took a seat, extending his long legs beneath the table and leaning back onto the chair. Like his jeans, his boots had seen better days. The toes were scuffed and the heels well rounded.

Several hours ago, on that back road, for a few brief minutes, her lungs had rejoiced with the exhilaration of freedom. Now with each pulse of her digital watch, the stale air surrounding her grew thicker, like sewer sludge. "The captain said I could see Luka if I cooperated and allowed my prints to be taken."

"You will, but when I say so."

She tamped down her temper. Showing her anger would do her no good. "Why are you keeping us?"

"I think the captain already covered this. You were found with a kidnapped girl, Katrina. Does Gorgon know she's gone?"

She fought to keep her surprise from reaching her eyes. He knew the name given to her by Gorgon.

Nicole smoothed her moistened palms along the

seams of her skirt. How well did the marshal know the bastard who now faced the devil? William Haus could be a cop on the take, working for the Novokoffs. The family had many connections. She knew this by their conversations. The Russian bastards thought she'd paid no attention to them, but over the years she had learned bits of their language—enough to understand most of what they said. She had to be careful. "How do you know my name?"

"We have our ways." Drawing his legs back, he shifted up and forward in the chair. "Look, I don't have time to waste. I have a woman who isn't responding after she put a bug on Susie. Gorgon took the girl, but before we could move in on him, all hell broke loose at the SOB's place. Then you show up here with Susie. You want to tell me what happened tonight?"

He sounded sincere. Nicole kept her facial expression blank. How could she be sure Will Haus told the truth?

She decided to play stupid. "I don't know what you mean."

"I'm sure you do." Will tapped the desk in front of him three times. "Here's how I think things went down. Gorgon brought Susie home, which pissed you off."

He said the word home like she'd played house with the Russian bastard. This cop who glared at her with disdain had no clue what a living hell she'd survived.

"He never brought any other girls home before, right?"

"You don't know what Gorgon did or didn't do."

"I know when he takes a piss."

His frankness made her blink. If that was so, why had he and his agency not saved her? "I don't believe you. Who are your inside people?"

"I can't tell you who they are. You're Gorgon's

woman."

"I am not his woman." Fury burnt her tongue and she clamped her lips tight before she'd let her secret slip.

"Really? My man said just the opposite."

The way his eyes filled with repugnance and fell away from her made Nicole feel unclean. She ran her hands up and down her arms as if she could brush away the filth of her past.

William Haus sighed before looking at her again. "Look, we can do this dance all night, days even, but we're not going to. I've got a feeling my people might be in big trouble. Tell me what happened tonight."

"You could work for the Novokoff's." The words had tumbled past her lips and she saw the agent's face turn stone-like.

"I want the son of a bitch dead."

His cold tone caused her hair to prickle on her arms.

Nicole refused to lower her gaze from his. She dipped deep into that well that had given her the strength to kill Gorgon and grabbed the courage necessary to stand her ground. "That is a nice speech, but why should I trust you?"

"I could've whisked you away from here to a high security jail and locked you up. I could've taken your son into protective custody where in two days he'd disappear, and believe me, you'd never see him again. But, as you can see, you're here and your son is down the hall, and I'm giving you a chance to tell your side of the story."

Will's words cut into her soul. She would go insane not knowing where her son was. She'd die without him. "How do I know Luka is still here?"

"Okay. You need proof. I get that." The chair scraped the floor as he rose. "Come with me."

Opening the door, he motioned with a simple nod for her to exit the room.

She hesitated before rounding the table and passed by him.

"This way." He latched onto her left elbow.

Nicole's nerves tingled under his touch.

As they walked a short distance through the hall, she noticed the earthy smell of his cologne. The scent reminded her of a warm sunny day at the beach. Nicole peeked at William Haus from the corner of her eye. A two-inch, jagged, white scar cut through his whiskers near the back of his strong jaw and extended down his throat. She wondered how he'd been cut.

Ahead, an officer stood guard at a door.

"The boy inside?" Will asked him as they approached.

"Yes, sir. Officer Wagnall was great with him. She read him to sleep."

Nicole's pulse quickened knowing her son was on the other side of the door. She swore Will had to have felt the rush of her blood because he shot her a glance before he said, "Open the door a second."

The officer did as he was told.

Seeing Luka curled up on a couch, Nicole's heart cried out. She wanted to run to him, gather her son in her arms and feel Luka's heartbeat against her palm but Will's strong grasp kept her rooted in place.

After a few seconds, the officer closed the door and Luka disappeared from her view. She looked up at Will. "Thank you."

Without acknowledgement, he turned her toward the interrogation room and once the door closed behind them again, he hooked a thumb through his belt loop and said, "Okay. You saw I haven't lied to you."

She drew a breath of warm air. Beads of perspiration formed on her upper lip while her stomach rolled tighter. "If I tell you what you want to know, will you promise to keep Luka and I together—somewhere safe from the Novokoffs?"

"Why would you need protection from them?" Confusion wrinkled Will's brow.

Ridding the earth of Gorgon's presence was the right thing to do. There wasn't a bit of doubt in her mind that she'd done humanity a favor, or an ounce of regret, but would this cop see Gorgon's demise the same way? Or would he call it murder? What jury would convict her of the crime, if she killed him in self-defense? None.

"Are you going to answer me?" he asked, breaking into her thoughts.

"Because Gorgon is no more."

The marshal stepped up to the table between them. "Are you saying Gorgon is dead?"

She nodded without hesitation, not wanting to give herself a chance to back out of the confession.

"You killed him."

"It was self-defense. Luka and I must disappear. The Novokoffs will kill me. Can you help us?"

"How do I know you're telling the truth?"

Katrina folded her arms over her chest and tilted her head to the side, looking down her nose at the officer with every ounce of confidence she could muster. "Until your man tells you it is so, you must trust me."

Chapter Six

"I told Gorgon a thousand times that woman would be the death of him. I could see it in her eyes. She is the devil's bitch." The heels of Yegor Novokoff's Italian loafers slapped the vinyl flooring like rapid gunfire as he stalked through the halls of the local hospital with his bodyguard close behind him. "Would he listen to me? Nah. Gorgon always thought he was a smart boy. He's an idiot who thinks with his dick. Tonight he's proven me right."

His own use of the past tense and the very thought of his son dead, strangled his rant. He fought to keep the pain attacking his heart at bay. He was the head of the Novokoff family, and needed to be strong and think clearly about the revenge the family would take against the attacker of his eldest child.

Rounding the corner, he entered the puke green cubical known as the emergency waiting room and pulled up short. The optimistic view he clung to fell into the burning acid churning in his gut. Sofia, his wife, sat hunched over, leaning against her sister. Tears streamed down Sofia's thin cheeks and her complexion was washed of the ivory tone he loved. The smiling green eyes he looked into every night over the past forty years, before he closed his own, were dull and erased of any Sofia's witty humor.

His Sofia, she seemed to have aged twenty years since this morning when he'd kissed her goodbye and left to take care of a business matter gone awry in Atlantic City.

Yegor drew a quick breath, trying to calm the tremor that quaked the morrow in his bones. He had to be strong for the dozen or so family members that had gathered, and for his Sofia.

He stepped forward and Sofia's red-rimmed eyes lifted from their study of the space beyond the commercial carpet.

"Yegor, our boy." She pushed from the chair and teetered toward him.

Yegor rushed forward and gathered Sofia into his embrace just as her knees gave out. Her breath warmed the hollow of his neck and he found comfort resting his cheek against her silky, brown hair. He rubbed her back. She felt thinner than he remembered and he loosened his hold, thinking he might break her brittle bones if he cradled her too tight.

Sofia's tears moistened the breast of his golf shirt. "Shhh, my love. You gave me a strong son." He planted a reassuring kiss on her temple and continued to rock her for a moment longer before he peered up at the stone-like expression of his man, who'd stood guard over his son tonight.

Marco blinked.

What had gone wrong? He would question the man soon, but not now. Not in front of Sofia. Not until he knew his son would live. And God help Marco if he'd screwed up. "What say the doctors? Are they the best?"

"Ya. I made sure they understood. Only the best." Marco glanced at his wrist. "They've been in surgery for almost two hours. We should know soon whether—"

Yegor cut him off with a glare. "Go find a nurse, someone who can give us news." He waved Marco off and then turned to his wife.

Her soft hands cupped his face as she stared up at him. "This is not supposed to happen, Yegor. A mother is not supposed to bury her children. They are to bury her."

Not only a mother, he thought. Yegor bit back his own fears, grasped her by the forearms and said, "Don't talk as if Gorgon is already with his maker. Sit. We will know soon when we can see our son."

He helped his love to the same chair she arose from a moment earlier. Then he thanked his sister-in-law when she vacated her chair, allowing him to sit next to his wife. He nodded his appreciation of support to the family members who filled the room and who witnessed his and Sofia's pain.

Did he look as frightened as they?

Sofia sought and gripped his hand so hard he felt the circulation to his fingers dwindle. "You must have faith in our Lord," he whispered.

"The doctor said Gorgon's chances were very small. The stabbing had done much damage and Gorgon—" she sobbed. "He had lost too much blood."

"The doctor doesn't know what a fighter our son is. Gorgon will live to seek his revenge. Mark my words."

"And if he doesn't?" Sofia's fingers tightened around his and she stared deeply into his eyes. "What will you promise me?"

"I promise, his murderer will know our revenge."

Chapter Seven

Will shoved open the door to the observation room. Gary waited inside. "Where's Ebberts?"

"A couple tractor-trailers played chicken and got tangled up in a fog patch. He had to handle a few things. I guess Interstate 80 is shut down on the east bound side just west of the Hazelton exit. So what do you think? Do you believe her?" Gary indicated Katrina through the two-way glass.

Will pursed his lips for a second before answering, "Why would she lie about killing Gorgon?"

"Why would she kill him?"

Will shrugged. "He pissed her off. Someone paid her. I don't know."

"Oh. Oh. Wait. Do you think they found the trace-maker on Susie and know about Kyle and Jolene? This all could be a ploy to expose them?" Gary's finger waggled in mid-air while he continued. "Think about it. We catch a break to nail Gorgon and the opportunity is snatched away from us. Then Katrina shows up with this story. You really think Gorgon's men would let her out without his approval. I mean from what Intel has told us, Gorgon kept her on a six inch leash. And here's another thought. Maybe the Novokoffs are trying to find Louie Betts."

"Why would they want to find Louie? The guy was Minkon's man."

"The Novokoffs owe the Minkons a favor?"

Louis Betts had been part of Minkon's New Haven, Connecticut gang until a few months ago. Something had finally ticked Louie off enough to walk into the marshal's field office, in Scranton no less, and turn himself in. In turn for his testimony against the Minkon's connection in a money laundering scheme involving a well-known charity, Louie had been given a new life as a short-order cook in Dust Bowl, Kansas. It was what Louie wanted. Go figure.

Will thought about what Gary said a moment longer before answering, "I don't think so. Gorgon wouldn't allow his own kid to be used."

"It's a big debt. Besides, Gorgon uses kids every day. I wouldn't put it past the son-of-bitch to use his own son. He probably considers it on the job training."

Gary had a point. From what he knew of the man, Gorgon had no conscience. "Katrina waltzes in here with the kid in tow, hands us a sob story, we're stupid enough to wisk her away just like we did Louie and she learns what? Squat," he said more or less to himself, thinking of ways to shoot holes in Gary's train of thought. He looked at Gary. "They're not going to find Louie that way."

Gary paced to the other side of the room and turned. "Maybe Gorgon thinks she can gain someone's confidence in order to learn Louie's whereabouts. I mean, look at her, man. Gorgon has some serious taste."

Katrina was beautiful. No arguing with his friend there. She had long legs and a heart-shaped bottom displayed nicely by the Daisy Duke jean skirt. "Wouldn't do her any good. No one at this level has a clue where Louie was placed."

"Except you and I."

True. He and Gary were the only field agents who knew the final location of their WPIs, Witness Protection Inductees. Just in case, they had to act fast and move them.

Will raised his brow at Gary and his partner splayed his hands across his heart. "I'm not going to say squat."

"Good. I'd hate to make a noose out of one of your loud ties."

"My wife picks my ties."

"I doubt that. Sharon has better taste."

"True."

They both faced the glass.

"So what do we do with her?" Gary questioned him while staring at his reflection.

"We play along."

"Meaning?"

"We give the lady what she wants." He turned to his partner. "We take her and the boy into protective custody, but this time we don't follow the normal procedures. One of us is going to stick by her like a fly on honey."

"Why one of us? Why not Chase or Aden?"

"Come on, really? You want junior agents to take watch over Gorgon's woman?"

"Okay, if not them, which one of us do you think is going to be the nice cop and be her pasty? Not me."

"Again with the fingers," he said seeing Gary's wagging digit. "Why not you?"

"Come on, man. Again, look at her." He pointed toward Katrina with his whole hand. "She works for Gorgon which means she'll be willing to do just about anything to get the information she wants."

Will's body reacted at the vision of a bare-assed Katrina which popped into his mind. His strained chuckle made him rush to clear his throat and the picture from his thoughts. "You afraid of her?"

"Not of her. My wife. Sharon would kill me if she got wind of me playing footies with a prostitute. You know Sharon knows how to use a gun. She hasn't been retired from the agency that long." He patted Will's shoulder. "You're not married. If Katrina's plan is to pin someone to the sheets, you're the better candidate. Time to get back in the saddle, Will."

Will killed Gary with a glare before turning back to the mirror. A year had gone by since Laura walked out on him. And their love life had headed south months before that. His cock stirred while studying the outline of Katrina's breasts and he chided himself to cool his jets. This was a job. His gut told him Katrina was hiding something. If getting seriously laid was what it took in order to find out what she was hiding, he guessed he could sacrifice a few seed for his country. "All right. Let's set this ploy into action. Maybe I can find out something more about the family and their work."

"Oh, please." Gary chuckled. "Don't act like you're going to your death."

The door opened and Ebberts entered. "Did she talk?"

Gary snorted. "Boy. Did she!"

Ebberts's glance jumped from Gary to Will. "What did she say?"

"We need Katrina's car to disappear," Will ignored Ebberts's question. "You've got any ideas how to do that?"

"Why?"

"She says she put Gorgon in his grave," Gary answered.

The older man's eyes snapped wide. "No, shit."

"Exactly. If she's telling the truth, the Novokoffs will turn over any straw bale, looking for a clue as to where Katrina was last seen. To protect everyone in the area, the vehicle should never be found. But, if by chance the thing is ever found, it's got to look like she dumped the car."

Ebberts combed his hand over his thin hair. "There is an old quarry not far from here. We could ditch the car there."

"Any divers use dive there?"

The captain shook his head. "This one is too dangerous. It's surrounded by about one-hundred feet of huge round boulders. The four wheelers don't go near the place. There's only one way in and out——through a locked gate."

"Sounds good. Where's the car now?"

"I had sedan towed into the lot out back."

"Who did the towing?"

"Local guy."

"We'll need his name. He might have to disappear for a while."

"You're kidding me?"

"He doesn't joke around when dealing with the Russian mafia," Gary said over his shoulder while he gathered his file.

"The Novokoffs will not stop until they find her." Will turned to Gary. "I'll head out with Katrina and her kid in your car. You go with Ebberts and ditch the car."

"You got it."

"Why not take her in your helicopter?" Ebberts asked.

"I have my reasons. The less you know the better off you are. The young cop that brought Katrina in, how trustworthy is he to keep his mouth shut?"

"I haven't had any problems with him."

"This is serious shit." Will threw him a stern look. "One peep in the wind and he and his family could disappear. I can't stress that too much. The Novokoffs are ruthless. They'll stop at nothing to find Katrina."

The captain's throat muscles worked before he spoke up. "At this point, the only ones here who know who she is are the three of us. I haven't said anything to anyone."

"We should have a story," Gary piped in, glancing up from his phone.

"Yeah," Will said, scratching his chin. "Captain, how

do you get your fingerprint info back?"

"We're still old-school. Our reports come across a fax."

"Okay, stand by your man receiving Katrina's fingerprint info. As soon as the fax comes in, snag the thing. We're going to leak that Katrina and the girl are related—make Katrina her aunt. Call her Barbara. We'll take Katrina-Barbara into custody as if this is a family feud child abuse situation. We leave the mafia out entirely. We'll walk out of here as if we're handling business as usual."

Will looked through the two-way mirror and studied the woman who now held her head. The light reflected shades of brown, gold and red in the long strands that splayed over her shoulders and brushed the table top.

As if sensing he watched her, Katrina looked up and stared at the glass like she could see right through the pane. She brushed her hair back, her breasts jugging forward with the movement.

Will held his next breath, tempering his reaction to the sight of her nipples pushing against the thin fabric of her white blouse.

Gary's hand clamped onto his shoulder. "Some guys have all the luck."

Will shot his partner an evil side-glance. "Did you ever hear of a black widow? I probably won't sleep for a couple days."

"If I were you, single I mean, no attachments, I wouldn't either. Take your vitamins."

Chapter Eight

The scent of oil permeated Nicole's subconscious and laced her tongue. Stones pinged against the SUV's underside. Then Nicole was jarred against the door and her eyes popped open. She jolted up-right in the front seat. With her right hand, which tingled from lack of blood flow, she blocked the razor-sharp splinter of sunlight reflecting off the side mirror. The rain had stopped. She moved away from the bright beam and swiped strands of her long hair away from her face.

The SUV's digital clock read 8:17 AM. They'd been driving a little over two hours. She'd dozed off. Stupid, stupid, stupid, she chided herself while she clamped her lips closed. She had to stay awake. This agent, who drove them to wherever they were going, said he was one of the good guys and she wanted to trust him but until she was sure she and Luka were safe, she didn't dare let her guard down.

The adrenaline rush which had coursed through her veins earlier had run its course, leaving her feeling exhausted.

Nicole arched her back and stretched her arms forward. The movement caused the faux leather seat under her to crinkle. Her mouth tasted like stale crackers. She needed something to drink and a couple of aspirins to nip the throb in her temples.

Out of the corner of her eye, she studied the stern unshaven, jaw line of Marshal Haus. The jagged scar on his neck was more visible in the morning light and again she wondered how he'd received injury.

Haus hadn't said much more than a grunt to her since they started out. The man didn't like her. Not liking her was understandable, considering the monster she had associated with over the past eight years. To the marshal, she was Gorgon's woman.

She could change his opinion of her with one confession but she wouldn't, not yet. Not until her and Luka were settled into a new life. The government might not put her in the WP program if they knew she had a family to go home to. And surely, after they had placed her and Luka and given them new lives, the government wouldn't pull them out.

She had to remain silent.

Nicole turned toward Will, glancing at Luka who slept in the backseat and asked, "Where are we?"

"Central PA," he clipped, without looking in her direction.

"You are being pretty vague. Can you not be more specific?"

He ignored her and veered the steering wheel to the right.

The seat belt pressed against her breast bone and her stomach as the vehicle came to a rest in front of a building that looked like a white stucco ranch home gone wild. On its roof, a sign depicted a snoring man, hosting a long, white beard. Under his bed it said, 'Blue Mountain Roadside Motel, Twenty Units.'

As the cloud of dust settled around the tires, she peered over the SUV's steel-gray hood and noted a cardboard sign, leaned against the front large pane window near its bottom right corner. The poster, held in place by two long strips of yellowed tape and less-than-white mini-blinds, stated, not to the world but to those who came close enough, in dull, red letters, that rooms were vacant.

The vehicle's side windows whirled down and the aroma of fresh cut hay spilled into the cab. Nicole relished the scent of freedom for a half of a second before she glanced to her right and then left past Marshal Haus, who jammed the SUV into park. There was one other car parked in front of the left wing of the motel, so, if she had to guess, at least nineteen rooms were empty.

"Why are we stopping here?" She watched Will remove his sunglasses and toss them on the dash.

"It's as good a place as any to wait."

Her pulse jumped. She had no clue where they were. He said central Pennsylvania, but for all she knew they could be back in New Jersey. New Jersey was known as the Garden State and produced tons of vegetables, including sweet corn. They could be within the Novokoff's grasp. She grabbed the armrest with her right hand. "Wait for what?"

"My orders."

"From?"

"The home office telling me where the drop off point will be for you and the kid." He tilted his chin toward her door. "Relax. You're safe."

She knew her fingerprints would give up her identity sooner or later. Her mother had them taken years ago when she was in elementary school during child protection program. Would the marshal's office check her prints against the fingerprints of missing children? Not likely. At least not right away, but, in time, they would. "How long will we have to wait?"

"We're code black for the next forty-eight hours. Meaning no cell phones, no contact unless—" His gaze jumped away from hers.

"Unless?" Her mind leapt between different circumstances that would cause him to hesitate to complete his train of thought and her instantaneous angst caused her to reach out to him.

He drew his arm away, not as if she'd scorched him with her touch, but in a cool-decisive motion that said I don't care to be touched by you. "We run into trouble, which we won't. We weren't followed."

"Is going code black normal procedure?"

His cool, blue eyes narrowed. "Yes. Why?"

Nicole shrugged. "I thought we'd be taken to your headquarters for maybe a day and then placed into our new lives."

He shook his head. "Putting someone into the program doesn't happen that fast. We could be here a week, maybe two."

Nicole's eyes widened. "Two weeks?" She had imagined that in two weeks she and Luka would pretty much be settled into a new home somewhere far away.

"It takes time to build new backgrounds," Marshal Haus said, breaking her muse. He turned off the ignition and pulled the keys. "Stay here."

"Can I come with you?" Luka asked from the back seat.

Surprised by Luka's voice, Nicole turned on her seat. Her son was safe, strapped into a booster seat behind the driver's seat. The agent who owned the vehicle had kids. What was his name? Gary?

Gary had carried Luka from the police station to the car with such care. After securing her son in the seat, he had turned and smiled at her—something Will Haus had yet to do. But, now, he hosted a nice smile, exposing a tiny dimple, while looking at Luka via the rearview mirror.

"No. You need to stay here, with your mom, for a few minutes." Will's face hardened as his eyes shifted from the mirror to her. "Don't leave the car. I'll be right back."

The clack of his seatbelt clipped the air a second before the door creaked open. He stopped in mid-slide off the seat and turned back to her. "By the way, I'm Uncle Will, your brother's best friend." He tilted his head toward Luka. "I thought he'd ask— I didn't want him to think, you know."

Her cheeks warmed under his stare. She knew what he meant. Will didn't know she had a brother or that she missed him and her sister so very much.

"I'll be right back." He climbed from the SUV, leaving her with a hundred questions on the tip of her tongue.

As soon as the Marshal disappeared inside the motel's lobby, Nicole scanned the immediate area around the SUV for any sign of anyone watching them. Seeing no one and that all was quiet, she twisted on her seat and faced Luka. "So what did Uncle Will and you talk about?"

"He calls me kiddo."

"He did?" Surprise tinted her tone.

Luka's feet wiggled while his head bobbed up and down. "He says I can have chocolate chip pancakes for breakfast. I told him they were my favorite. What are you going to have, Mommy?"

Nicole stared beyond the gray pebbled parking lot and saw nothing but lush fields hosting waist high stalks of corn. There wasn't another building in sight in any direction. "I don't know, honey."

"I told Uncle Will you really like blueberry muffins. He said you could have them."

"Is that right?" Imaging the stone face agent had actually talked to Luka on his level was hard to do.

"Ah huh. He's going to have bacon and eggs and potatoes and—"

"You two had quite a conversation didn't you?" she

cut him off while wondering why she hadn't heard any part of her son's conversation with the Marshal. Killing Gorgon and escaping the Novokoffs had left her exhausted. She wiped her palms across the stiff denim material covering her lap. Even though she had washed her hands several times since, she could still feel the stickiness of Gorgon's blood between her fingers.

"Ah, huh. How long will Uncle Will be in there?" Luka arched up on his seat, trying to peer over the driver's headrest.

"A few minutes."

Failing in his attempt to locate Will, Luka huffed and dropped back onto his seat. "I'm hungry."

"Don't kick the seat." She pushed his foot away.

In the distance, she heard the soulful wail of a locomotive. She'd never rode a train, or a plane for that matter. There were a lot of things she had missed out on because of Gorgon's sick need. Getting her driver's license, going to the drive-in with a boy, summer days spent at the amusement parks, holidays, birthdays, the prom, her graduation and college. She had so wanted to go to college and maybe one day become a veterinarian.

The memory of her Irish Setter rushed at her before she could put up the barrier, blocking her past. Her chest constricted as tears moistened her eyes. Kelly would be ten years old now. Would he still be alive? Would he recognize her, if she went home?

Her heart grew heavier with each memory of home, friends and family. She longed to be home and safe. But, going back now wasn't an option for her. She had to remain strong. Doing so was the only way to keep her family safe.

The vehicle moaning under Marshal Haus's weight and the rocking of the cab pulled her back to the present. She hadn't seen Will exit the building.

A line crossed his brow. “Are you okay?”

“Yes.” She turned toward the passenger window, pinched the bridge of her nose and drew a slow, long breath of fresh air. “Allergies, I guess.”

She grabbed her purse from the floor and started to dig for the small container of aspirin she carried. “I’m getting a headache. Is there a vending machine inside, where I could get a bottle of water? Luka’s thirsty too.”

“I didn’t see one.” He stabbed the key into the ignition, turned it, and the engine purred to life. He turned on his seat and looped his arm over the back of hers. She caught his appraisal of her thighs and warmth stirred in her core. He backed the vehicle away from the building and Nicole tugged her skirt down.

Will steered toward the lot’s exit and Nicole pushed away the sensual musings creeping into her mind. She sat straighter on the seat and thought about the situation at hand. Had Will gone inside just to make a call? One she wasn’t supposed to hear. “I thought we were going to stay here. Where are we going?”

“We’re coming back. The guy inside said there’s a restaurant about a mile down the road. I promised the kid pancakes if he’d let you sleep. He did. I keep my promises.”

The man had swayed Luka’s allegiance with a promise of chocolate chip pancakes. She had to talk to Luka later and make him understand how important it was to keep their secrets. “Do you really think going into a restaurant is wise?”

“Mommy, look.”

She dashed a glance at Luka, whose dark irises sparkled with excitement. He pointed at a small herd of cows munching in green pasture. “I see. Can you count them?” And then to Will she conveyed her angst in a hushed tone, “I mean, what if you know who comes looking for us and someone remembers seeing us."

"I'll get the food to go. We can eat back in our rooms."

"You got more than one?"

"Yes. Two." He glanced her way. "Don't worry, they're connecting. The door will stay open. I'll be right there if you need me."

"Of course." He trusted her enough to give her and Luka some privacy. Or was he testing her?

Nicole stared at the highway ahead watching telephone pole after telephone pole whiz by. He could watch her all he wanted. She wanted nothing more than her freedom from her past. And Luka. She'd never leave him.

A billboard advertising Hershey, Pennsylvania loomed ahead. She'd been there once with her grandparents. Nicole relaxed against her seat and sent a thank you to God. The agent had told her the truth about where they were.

"Luka does not warm up to too many people."

Will glanced at her twice before he answered, "What warm? The kid's stomach growled. I asked if he was hungry. He said yes and asked for chocolate chip pancakes. That's all. There was no warming up to anybody."

Nicole couldn't help the smile that pulled her lips into a grin. A crimson blush surrounded Will's tee shirt's collar. The big bad cop had a soft spot. Being in the presence of a decent man was comforting. "I hear you, kiddo."

***

This assignment was going to kill him, or maybe get him laid. Maybe both. Will dug the motel keys out of his jean's front pocket and unlocked the room's door, while holding the bags containing their breakfast. He needed some space between him and Gorgon's woman in order to cool the fire her curves and long legs caused in him.

Thank God there was a kid with them, otherwise he might toss Katrina on the sheets and bang out of her the information he needed concerning the Novokoff's operations.

The door to room number eighteen stuck, giving way after a shove of his shoulder.

"This place needs updating," he said scanning the orange and yellow shag carpet and the pine paneling. Framed pictures of pale blooms splattered the walls.

"Clean is what matters." Katrina passed by him, her scent masked by the Lysol tingling Will's nostrils.

Fighting to keep his eyes from following the sway of Katrina's hips, he entered the small room and dropped the bag containing the kid's pancakes and Katrina's muffin on the cheap, round table, marked with about fifty years of water rings. "Here you go. I'll keep the key to the room." He shoved the key back into his pocket.

The kid raced around him and bee-lined to the television. "Can I watch cartoons, mama?"

"Yes, but first we must eat. Before the food gets cold."

"There's a microwave on top of the refrigerator."

"I see." Katrina hoisted the gym bag from her shoulder and tossed it on the sun-kissed-colored bedspread.

Will had searched the black bag before they'd left the station and knew the case contained clothing, necessary personal items for both her and Luka, a few books and a video game for the kid and a little money. Not a hell of a lot of cash, if you were going to start a new life.

She slid the cardboard tray holding their cups of coffee and Luka's milk onto the table alongside the bags and then turned her eyes up to him.

His blood simmered. He could leave them for a minute—the time it would take him to unlock his room's door and the connecting door. Katrina wanted something from him. She wasn't going to run.

"Okay then." He snatched his cup of coffee and with the bag containing his breakfast bagel in hand backed away from her warmth. "I'm going next door."

"You are not going to eat with us, Uncle Will?"

"No, I'll eat in my own room, kid."

Katrina coughed. "Stay. Our family always eats together and you are Luka's Uncle Will now."

Will stood in the threshold with his room key and breakfast in hand. The kid's hopeful stare held him in place. They were double teaming him. A smile pulled at Katrina's lips.

He had two questions. One. What was her game? And two, was he man enough to handle her. Latching on to her gaze, he nodded. "Let me wash up. I'll be a minute."

"Good." She turned. "You can let your drink and food here. I will not touch them," Katrina said, turning and tugging on the overstuffed chair standing in the corner. Her ass waved at him while she back peddled, pulling the chair along, and almost smoked her last comment over his head. He hadn't thought about her trying to drug him. Why had she?

He had to get his head together.

"Okay." He tossed the bag back onto the table, but kept his coffee. "I'll be right back. Dead lock this door behind me."

Katrina stopped her rearranging of the room and tossed her long locks over her shoulder. She scanned the parking lot via the room's one window. "I thought you said we weren't followed?"

Was that real fear he saw in her eyes or was she that good an actress?

"We weren't. Just lock the door. And close the drape."

"You are not making me feel safe," she said, walking toward him.

"You are. Just precautions." Will slipped out and closed the door. When he heard the dead bolt slide into place and saw the drape draw closed, he turned and scanned the area surrounding the tiny motel before he unlocked the door to his own room. Barring the door behind him, he used the john and washed up. Within a few minutes, he unlocked the dividing doors between the rooms and carried his coffee inside. The room smelled of maple syrup. Katrina had made use of the tiny microwave.

Luka sat on the bed's edge in his place to eat, but was twisted around watching a cartoon. Katrina sat on the hardback desk chair pulled up to the table with her hands folded in her lap. Her stare concentrated on the wall beyond the television.

Their food containers sat in front of them. His bag, unopened, sat in front of the cushioned chair.

He cleared his throat and Katrina's gaze popped up to meet his.

"Good, you are ready. We eat."

"Yeah. My pancakes," Luka cried while wiggling into position on the bed's edge.

"You didn't have to wait." Will crossed the tiny room in a few strides and took his seat.

Katrina had plastic knives and forks placed on top of napkins to the right of their food.

Luka extended his hand to Will. A second later

Katrina extended hers and then bowed her head. Did she really think he would believe God had a place in her life?

Okay, he'd play along. He placed his coffee on the table and took Luka's small hand.

Watching Luka stare at the Styrofoam box in front of him, Will couldn't stifle his chuckle. "Why don't we just eat?"

Katrina wiggled her fingers at him. "No. We say grace first."

She brushed her soft fingers against his extended palm and an electrical volt ran up his arm. He glanced at her, expecting to see her smiling, but her head was bowed and her eyes closed. Her pouty lips moved in silent prayer. Was she pretending she hadn't felt a thing?

When would Katrina make her move on him? He had to get a grip. They hadn't been alone for six hours and already he was as jumpy as a teenager about to get laid for the first time and Katina was as cool as snow on ice.

He could relax, for now. She wouldn't jump him during breakfast. Will dropped their hands and said, "Amen."

"We have not finished with grace."

"I said mine silently. The kid is hungry. Let's eat."

Luka didn't have to be told twice. He dove into his pancakes.

A few minutes later, Luka turned away from the cartoon he was watching and asked, "Uncle Will. Why haven't you come and visited us before?"

"I'm—"

"Uncle Will has been away for a while," Katrina interrupted.

"Where?"

"To a far off land. Now eat your pancakes. I can't microwave them again. They'll get as hard as rocks and you'll break your teeth trying to chew them."

Will swallowed his bagel in several bites and downed his coffee, after which he made the excuse that he had some work to do, and left Katrina and Luka alone.

He entered his room, leaving the adjoining door ajar. He snatched his cell from his belt, intending to tell Gary to send someone else, but in his mind he heard Gary's chuckle and the cry 'Wuss'.

The phone clicked against the glass covering the nightstand. He was no wuss.

Will stalked into the john and shut the door where he stared into the mirror at his refection. If Katrina was telling the truth about killing Gorgon, he'd protect her with his life. If Gary's hunches were right and she was trying to get information, she'd get nothing out of him.

His sacs tightened picturing Katrina on her knees in front of him, her soft hair wrapped in his hands while her soft lips were working his cock. Well, she'd get something from him. How long had been a while since he had a woman do him? A long fuckin' time. His release could be quite a load.

Will hit the faucet and splashed cool water on his face. Sex with a prostitute wasn't his style. She was Gorgon's woman. He was a sick son-of-a-bitch. Maybe there was another way to bring Katrina over to their team. Her kid.

Chapter Nine

"Luka!" With a start, Nicole sat up from the bed, holding her forehead. Had she been drugged? Her vision was fuzzy. She swiped her eyes and blinked. No. She was just exhausted and stressed. She slept very little last night-reliving over and over the horror of the prior night. The nightmare had kept her tossing and turning.

The bathroom door was closed.

"Luka."

No answer. The television was turned down low. He should be able to hear her. Her breath caught. She scrambled off the bed and stalked to the bathroom. He wasn't inside.

He was with Will. She couldn't keep her son away from the man. She yanked open the connecting door, expecting to see the pair continuing their intense game of 'Go Fish' from last night, but the room was empty. They were gone.

"Luka." Nicole's acid burned her rolling stomach while her last breath remained trapped in her lungs. Her greatest fear had come true. Will did work for the Novakoff's.

Where would he take her son? How would she follow them?

She slammed her fist against the door frame. God. She was so stupid. Will had bought them the biggest, most delicious pizza and like a fool she had stuffed herself. Then, while lying on the bed and feeling Luka's warm body next to hers while he watched television, she had fallen asleep.

Nicole glanced at the digital clock on the nightstand which read 1:42 PM. She had slept for an hour—long enough to lose her son.

She stuffed her feet into her sandals and dashed to the door. She had to find them and stop Will from giving Luka back to the Novokoff's. How? She had no idea where they had gone. If she went back to the family, they'd kill her.

Her fingers curled into fists. Then she'd die trying.

She raced outside into the blinding late afternoon sun and skidded to a halt. The SUV was still parked in front of room fourteen, several doors down. She knew why Will had moved the vehicle there. However unlikely, if the Novokoff's did find them, they'd assume she, Luka and Will were hiding inside room fourteen. The racket they'd create storming inside the empty room would give Will enough time to react.

But why do that if he was one of Novokoff's men?

"Mama."

Nicole's heart soared hearing Luka's voice. She spun around and saw him running across the parking lot from the far side of the building. His bare chest was pumped and glistened. A motel towel draped his shoulders. Behind him, a shirtless Will followed. "Where were you? I was so scared."

Her son slid to a stop in front of her. His eyes shimmered with joy. "Uncle Will took me swimming."

Nicole dropped to her knees. She grabbed him by his thin arms, pulled him to her and hugged him tight. Tears welled up in her eyes as the tips of Will's boots came into her view.

"He swims pretty good for a four year-old."

She stood, still clutching her son. "You son-of-a-bit-" Nicole bit her tongue, feeling Luka's head turn up against her stomach. She fought to calm her shaky voice.

"I thought you took him."

"Didn't you read the note I left you?"

"What note?" She glanced toward the open hotel door and shook her head.

"I laid the pad on the nightstand next to the bed. The kid was bored and you were zonked out. So we went for a walk and found a small pool out back. It's the owner's private pool, but he said I could take the kid swimming."

"Just like that?"

Will shrugged. "I'm a nice guy. People like me. What can I say?"

Her throat clogged with emotion and she trembled. If she had lost Luka, she would've died.

The marshal's eyes narrowed as he dipped his head to the side. "Are you okay?"

Her heart continued to pound. A dusting of blonde curls covered Will's broad tan chest and drifted into a V under the waistband of his jeans, which hung low on his trim hips. She'd never been this close to a shirtless man besides Gorgon. Will's presence warmed her blood. She met his concerned stare just as he reached for her and stepped back. "I'm fine."

"Guess what, mom." Luka tugged the hem of her top.

"Uncle Will said we could go to a park."

"What are you talking about?" She looked up at the marshal.

"Hershey Park is about twenty minutes away." He hooked a thumb over his shoulder, making his bicep bulge. "I thought if you're up to it, we'd take the kid there and put him on some amusement rides. Maybe grab dinner at the park. No use sitting around the room all day and night."

"But what if—"

He cocked his head to the side. "Do you really think you know who will be looking for us there?"

"Who is looking for us? Daddy?" Luka asked.

"No—"

"No one you know, kiddo," Will responded the same time she had. Will rubbed Luka's hair, leaving the rusty strands a mess. Then he turned his amused gaze to her. "What do you say? It's better than sitting around here watching the clock tick."

"The clocks are digital."

"Okay then, flip or bleep or whatever. What do you say?"

"Say yes, mama. I've never been to a ride park." Luka jumped up and down in front of Nicole.

Her son's excitement was contagious. There was no way she was going to say no. Will was probably right. Novokoff's men would not search for them at an amusement park.

She glanced at Will while grabbing Luka's shoulder to make him stop jumping. Exhaustion dulled Will's blue eyes. Tiring Luka out was a good idea, and doing so would take both of them. She grabbed her son's chin and turned his attention up to her. "On one condition. You must hold my hand the whole time."

"Even on rides?"

"Okay, not while you're on rides. But before and after."

"Sounds like a plan," Will said, winking at Luka. "Let's get changed, kid. The bus leaves in ten minutes."

She had a feeling she was played by the two.

"Yeah!" Luka took off like an Olympian in training and entered the motel through the door she'd left open.

Will turned on his booted heel to follow. Nicole reached out. Her fingertips hovered above his shoulder blade. She never touched the bare skin of any man other than Gorgon. Will took his second step and she grabbed his arm. "Why are you doing this?"

Will yanked out of her grip as if her touch scorched him. He turned and the odd glint in his eye changed to a twinkle.

"Don't you think an uncle has the right to spoil his nephew once in a while?"

"But you're not Luka's uncle."

With both fists, he grabbed the towel slung around his neck. His ribs expanded as he drew a breath. "Look, he's a kid. He has enough energy to power the next space shuttle to Pluto and back, and he was bored watching you sleep. I need sleep. So why don't we take him to the park, double team him, wear him out and then tonight we can all rest."

She was right about Will needing sleep. He had been up all night and after taking on her case all day, driving them here, keeping watch over her and Luka. "You're right. I'm sorry I know you're just trying to help us."

"Good, let's go." He frowned and headed toward the motel.

***

Four hours later, Will's turn to sit came again while Katrina kept her son busy, within his view. Carrying two bags of half eaten cotton candy, Will dropped onto a bench labeled chocolate stop #5 while Katrina raced after Luka.

He reached down, and through the material of his jeans, adjusted his Glock back into position which had been jostled to the side on the last ride.

Straightening, he noted Katrina and Luka now stood in line for the park's smallest roller coaster while dusk hung heavy in the summer sky to the east behind them.

Will squinted at his watch. The hour confirmed that the gritty feel of his eyes was indeed a sign he'd been up for near thirty-six hours. He stretched his neck and shifted his weight on the wooden seat, fighting off the exhaustion that settled in on him with the setting sun's last warm rays.

Through the array of carnival hum, he heard Katrina's laughter and he zeroed in on her. She was a puzzling woman. One moment she came off as a strong, sexy siren, standing so close to him that her heat singed the hairs on his arms and caused his blood to boil with forbidden desire, and the next moment, she kept her distance, and with down casted eyes, acted as if he might hit her for no reason at all.

He pressed his spine against the hardwood slats, squared his shoulders and inhaled a deep breath of French fries. He had to remain sharp. Katrina was dangerous.

Will studied Katrina's profile as she trapped Luka's chin between her thumb and fore-finger and with a tissue began to wipe away something from the corner of the kid's mouth. He couldn't find a single flaw in the innocent mask she wore.

After she'd finished caring for her son, Katrina stashed the tissue back in her purse and then reached up and adjusted the ponytail she'd trapped her long hair into before heading to the park. As if sensing he watched her, she glanced over her shoulder still wearing her beautiful smile and flagged a little wave in his direction.

There had been moments throughout the afternoon just like this one where Katrina seemed almost childlike—as if she were enjoying the world for the first time. He recalled the way her eyes rolled in bliss while wrapping her first bite of cotton candy around her tongue. A moan of ecstasy had escaped her.

He had mustered every ounce of willpower and pulled his eyes from her enjoyment of the sugary fluff. Her pouty lips parting, her tongue swirling around the candy and the smacking sound she made as she licked her fingers clean, had almost driven him to fall to his knees in front of her.

Katrina's elation over her first bite could've been an act but he didn't think so. She ate the confection as if she hadn't had anything so sweet in a long time. Looking at her, he doubted she ate many sweets at all. There wasn't two ounces of fat on her trim frame, except for the two perfect breasts displayed nicely by her little white top— a linen blouse with a top button that kept popping open, exposing the curve of her right breast. A white top that stopped short of touching the band of her tiny jean skirt, just enough to show a peek of her tan belly whenever she lifted her arms even slightly, like right now, as she again adjusted her ponytail.

She was playing with him.

Will's loins tightened, thinking how the curl of her hips would fit both into his grasp and against his own.

"F U Dork," someone cried.

Will's heavy lidded eyes popped open and he twisted around on the bench in time to see a pimple faced adolescent race through the mingling crowd, waving a red tee shirt above his head like a hard-earned trophy. Two seconds later and not far behind, five other unsupervised boys, one missing a shirt, raced after him.

Scanning the crowd for anyone who might also be watching the group with interest, the hairs on the nape of Will's neck prickled. He relaxed, noting the only ones who paid any attention to them were those who the boys elbowed.

Will rested against the hard wood, seeing the world was okay and shook his head. Didn't the parents realize assuming the world was a utopia was dangerous? He figured the boys were maybe thirteen or fourteen years of age—an age where their parents felt safe leaving them on their own. God, they couldn't be more wrong.

Will glanced at Katrina where she and Luka neared the front of the line. He'd like to put every one of the boys' parents into a room with Susie Lakes's mother and father just for five minutes and then they'd understand how important diligence was in their child's safety.

One never knew how heavy guilt was until they carried the shame. He wouldn't wish the burden on anyone.

He squeezed his eyes closed and swiped away the memory of a perfect spring day blackened by evil in a place where it had no business.

He jumped at the weight of someone joining him on the bench and dropped the bags of cotton candy, reaching for a gun that wasn't at the small of his back.

"Oops. Sorry, I didn't mean to startle you."

Katrina reached for the candy at the same moment he did.

Even her pink painted toes peeking out of her sandals were perfect.

Perfectly done. That is what he meant.

His mind swirled like the lights circling the rails in front of him. Between his lashes, he met the bits of warm amber glowing in her midnight irises. Close enough to feel her breath, he noted a tinge of purple under the makeup covering her cheekbone. Her rosy lips lifted into a smile and his breath grabbed his chest with sharp claws.

She willed him closer. The pull, as old the world itself, caused him to lean towards Katrina.

She didn't move, but instead waited, watching for his next move.

He studied the little mole above her full upper lip. A sudden desire to feel the soft cushion of Katrina's lips pressed against his caused a battle inside him to lean toward her. He'd bet a week's pay she tasted like pure honey laced with cotton candy.

Her fingers brushed the back of his hand and an electric charge zapped its way to his groan.

Laughter erupted from the crowd behind them.

Will snapped back. He wouldn't allow himself to be fooled and sucked in by her innocent act. He was the cop trying to knock her off keel.

Summing all his willpower, he pushed to his feet, forgetting the bags that lay at them. "I ah…" He stammered for words while noticing the length of her legs, again. Damn, she was beautiful.

Katrina picked up the bags and tilting her head to the side, stared at him with a curious expression.

Will turned away and raked his hand over his long hair. He couldn't do this. From the moment he'd seen Katrina, his blood had simmered and with each passing moment they were together, the heat rose. He had to keep his distance.

He stared beyond the twirling mechanics and was deaf to the screams they caused. Gary should've handled Katrina. He was the charmer. He was the one who was married and used to a woman's wiles. Even without the threat of his wife putting a bullet through his cock, Gary wouldn't tumble into bed with Katrina.

He, on the other hand was the bad ass cop, used to getting the answers he needed through force, any force. And, he hadn't been laid in well over a year. He had to keep his head on straight.

There he had his answer. He had to keep his distance and his head on straight, and forget about the strain causing his jeans to feel too tight in the crotch. He turned and looked down at her. "Where's Luka?"

She pointed ahead. "On the roller coaster. He's next to the little blonde. It seems I'm just a tad too large for the ride." She smiled.

He didn't return the gesture. There was nothing large about Katrina. "Right."

Her brows pulled together. "What's the matter?"

"Nothing." He shook his head, feeling as if he was under a microscope.

Her eyes narrowed further. "I don't think it was nothing. You looked so sad."

He wasn't about to tell her about his personal demons no matter how sincere she seemed. He walked four feet to the roller coaster's guard railing. A moment later she stood next to him.

"What were you thinking about when I sat down?"

"A bunch of kids ran through here unsupervised. If their parents knew how their world could crash without notice—" The words had tumbled out of his mouth. He didn't want to put her on guard. Damn, he was tired.

"If someone like Gorgon got their hands on them," she finished his thought.

"Yes."

The delight that radiated from her face a moment ago disappeared. He saw the understanding in her eyes before she lowered them again. "I know."

She was putting on a good act. Thinking about the deeds she must've witnessed. Disgust left his mouth sour and his skin now crawled at her closeness. He wanted to move away, but he stood his ground. How did she live with herself? "Of course you do."

He looked down his nose at her and ignored the hurt in her eyes. "Answer one question. Why Susie? Why did you save her?"

"I had to. I couldn't let her behind, with him. She reminded me of me when I was—" Katrina bit her lip. Tears clung to the edges of her eyes as she backed away.

What wasn't she saying? Will drew a breath of night air. An amber moon sat on the mountains to the east.

Susie reminded Katrina of her. He didn't see the resemblance. Susie was blonde, fair. Katrina was just the opposite. Auburn hair and had a bronze complexion.

The roller coast in front of him slowed around its last winding turn.

Will turned and saw Katrina had taken a seat on the bench again. The pink and blue bags lay beside her. Her eyes were lowered to her lap and her fingers worked the hem of her blouse. Was she ashamed of her actions?

A tear fell to her cheek and she swiped the moisture away.

He wasn't the forgiving type, but his heart mellowed watching her. Fuck, he needed a stiff drink.

Under the blinking lights, he checked his watch. He needed to check in again with Gary in about an hour.

Will crossed the short distance to stand in front of Katrina. "The ride is slowing down. I think it's time we head back to the motel."

Katrina snatched the bags off the bench, stood, brushed by him and stalked toward the ride. The moment Luka cleared the exit gate, she clamped onto his hand and marched toward the park's exit. She never looked back to see if he followed. Will had a feeling she didn't care.

Chapter Ten

The night air rushed into the cab, feathering Will's hair. He drew in and exhaled several long, shallow breaths in an attempt to weaken the angst prickling his gut. Silence reigned in the SUV. Not even Luka spoke.

In the rearview mirror, Will noted the kid's lashes rested against his cheeks and his head lobbed to the side. That explained Luka's silence. He darted a glance at Katrina from the corner of his eye. Wearing a frown, she remained a statue, leaning against the passenger door. Probably sensing he was watching her, she folded her arms over her chest and turned to stare out her side window.

Will stretched his fingers one by one and tightened his grip on the steering wheel. Damn. He hadn't meant to alienate her. He needed to stay on her good side so she'd talk, or make her move on him. Those boys at the park reminded him of his friends and a loss he would never get over. He'd let his loathing for the people she associated with get the best of him.

Katrina's safety belt clinked the moment his tires crunched the pebbles covering the motel's parking lot, and before he could turn the key and cut the engine, she'd already jumped from the vehicle, shot around its rear-end and opened the back door.

He stepped from the vehicle as Katrina lifted a drowsy Luka out of the child's safety seat and stalked off, leaving the backdoor to his attention.

Silently, Will unlocked their room and once inside, she back-kicked the door closed with enough force to shake the jamb. A half-second later he heard the dead lock slide into place and the safety chain rattle.

Well, he guessed he didn't have to worry about getting seduced tonight. He shrugged. Just as well, he wouldn't be at his best. He was too damn tired. He unlocked his door and hit the light switch in time to see the door between their rooms close. Again he shrugged.

After dead bolting his own door, he checked the connecting door. It wasn't latched, just sitting within the jamb. With his ear to the door, Will heard water running and Luka's protests at having to take a bath. Figuring he had a few minutes to himself, he decided to wash off the last twenty-four hours of grime and slip into clean clothes.

The hot stream smacking him in the face and whooshing down his frame was exactly what he needed to clear the sleepy fog from his head. A few minutes later when he stepped out of the shower, he knew he'd be good for another hour, maybe two, but sleep would call to him again.

Will slipped on his jeans and stopped by the adjoining door and listened again. He heard splashing and Katrina's laughter mixed with Luka's. The disdain poking him earlier during his and Katrina's conversation at the park slipped another notch. In many ways Katrina was just like any other woman.

With that thought, he headed outside, needing to clear his head of the many cute snapshots of Katrina he witnessed today, especially the one as she swirled her pink tongue around the cotton candy. He focused on checking the grounds and he had to checkin with Gary before closing his eyes for a few hours.

He circled the motel twice, inhaling the scent of fresh cut hay before taking a stance in the shadows near the corner of the motel and plucking his phone from his pocket.

"About time you check in." Gary must've been sitting on his phone because he answered on the second ring. "What the hell have you been doing? I've been trying to get a hold of you for the last twenty minutes. Your phone went to voicemail. I thought maybe something happened."

Had he been in the shower that long? "So you do worry about me?" Will smiled, imagining the cherry red apprehension rising above Gary's starched golf shirt's collar. "Has Kyle checked in?"

"Yeah. Both he and Jolene are fine. Boy, do I have news."

Will heard a thud and knew the noise was caused by Gary's case file hitting the desk. The guy carried his papers everywhere.

"She was telling the truth."

Will pushed off the wall and headed toward the road. Except for the tree toads chattering and the hum of the motel's rooftop sign, the night was as still as a graveyard at midnight. His grip on the phone tightened. "You're not pulling my goddamn leg, are you? She really killed Gorgon?"

"She tried."

"He's alive? What the hell happened?" Will edged the corn field, scanning its murky, narrow rows for prowling silhouettes.

"Kyle couldn't go into details. He's in hell's kitchen. Katrina did a number on Gorgon. She sliced and diced him pretty good and left him for dead. He's in Mercy Hospital, critical condition. I have people in place there already, trying to get more information. Last report, it's still touch and go. Yegor and the Mrs. are there too, keeping a watchful eye over the bastard." Gary drew a quick breath. "You were right to get her out of here. The street grapevine is already hot. Old man Novokoff didn't wait for the outcome. He's offered a five-hundred thousand dollar reward to anyone who brings his grandson back to him unharmed and another five for Katrina's head."

The small boulder at Will's feet became Katrina's head. Her glossed over eyes stared accusingly at him. Some might not agree with him, but he didn't think the woman deserved that type of ending. She had redeemed herself somewhat by saving Susie and trying to rid the world of Gorgon. "Christ, the whole underworld will be looking for her."

"I got a feeling if Gorgon kicks, that reward will double. We're not only going to have every slime ball looking for them, but also every bounty hunter who has financial problems, and you know there are a lot of them out there who don't give a rat's ass about right or wrong. They're in the profession for the money."

Gary was right. A couple million dollars was a hell of a lot of cash. Hell, they wouldn't have to kill Katrina for the reward. Just drag her ass back to New Jersey and throw her at Yegor Novokoff's feet. The old man had trained his son in the art of torture. Yegor would take great pleasure in ending Katrina's life himself.

Will's mind spun. How in the hell was he going to keep Katrina and Luka safe? His gut told him the net meant for Katrina was already crisscrossing the country and getting larger by the hour. He stared at the long, dark road heading west.

"Will, are you there?"

He blinked. "Yeah. She turned against the Novokoff's for a reason."

"That's what I was thinking. Find out why. Offer her a deal. Make her believe we can only help her if she helps us. She's the key to shutting down their whole fuckin' operation."

"I'm already on it. I'll call you when I know something," he said, turning toward the motel. For three long years his team had worked on this case. Most days they took two steps forward and three back. Now, in under twenty-four hours, hell broke free and the icy grip round his heart began to melt.

Inside, he knocked three times before opening the connecting door and stepping into the dimly lit room. Katrina led a sleepy-eyed Luka dressed in his PJs out of the bathroom. "I need to talk to you."

Noting his frown, Katrina's step faltered. She knew something was up.

She grabbed Luka by the shoulders and ushered him toward the bed. As she passed by Will, she whispered, "Give me a minute."

The boy was an innocent. "Sure. Night, kiddo."

"Can we go swimming tomorrow, Uncle Will?" Luka asked on the tail of a yawn.

"We'll talk in the morning."

"K'ay."

Will nodded to Katrina and backed through the door, leaving it ajar a few inches. A minute later he heard Katrina guide Luka through a child's prayer. What kind of woman could lie with the devil and yet teach her child God's word?

The woman confused the hell out of him.

Will put his foot on the edge of the bed and tucked his pants leg up over his gun. He unsnapped his leg holster just as he heard the door behind him creak open. With his gun in hand, he let his pants leg drop and turned to face Katrina whose worried gaze dropped to his weapon.

She pushed the door behind her to its jamb. "What's wrong?"

"I have some news," he said cutting to the chase.

"You've found us a home?" Her face beamed with hope as she stepped toward him.

Will stiffened. She was anxious to disappear. Now he understood why. He'd seen Gorgon's handiwork. Tossing the leg strap onto the dresser, he tucked his gun into his belt. "Not yet."

Katrina brushed back her hair. "Then what's going on? You look worried. What's happened?"

The tiny room enclosed in on him, along with the scent of sunshine and cotton candy, as she stepped toward him. Will detested the hot rush that Katrina's closeness sent coursing through his veins, but he held his ground anyway, folding his arms across his chest. "We want to offer you a deal."

"I don't know what you mean." Her brow furrowed under her fringe of bangs. "A deal for what?"

"We'll put you and Luka into the witness protection program in exchange for information and your testimony against Gorgon and his family."

"Gorgon is dead."

Will shook his head while gauging her reaction to the news he was about to share. "No. He's alive."

Nicole's hand covered her mouth and she backed away until the wall stopped her retreat.

"No. He can't be." Her throat strained against the rising, hot bile. Feeling like a caged animal about to be slaughtered, she searched for an escape. Will stood between her and the outside exit. She edged toward the adjoining door. She wouldn't leave without Luka.

"Katrina." Will's stern look warned her not to run.

Her lungs burned. She labored to drag in quick breaths, but even those weren't enough to keep the darkness from edging in on her.

Will stepped forward and a moment before her knees

gave out, he caught her by the elbows.

"Come here. Sit down." His strong arm encircled her waist and provided support while he helped her to the bed. The mattress springs creaked as she sunk onto its edge.

"He can't be alive. I kill—" Nicole's cry caught in the vise closing her throat and her hands trembled so hard she couldn't seem to fit them together. She shook her head in disbelief. "It can't be true. Gorgon can't be alive. There was so much blood." Gorgon's blood had seeped into the bedroom's hardwood floor, overflowing the cervices. Its phosphorus smell haunted her memory. Bile rumpled in her stomach and caused her to blurb. "Oh, my God." She could feel the stickiness of his blood between her fingers. She scrubbed her hands across her lap, first the bottoms and then the tops. She pleaded with glistening eyes before saying, "I swear. You need to believe me. I saw him. He was dead."

"I'm told you did a number on him. Word is Gorgon still might not make it." Will studied her for five rapid heartbeats before his fingers curled into fists along his sides.

Was he mad at her? Because she didn't finish the bastard off?

Will wavered in his stance.

Was he going to hold her and console her? God, she wanted to feel safe and she had a feeling she'd have no fears within his embrace.

Instead of stepping toward her, he turned on his boot heel and crossed to the dresser, tapping the wood with his knuckles before looking at her again. "There's more."

A grave feeling snaked its way along Nicole's spine. She inched back on the polyester, flowered bedspread and braced for the additional good news Will had to share. "What?"

"Old man Novokoff has offered a half of a million dollar reward to anyone who returns his grandson to him and another half million…"

Will's gaze fell away with his words.

An egg sized lump formed in her throat and Nicole swallowed around blockage. "If they kill me."

He nodded once. "Yeah."

She'd known Yegor Novokoff would do this. If she were in the old man's position and someone had hurt Luka, she would go after them with a devil's vengeance.

The question now was what was she willing to do to protect her son? The marshals wanted her testimony. She couldn't testify. Silence was her family's best defense.

If the law wouldn't help her, then here was only one way for Luka and her to be safe.

Nicole slid off the bed and walked to the adjoining door with her resolve in place. Holding the knob, she kept her back to Will. How could she make him understand how important disappearing was to her without telling the truth? She turned to face him. The muscles in her neck worked before she spoke. "You were right. Gorgon had brought the girl home to replace me as his mistress."

"He told you that?"

"No. I just knew he was going to—" She lifted her face and stared at the ceiling tiles while trying to control the anger and the fear produced by the memory of that night. A hot tear drifted down her cheek. "He told me to prepare her for him. I couldn't do what he asked. I couldn't let him do to Susie what he did to me. What he made me do… I just couldn't."

"Did he attack you when you didn't do as he said?"

Nicole swiped a tear from her cheek and ran her tongue across her dry lips. "Yes. Everything happened so fast. I grabbed a letter opener from the desk and stabbed him," she lied. She had to. "I had no choice. He was going to kill me and give Luka to his wife. I have no doubt in my mind." She locked onto Will's gaze. "Gorgon can't know where I am. He will kill me. Please, you must hide us."

"I have my orders. We can only help you if you agree to turn evidence against the Novokoffs."

Not a spark of caring flashed in his cold, steel blue eyes.

Nicole's heart plummeted toward the floor. Will had his orders and she was the caretaker of her family's lives. She had to do what was best for everyone, no matter how much her only option would tear her apart inside. "I can not."

Will crossed his arms over his broad chest. "I don't see that you have a choice."

His pupils widened slightly telling Nicole his cool mask was a bluff. She stepped closer to him. "I do and I wouldn't."

Will blinked.

She left the room with an escape plan already in mind.

Chapter Eleven

Under the dark shadows, Luka reminded Nicole of Gorgon, which tightened her already wrung out stomach. She repositioned herself on the bed, propped her head in her hand, and smoothed the hair from his brow, careful not to wake the sleeping child.

She prayed Luka would do something with his life that he'd love and that would earn him respect. But as long as he was with her, chances of that happening were slim. They'd always be on the run.

A tear fell over her lashes and followed the path of several others. Her gaze traveled over Luka's small frame to where the child's tiny toes wiggled out from under the crisp, white sheet. SpongeBob's toothy grin sat above the blanket and spanned Luka's rounded belly.

Nicole smiled in spite of the desolation encasing her heart. Gently, she pulled the sheet up over SpongeBob and slipped from the bed. She had no choice. There was no other way. She had to leave Luka behind.

The connecting door between her and Luka's room and Will's stood ajar.

Wearing her underwear and a tee-shirt, Nicole tiptoed toward Will's room and listened. His soft, deep snore satisfied her that he slept. She took care gathering her things because she had a feeling Will was a very light sleeper. If he caught her trying to leave, he'd have no choice but to throw her ass in jail.

Nicole slipped into her jean skirt and grimaced at the zipper's song that raked the silence. She tiptoed to the door again and checked Will. He still slept soundly.

She padded on tip-toes to Luka. The awful taste of sorrow coated her mouth while she allowed herself a full ten seconds to etch Luka's angelic face into her memory before she pecked his forehead, spun away and snatched her bag and sandals off the floor. Then, using her body as a muffler, she unlocked the door and slipped out into the cool, dark night, locking her whole world behind her.

Thinking only of Luka's future with a new family, she ran around the corner of the building toward the backside of the motel. When Will realized she was gone, he'd assume she would've looked along the highway for a means of escape. He'd be wrong.

She hurried across the motel owner's yard. Cool, fresh cut grass clung to her feet. Chlorine tickled her nostrils as she raced by the pool where Will had taken Luka swimming twelve short hours ago. Behind her, from inside the owner's house, a dog howled. She had to hustle before the dog woke his master and she was spied.

Huddling next to what once was an outhouse, Nicole dropped her sandals to the ground and while keeping an eye on the surrounding darkness she wiggled her feet into them. Then she raced through the hip-high grassy meadow, checking over her shoulder every few seconds for signs of anyone chasing after her.

At the wood line she caught her breath and then whispered to Luka, "I love you, sweetheart, and I promise, one day I'll find you. I promise." Blinking away tears that threatened to fall, she inhaled the scent of moss and flowers. To stay on course, she had to follow a star, and the sky was filled with them. Nicole turned and headed northwest, disappearing into the forest.

***

"What the hell do you mean she's gone?" Gary's

bellow battered Will's eardrum and made him yank his cell phone away from his ear. "How the hell did you let that happen?"

He hated that he'd fucked up. He didn't need Gary to add to the tension jack-hammering his temples. Will paced the concrete sidewalk outside the rooms. Luka still slept, curled up in the blankets with not a worry in the world. "I needed to fuckin' sleep, okay. Katrina slipped out without me hearing her. Last time I checked in on her was around two. Both her and the kid were sleeping." Or she had been pretending to be asleep. Damn. He should've handcuffed her to the bed, but he didn't want to send Luka into therapy.

"She left the kid?" Gary questioned. "Some kind of mother she is."

"She's not like that." Will scrubbed a hand over his face while recalling the loving touches Katrina gave her son. What the hell was he going to tell the kid when he woke and saw his mother was gone? "We forced her to do this, you know."

"What do you mean?"

"She pleaded with me to put her and the boy under protection last night. She was pretty insistent. I played hard-ball and said no, not without her testimony against Gorgon. I guess she figured if she left we'd have no choice but to take the boy."

"So you think she ran to save her son."

"Yeah. I do."

"Why the hell wouldn't she just testify? She could've stayed with him."

"I don't know. She said she couldn't. She's hiding something."

"You need to find her, Will."

"I know, but I can't go trampling around the countryside with the kid."

"I'll send someone out to pick him up."

"No." Will stopped in mid-step, imagining Luka's frightened expression. "You come. I don't want anyone to know where we are. If word got out and Katrina hasn't made it too far, she could be found before the sun sets again. We can't blow the case. Besides, Luka saw you at the station. I'll tell him you're my step-brother."

"Step-brother?"

"He'll buy it. I'll explain later. He's a good kid. He'll be okay going with you. He trusts me." Will grabbed the doorknob. "In the meantime, I'll get him up and take him for breakfast. I can look around town for Katrina."

"What are you going to tell the kid?"

"Damn if I know."

"Okay. I'll be there in a couple hours."

"Bring my car. She doesn't know it. You can take your SUV."

"Okay."

"One more thing," Will said, stopping Gary from disconnecting. "I don't want child services brought in just yet. Can we bend the rules on this one? Do you think Sharon would watch over him?"*

"I'll ask her."

Twenty minutes later, Will had Luka in the back seat of Gary's SUV and they were headed toward town. Luka looked forward to chocolate chip pancakes while Will searched every ditch and corner for Katrina.

Chapter Twelve

He felt heavy. Pressure swelled against Gorgon's right bicep, causing his fingers to tingle. A moment later the force dispelled and his blood rushed through his veins in a free fall. He blinked against the brilliant light surrounding him, failing miserably to open his eyes. Had he died?

If he had, with wings, wouldn't he feel light?

Maybe heaven wasn't in his destiny.

He was so thirsty. Maybe he was in hell.

No. Hell was hot and a deep seeded chill encased his bones, causing him to shiver.

"Yegor, our son wakes."

His mother's cry grabbed onto his waning consciousness like a life-line tossed to a drowning soul in a heaving sea and pulled him from the thick, opaque sluggishness that weighed both his mind and body.

To his right, a steady bleep kept rhythm with the rise and fall of his chest. The air filling his lungs was fresh. He was reminded of a frosty Serbian dawn, yet, a wash of bad antiseptic moistened his tongue as he licked his parched lips.

"Gorgon, do not worry. We are here with you." His mother's soft hand warmed his left forearm below his elbow.

Worry. Why should he worry? His mother always vexed too much over him. He reached to calm her fear and stinging zapped through his right hand and up his arm. He bolted forward in reaction and hot fire ripped through his gut. His shriek rolled over a raw throat and escaped him between clenched teeth.

Tears burned his closed lids.

A familiar force at his left shoulder pushed him back.

"You must lie still," his father's order cut through the fog. "That's it. Relax, son, and breathe deep. The doctor said you must not move."

The constant beep-beep vibrating his left ear drum raced against his heartbeat. Beads of perspiration spouted on his forehead and upper lip.

"Breathe deep."

Gorgon listened to the voice that had never led him astray and sucked in puffs of antiseptic spiced air.

The doctor? Where was he? What the hell had happened to him?

Gorgon felt his father's strength and forced his eyes open. He twisted his neck to the side and blinked. "The light," he managed to croak across dry lips.

"Sophia, pull the string. The damn light is blinding him."

Following the click, the radiance pushing against Gorgon's lids faded. "Where am I?"

"Mercy Hospital," his mother answered as her hand again found his arm and brushed against the grain of his hair.

"Why?"

"You don't remember?" Yegor asked.

Gorgon squinted, his brows knitted, at his father's concerned stare. The gray at the old man's temples seemed to extend further into his brown hair and the tiny lines edging Yegor's dark eyes had deepened since yesterday.

He shook his head and a pinball of throbbing spikes rolled between his dark eyes. Every nerve of his body zinged with pain. He had to lie still. "No."

"Katrina did this to you. The doctor said you were

lucky, but the fear of infection is still great. You must rest."

Yegor's gaze shifted and he pointed to Gorgon's lower abdomen. Tubes revealing a vile discharge ran from under the white coverlet and down the side of the bed. The other tubes connected to his body brought fresh air and liquid to him.

"That bitch." His mother's soft fingers became talons biting into his flesh. Her green eyes shimmered with fiery tears. "I will not rest until she is dead for what she has done to my baby."

"Katrina." He looked between his parents. The name that had always brought him joy now made the fire in his gut twist with searing anger. Gorgon closed his eyes and rested his pounding head against the stiff pillow. The night came back to him in flashes. In his mind's eye, he saw Katrina's hard-hearted expression, shed of any respect or fear for him. The callous angles of her face were filled with contempt and… He ground his teeth. Something more. A new found dignity.

Gorgon jerked and curled his fingers into a fist while he recalled the blazing knife twisting his intestines like a twirl of pasta.

The beeping of the machine behind him increased. His father had warned him many times to rid himself of the cunt, but no, he let his heart or maybe his cock, rule his thoughts. Katrina was an angel at sixteen. His kitten. She bore his child.

He shrugged off his mother's hand and glared up at his father. "Where is she?"

The old man shook his head. "We do not know, yet."

"And Luka?"

"He is gone too."

Even though he had set his jaw for the truth, Gorgon's head dropped back against the pillow and his heart froze in his chest. His father was not blaming him for the loss of the family's heir. He should. But then a father forgives a son's shortcomings and allows him a second opportunity to prove himself. A second. Not a third.

"How long have I been sleeping?"

"Three days," Yegor said.

"Three days." His eyes widened, imagining the distance Katrina could've covered in the time. Her and Luka could be anywhere in the world by now, but he knew they weren't. She didn't have the resources to escape the boundaries of this country. Where would she hide? "Set me up."

"The doctor—"

"Now," Gorgon cut his mother's protest off while ignoring the pricking in his hand and fumbling for the control hanging on the railing.

"Help him, mother, before he hurts himself."

His mother's eyes narrowed with concern while she pressed the control's button. The bed grinded under him and slowly slid back and up.

Gorgon clamped his jaw and refused to show any weakness as he shifted and straightened on the mattress. "Have you sent men to watch her family's home?"

"Yes. She is not there and she has not contacted them, so I imagine she has not gone to the police, yet."

"She won't go to the police. Katrina knows there are those we own. She is not a stupid woman."

"I have paid someone close by her family who will have no problem letting us know if she does call them, and then we will move quickly to learn her and Luka's whereabouts." Yegor stared down his nose at him. "Do not worry, my son. We will get Luka back. There is not a place on this Earth we will leave untouched. I've offered a huge reward to find them. Someone will turn them in."

"How much?"

"Five-hundred thousand. Another five for Katrina's life."

"That is not enough. Raise the reward to a million for Luka."

"A million dollars?"

"Ya. And another million for Katrina's safe return to me."

"Oh my God," his mom cried. "You do not want that woman back?"

Gorgon flashed a silencing glance at his mother before turning back to his Da. Gorgon knew his stare was as cold as his icy heart. "I want to cut her as she has done to me. I will not fail to take her life."

Yegor Novokoff straightened, squared his shoulders and dipped his head with a quick nod. "It will be done. In the meantime, you must rest and heal. Luka will need you strong when he is returned."

If Luka is returned. The thought of not ever seeing his son again pierced Gorgon's heart before he could shield it. He closed his eyes. A smile tugged at his lips while he imagined Katrina's fear when he stood before her again with the knife that would end her life.

Chapter Thirteen

Only her third day working at the small truck stop in tiny town, Tennessee and her eleventh day on the run, missing Luka, and already Will found her. How the hell did he track her to this little town tucked between swells in the Smokey Mountains?

Nicole's heartbeat throbbed in her temples while outside, a thunder storm of biblical proportion rolled in from the west casting an eerie coat on the Sunday morning twilight.

Damn. She squashed the pen and pad she held. In another two hours she'd be done with her shift and out of here. In three, she'd be curled up in her bed in the little apartment she'd rented above the Jacobs' garage, dreaming of Luka.

She had to get out of there. But how?

Nicole ducked below the restaurant's kitchen window, careful to keep out of Will's sight and darted to the swinging door, which led from the kitchen to the restaurant. She cracked the steel passage open enough to hear the conversation between Will and Crystal, the other waitress on duty.

Peeking at Will, Nicole's stomach did a happy flip and she chided herself. There were a million good looking guys in the world, why was she attracted to the one man she had to dodge.

"She might be using the name Becca Smith," Will said to Crystal.

The truck-stop waitress who'd worked the establishment since the owner opened his doors, splashed coffee into the porcelain mug sitting on the counter while staring at the photograph Will presented.

Crystal snagged the picture and held three by four photo so Nicole could also see her image. How the woman knew where she stood was a mystery, but Nicole had learned over the past three days that little got by Crystal. She seemed to have 360° peripheral vision.

The snapshot, showing part of her face, was taken of her outside a theater in New York City. Gorgon had taken her to the play as a Christmas gift. The play had been magical. Gooseflesh snaked up Nicole's arms. The thank you he expected when they'd returned home had been anything but.

"This isn't a good picture."

"It shows most of her face. Take a good look."

Under the high-hat lighting, Crystal repositioned the pictures several times and squinted. "Yeah. I think the same woman was in here last week."

Will's tired gray eyes flashed blue with new life. "When?"

Crystal handed the picture back to him. "I could be wrong."

He tucked the photograph back into his wallet and laid his wallet on the bar. Will took a few sips of coffee while studying Crystal over the lip of the mug with eyes that now mirrored the disquiet sky beyond him. He was gauging whether the woman told him the truth.

"On Sunday night around midnight." Crystal posted her free hand on her hip and shifted her slight weight to her other orthopedic shoe, causing the sole to make a sucking noise against the vinyl flooring. "Wait. No. It was a little after eleven, right after I came on duty. The girl turned a few heads. The way she was dressed in a little top and a ribbon of a jean skirt, I thought maybe she was working the lot, but I've never seen any of the lot lizards make that kind of money."

Will's brows pulled together. "What do you mean?"

Crystal jabbed her chin toward the hallway to the left. "She used the restroom and changed into a pair of designer jeans and leather jacket. Looked kind of expensive, and her watch was not a Timex."

Will looked up from the jangling charm bracelet on the women's thin wrist. "Was she alone?"

"Yeah," Crystal answered over her shoulder while she returned the coffee pot to the burner.

The older woman caught Nicole peeking through the door's crack and winked before turning back to Will. Grabbing a menu, Crystal dropped the vinyl covered booklet onto the counter. "She ordered a sandwich and an iced tea and set up camp in a booth for about two hours. Do you want something else with that coffee?"

"No." Will shook his head. "Coffee is enough. Thanks. What did she do for two hours?"

"The truck drivers are grabbing breakfast at that time before they hit the road heading up into the New York markets, so I was pretty busy, but as far as I could tell she just watched people. I was a little perturbed she took up a booth that long, but she looked like she needed to rest. I caught her dozing off once or twice. Better to doze off here than on the road." Crystal thumbed the gold cross she wore. "I don't need any strikes against me when I meet my maker by making someone hit the road when they shouldn't. You know what I mean? In the end, I made out."

"How's that?"

"She left me a ten dollar tip. Another reason I knew she wasn't working the lot. Those girls don't tip."

"Nice of her."

"Sure was."

Elmer, the short order cook, turned from the grill and

shot Nicole a wary look.

She placed her finger against her lips and shook her head.

He rolled his eyes and slid a couple of plates of steaming eggs and steaks under the overhead heat lamps. Then he slapped the counter bell signaling to Crystal an order was ready for pickup before returning to the food sizzling on the grill.

"Did you see how she left here?" Will asked drawing Nicole's attention.

"Nuh. All I see looking out these windows are semi's rolling by." Crystal pointed to the large pane windows across the room behind Will where outside, gray clouds churned. "Can I get you anything else? I have orders up."

"No. I'm good. How much for the coffee?"

"A buck fifty."

Will fished money out of his wallet and then slid the leather billfold into his back jean's pocket. "Here's five. Keep the change and here's my card. If you think of anything else, I'd appreciate your giving me a call."

"Thanks." Crystal looked at the card and her spine straightened. "U.S. Marshal? Did she do something bad?"

Will held his mug inches from his lips. "I'm not at liberty to say, but if you're a mother…"

"I am. Four daughters. My two oldest are in college. One's going to be a surgical nurse and the other an accountant," Crystal said with pride. "She got her head for figurein' from me."

"Then you would understand." Will gulped a swig of coffee, sat the mug down with a thud that reminded Nicole of a judge's gavel finalizing a sentence, and slid off the bar stool. "Call me."

"Sure thing."

Nicole slithered up the door's plane and stared through the tiny diamond-shaped window. Her breath fogged the pane in quick puffs while she watched Will's broad back disappear out of the exit.

Suddenly the swinging door shoved her backward and she scrambled to keep her footing.

Anger and resentment played across Crystal's face. "What the hell is going on, Becca? That guy is a U.S. Marshal. Jesus. I just lied to a fed."

She had to think fast. She crinkled her face into a state of confusion. "What? No. He's not a Fed."

"He gave me his card and told me to call him." Crystal held up Will's card.

"Let me see." Nicole snapped the card away from the waitress and glanced at Will's contact information before crumpling the paper into a ball in her tight fist. "He's no goddamn cop. That bastard made these up. Anyone can make a business card nowadays. The stuff is on Walmart's shelf," she stuffed the paper into her apron's pocket, hoping Crystal wouldn't think twice about the raised seal. "He wants to gain people's confidence so he finds me. I'm telling you he's my husband. You've got to believe me, Crystal. He thinks he owns me like a dog. He'll kill me if he finds me." She widened her eyes and grabbed Crystal's arm, hanging on for effect. "Isn't impersonating an officer a felony? Maybe I could have him arrested and have his ass thrown back into jail."

Ding. Ding. Ding. The bell behind them pinged.

"You two still have a couple hours to go? Let's get your asses in gear. Crystal, your order is up and getting cold. If you don't want to buy those truckers their breakfast you better get a move on," Elmer cried out. "And, Becca, you've got a couple of guys waiting at table six."

"Alright, Elmer, give us one second," Crystal ordered him right back.

"You've got to believe me," Nicole pleaded, twisting

her face with anxiety.

Crystal's gaze honed in on hers for a moment before she shoved a finger into her face. "You stay put. I'll get your table's order. You hear me?"

"I'm not going anywhere." She had to get out of there and fast. If Will asked around enough, he'd find someone who'd give her up. "I need a cigarette to calm my nerves. You got any?"

"You don't smoke."

"I used to." She lied. "I gave it up, but I really need to calm down. I'm freakin'." She hopped in place while trapping her lip between her teeth.

"Okay. In my purse." Crystal turned and picked up the steaming plates.

"Can you check out front and see if he's gone?"

"I'll ask Lisa at the fuel desk if she saw him leave as soon as I take table six's order."

The moment Crystal pushed through the swinging doors Nicole rushed to the lockers, opened Crystal's locker, and dug through her purse. Peeking over her shoulder and ensuring Elmer was busy at the grill, Nicole grabbed Crystal's pack of cigarettes and her car keys. Then she opened her own locker, grabbed and slung her purse over her shoulder. "I'm going out back for a few minutes, Elmer." Rushing by the steam table, she held up the cigarettes for him to see and jogged through the stock room to the back door.

With her hand on the push bar, she stopped. What if Will was watching the lot? She couldn't run like a scared mouse. If he had any inkling she was there, he would expect her to run and arrest her in mid-step.

Slouching back against the wall, between a stock shelf and the door, she folded her arms across her chest. Her heart ping-ponged against her arm. She had to calm down and think clearly. She drew a deep breath and then exhaled slowly. She had escaped both Gorgon and Will before. She could again. She would.

How had he found her? Nicole slipped Will's card from her pocket, unrolled the wad and brushed her thumb across the seal. Was Luka with him? No. Will wouldn't leave the boy alone in the car while he came inside. Her stomach tightened. Where was her son?

Maybe Will had already put him into the foster care system. Maybe he was already with a new family and on his way to forgetting her. The notion that her son was safe should make her happy, but somehow the thought had the opposite effect. Nicole leaned her head against the cool cement block wall and closed her eyes against the pain constricting her heart and threatening to test her vocal cords. She missed her baby so much.

She trapped her bottom lip between her teeth. As much as she wanted to remember every detail about Luka, she already knew in order to keep her sanity she had to banish them from her mind. Only in her dreams, when she was weak, did she allow herself to think about Luka. Then she'd wake sobbing and bury her wails in her pillow before she woke the elder couple who were her landlords.

"Are you alright?"

Nicole's eyes popped opened. Crystal stood in front of her. She hadn't even heard Crystal's squeaky soles. Damn. She had to stay alert.

"Yeah. Just scared. You know…of him." Nicole backhanded the tear that had escaped over her lashes and trailed along her cheek. Guilt edged its way to the forefront of her mind. The older woman had been nothing but good to her. Crystal worked too damn hard. Nicole dangled the car keys in between them. "I'm sorry. I was just going to borrow your car. I would've left it someplace safe and called you."

“Ah, baby. Everything will be okay.” The older woman pulled her into a warm embrace and rubbed her back. Nicole remembered her mom doing the same thing when she came home from school with a broken heart after Tommy LeBlanc dumped her. Things had worked out then too.

Hiccupping against Crystal’s shoulder, Nicole pulled back and swiped away any remaining tears. “I don’t know how. Did he leave?”

“Yes. Lisa said she saw him pull out in a little black car and head toward the interstate. He’s probably headed to the next town. We better get back out front. The boss just walked in. We don’t want to lose our jobs, right?” Crystal squeezed her arms.

She couldn’t go back to work. What if Will came back? Nicole faked a tremble. “I don’t know if I can. What if he comes back?”

“Okay, take my car and go home.” Crystal shoved the keys back into her hand. “I’ll get Elmer to give me a lift and I’ll pick my car up after my shift is over.”

“What about Mr.—”

“Don’t worry about him. I’ll cover for you. I’ll tell boss man you cut your hand trying to open a can of applesauce and I sent you home. He’ll be worried about his worker’s comp rates and just be happy you went home and not to the emergency room. Now go.”

Nicole gave the woman a hug. “How can I thank you?”

“What goes around comes around, honey. One day you’ll have to cover for me.”

Nicole laughed. “You got it.” Two minutes later, she pulled out of the lot while planning her next move.

Chapter Fourteen

The old air conditioner, which did little more than act as a fan pushing warm air into the room, rattled in the window, pulling Nicole from a fretful sleep. Under her long hair, sweat beaded the nape of her neck. She stretched and peeled away from the damp sheet under her. Through heavy lashes, she noticed a boot tapping the air at the base of the single-sized bed and her heart shot into her throat. Clutching the sheet to her bare breasts, she rolled and scrambled to the opposite side of the bed, only to be pinned, faced-down onto the mattress by the intruder.

"Let me go." She thrashed and kicked back, striking air. Her breasts squished into the mattress springs. She ignored the pain, reached behind her, and grabbed fists filled with the assailant's long hair. With all her might, she yanked hard.

"Owww."

She winced, her ear ringing with the attacker's cry.

He dropped his weight from his elbows, forcing the air from her lungs. His fingers locked around her wrists and tried breaking her hold on him. "Damn, Katrina. Stop pulling. You're ripping my hair out."

Every muscle of her body went stark still, except for her eyes-they widened. "Will?" Over her shoulder, she peeked through her auburn strands and caught a glimpse of Will's cheek plastered against her bare shoulder.

"Yeah. It's me. Christ. Now let go." His hot breath caressed her sensitive skin, sending tingles down her spine.

Nicole became aware of the softness of his hair between her fingers, his musty scent bombarding her nostrils on the cusp of each sharp breath she inhaled, and every inch of his hard body pressing against her backside. Warmth pooled between her legs and she closed her eyes against her body's reaction to him. "You first."

He let go of her wrists.

Nicole slid her arms close to her body and pushed against the mattress, trying to topple his weight from her, so she could roll over, but he kept her pinned in place.

The discounted, thin sheets she'd bought at the local Dollar-Mart and his clothing were the only barrier between his hot flesh meeting hers. The knowledge caused the room to grow warmer. "I let go. Now get off of me." She bucked against him. A mistake. She laid still.

"Not until you tell me what were you reaching for?"

"What?" She glanced at him and then scanned the nightstand next to the bed. "Nothing. I don't have a gun if that is what you're thinking. I was just trying to get away."

"Not until you promise me you won't try to run." Will arched up and bore his weight on his elbows. His strong thighs held her legs in place while his hard ridge pressed against her backside.

She fisted the sheet below her, trapped her lip between her teeth, and wrestled with the fire mounting low in her belly. Not to go dizzy with want, Nicole remained still. "I'll scream if you don't. My landlord has great hearing, and, he has a huge shot gun."

"You don't want to do that."

She struggled to push up on her elbows again. "Why not?"

"I'll have no choice but to flash my badge and haul your ass out of here, sheet optional."

"Ha. Ha."

"I'm glad you find the situation funny," his warm breath caressed her neck.

She struggled against his weight and her desire for him. "I mean it. I'll scream."

"Go ahead. I doubt anyone will hear you."

Brushing her hair from her face, she peeked over her shoulder and saw amusement dancing in his eyes. "Why's that?" she asked between clenched teeth.

"Your landlords, Malcolm and Hilda Handwerk, they're near eighty and both have hearing aids. Also, about twenty minutes ago, they left to go to the market and their closest neighbor is a half a mile away."

"How do you know who my landlords are?"

"It's my job to find shit out." His warm breath tickled her ear. "Now, if you promise not to run, I'll let you up. We need to talk."

She sighed. Her breasts flattened against the lumpy mattress as she caved. "What choice do I have?"

"We all have choices. Take your time. I'm quite comfortable."

Without seeing his face, Nicole knew Will grinned——from ear to dimple. Frustration should be what she felt, but with Will's hard muscles pressed against her backside, frustration wasn't the term she'd use to describe her condition. She'd never wanted a man before, but from the moment she'd laid eyes on Will she had wondered how delicious having him inside her would feel. If she rolled over under him, she could experience a man she truly wanted. She felt Will's hard reaction to her and knew he wanted her too.

But doing so would cement the notion in Will's mind that she was indeed a whore. She didn't want that. She closed her eyes and took in the memory of his body on hers—that would have to be enough. "I promise. Now, please, let me up."

"I knew you were a smart lady." The bed springs creaked and the air surrounding her cooled as Will pushed himself up and stepped back off the bed.

Lady. Will had called her a lady. The opinion brought a smile to her lips. The sheet wrapped her body as she rolled over. She scooted up and reclined against the headboard.

The wooden chair he'd brought into the tiny bedroom from the kitchenette moaned under Will's weight as he leaned back and crossed his leg over the other. His smirk hinted at his amusement while the razor sharpness of his blue eyes displayed his seriousness. "Now, should we start again? Good morning. Or, should I say good afternoon?"

Will looked somewhat rested. Had he grabbed a nap while waiting for her landlords to leave? "How did you get in here?"

"That lock wasn't much of a challenge." Will's gaze dropped to her breasts and the embers in her lower belly glowed anew.

Nicole drew the sheet higher and tighter over her pounding heart and tucked the cloth into her arms pits before swiping her locks from her face and behind her ears. "How did you find me?"

A smile pulled at the corner of his lips. "I followed you home from the restaurant."

Her hair tickled her bare shoulders as she shook her head. "Lisa saw you leave."

He sat forward and the chair thudded against the old wood flooring. Will propped his elbows on his knees and dangled his hands in between them. "I went down the street and waited."

"How did you know I was there?" She didn't think Crystal would give her up, but she had to ask. "Did Crystal call you?"

"No. Truckers talk. I questioned a few yesterday in Northern Virginia and they told me they thought you worked at Gilligan's."

Damn. Who would have thought he'd be able to track her through truckers? "Then you knew I was there when you questioned Crystal?"

"Yeah. I spoke to a driver who was fueling his truck before coming inside. He told me you were there."

"I don't understand." She shifted her weight on the mattress. "Why didn't you just nab me then?"

"I was curious."

"Of?"

"Seeing the setup you had. You know, to hide from Gorgon." The air conditioner rattled again as if on cue in order to demonstrate her new standard of living. "Who did you tell Crystal I was anyway?"

"My husband. My OCD controlling husband."

He smiled. "We have any kids?"

She knitted her brow together. "What?" Her cheeks warmed. "No."

"Good. I hate when kids are involved in a marital dispute."

His jest brought a smile to her lips.

Will's blue eyes glistened with amusement.

Kids. Nicole yanked the sheet free from the mattress and box spring and swung her feet to the floor, clutching the thin material in her fists. As much as she could over the past few weeks, which had been a few sparse moments, she'd kept her thoughts from turning to Luka. However, seeing Will she needed to know about her son. "Where's Luka?"

"Safe."

"Where?"

"Does it matter?"

She glared. "Of course it matters. He's my son. I

love him."

Will's right brow lifted quizzically. "If that's so, how could you leave him behind without saying goodbye?"

Will's words cut deep. Nicole fiddled with the cotton cloth covering her stomach and legs as she fought to keep her composure. Will thought she was a bad mother. At the time, she thought she was doing the absolute right thing.

Looking up, she let her heartache show in her glistening eyes. "Leaving was the only way I could think of to protect him."

Will studied her for a few quiet moments before he sat back with a sigh. "Why don't you get dressed and then we'll talk."

Without giving her a chance to argue, he rose and walked out of the tiny, paneled room, leaving the door ajar.

The urge to run rose in Nicole. She looked around at the faux-oak paneled walls. There was no way she could escape from this apartment without Will stopping her. Even if she did manage to slip out the bathroom window onto the garage rooftop and jump twelve feet to the ground without breaking her leg and without him hearing her, how long would it take before Will would find her again. Hell, she thought he'd never find her in this small town.

Nicole's nerves prickled as she slid off the mattress and stood on shaky legs. Could she do as Will wanted and become his witness against the Novokoffs? How could she protect her family from Gorgon's wrath?

Her choices were difficult. Either she gave up her family or protected her son.

Selecting a few articles of clothing from the small dresser, Nicole turned and with heavy steps entered her tiny bathroom. A few minutes later, dressed in jeans and tee shirt, she exited the bedroom and was met with the scent of fresh coffee. Sunlight poured through the front apartment windows that overlooked the driveway, casting columns of light across the square floral tiles of the kitchen counter.

Will's hand dangled over the open refrigerator door. The floor board under her foot creaked and he glanced her way. "I don't know about you, but no matter how hot the temperature is outside or what time of day, when I wake up I need my coffee."

"Yeah. Me too."

"Good." He smiled, flashing the dimple she'd love to tongue. "Do you take anything in your coffee?"

"Two sugars and a little cream." She shook her head, clearing her mind and crossed the few feet to the bar that served as her table. She watched as Will moved around the captain's kitchen like he owned the place, pouring the hot liquid from the coffee pot into two mugs and adding cream and sugar to one. He left the other black. Having someone take care of her was kind of nice.

"Here you go."

Across the bar, she accepted the mug Will offered her and took a sip, feeling the sweet caffeine rush against her tongue. She gripped the cup tighter. "Please. Tell me. Where is Luka?"

Will swallowed a gulp of his coffee before he said, "Gary, my partner, his wife is watching over him."

"His wife?"

"You don't have to worry. Sharon was with the agency until she and Gary decided to have kids. They have twin boys about Luka's age."

"Oh." Nicole stared out the window at the limbs of the maple tree and drank some more. The knowledge Luka was with someone who had law enforcement experience comforted her, but the thought of another woman caring for her son needled at her ego. “Luka has never been around other children besides his few cousins. Gorgon would not allow him to go to preschool.”

“He’s having a great time.”

Her heart jumped in her chest. “You spoke to him?”

“I call him every day.”

“Every day?” Why would Will take such an interest in her child?

“He thinks I’m his uncle’s best friend. Best friends do things like that.” Will stared into his mug. “The kid’s world has been toppled. Someone needs to reassure him everything will be alright.”

She knew Will hadn’t meant to hurt her but guilt struck Nicole’s heart, causing her to sit her mug down and slid onto the bar stool. Will was a good man. She was grateful he was the agent assigned to them. “Thank you for making sure he’s safe.”

He shrugged as if his actions were nothing. “You’re welcome.”

She rimmed the lip of the mug with her finger. “Where did you tell him I went?”

“I told him you and I were on a secret mission and would be back soon. He promised me he wouldn’t tell anyone.”

Nicole smiled imaging the sparkle in Luka’s eyes having a secret to keep. She studied Will’s face as she asked, “Why didn’t you just put him into the system?”

“That’s what you were hoping for?” His blue eyes narrowed, searching her for the truth of her actions.

“Yes.”

“You could do that? Not know where he was, who was raising him?”

“Anyone would be better than Gorgon.” Her mouth suddenly went dry and she swallowed another sip of coffee before saying, “I thought later I could learn where he was and watch over him from a distance."

"Well, your plan wouldn't work."

"Why?"

"We can't do that. He has parents."

Her stomach clenched. "You'd give him back to Gorgon?"

He sat his mug down and taking a stance, feet planted apart, Will folded his arms across his chest. "What choice would we have? Gorgon is his father, right?"

"Yes."

"If Gorgon wanted Luka back, we've have no choice but to comply."

"No. You can't." She jumped to the edge of her seat. "Gorgon is a monster."

"Unless we have concrete proof that Gorgon has hurt Luka, endangered him in any way or committed crimes, we'll have no choice but to return Luka to his father."

"I'm his mother."

"But you abandoned him."

"To keep him safe."

Will's hard gaze remained on her. He was right. In the eyes of the law, which he was, she had abandoned her son, even though in her mind her actions were just. If Gorgon lived, he could say she attacked him and took their son. Gorgon would get Luka and she would be locked away, never to see her little boy again. The pain she felt at the thought brought tears to her eyes.

"I know why you left, Katrina. I know what kind of man Gorgon is. I wouldn't want my child raised by him either, but as of right now, we have nothing against him to prove he is not the upstanding citizen he claims to be."

Nicole snorted. "Upstanding citizen."

"Help me help you, Katrina. You know Gorgon's operation don't you?"

Her mind whirled. She had to make a decision. Luka or her family.

Chapter Fifteen

Katrina's soft body under him had Will's libido jacked-up. Now, watching her, adrenalin kicked his psyche into overdrive like a smooth three fingers of aged whiskey. This was the moment he'd been working towards since he first saw Gorgon's mistress. He had her. She was going to spill her guts and they'd be able to shut down the Novokoff's operation and lock the bastards away forever.

Standing on the balls of his feet like a sprinter, he was all ears, anxiously waiting for the information he'd been searching for when Katrina's tan faded and her features distorted into shades of green. The mug she held trembled in her tight grasp and concern overtook his glee.

The exact moment he made the decision to rush around the counter separating them, she inhaled and said, "I need to tell you something." Her voice quaked.

Her eyes lowering disclosed that whatever she was about to tell him was huge. His gut knotted in anticipation and Will fought the urge to move toward Katrina, fearing he'd scare her into silence. "Go ahead."

Her mug clicked against the tile counter. "If I do, will you promise me you'll do everything possible to keep my family safe?"

If Gorgon and the rest of the Novokoffs were put away, there wouldn't be a threat against Luka, but he'd go with the flow. "Luka, sure."

"Luka too."

What the hell did she mean Luka too? He tilted his head to the side and narrowed his eyes. As far as he knew, Katrina had no one else here in the United States, but then there wasn't that much information on her in the file, other than she was Gorgon's mistress for the past five or six years. Who was she referring to? "You have other family?"

Katrina's eyes darted to the window. She seemed to stare a million miles beyond the quivering maple leaves outside for a long minute before answering, "Yes."

"Here in the United States?"

"Yes."

"Where?"

"You must promise me you'll keep them safe. Gorgon will not stop until he has Luka back. He will kill them all."

Will had no idea how many people he was promising to protect, but he had no choice. He needed to know what information she had. He was on the brink of shutting down Gorgon and his sick trafficking ring and there was nothing he wouldn't agree to. "I'll do everything I can."

The whirl of the air conditioner filled the silence hanging between them while she twirled the strand of hair that had hugged her neck. His nerves sizzled under his skin, but he kept a cool façade while he waited for her to continue.

"My real name is not Katrina."

Shoe leather slapped the floor as he dropped back onto his heels. Was this a con? Who was she going to tell him she was? He turned and sat his mug down into the apartment size sink before facing her. "Who are you?"

"Nicole Carson."

The name sounded familiar but he couldn't be sure. He'd have Gary run it first opportunity. "Nicole Carson," He repeated just to make sure he heard right.

"Yes. Gorgon gave me the name Katrina."

Will's stomach rolled as a bad feeling settled on his

shoulders. "Why?"

"I was abducted when I was sixteen." Her pink tongue swept across her lips. "On my way home from my after-school job eight years ago."

The hairs on the back of Will's neck prickled listening to the quake in her voice. He studied her facial muscles and eyes for any indication she wasn't telling the truth. He saw none. If she was indeed a victim, she would be the perfect witness to shut down Gorgon's whole operation and throw him and most of his family in jail until the flesh rotted off their bones. "Gorgon?"

"His men, I think. There were two of them. And a kid."

"What?" Using a kid sounded like something the Novokoffs would do.

Again she looked out the window. By the pale sorrow distorting the beautiful lines of her face, he knew Katrina—he meant Nicole—was recalling the exact moment her life had changed.

"Everything that happened seemed so ordinary. This mini-van pulled up beside me and the guy driving asked for directions to the school's soccer field. I knew the soccer association was holding their regional playoffs there so I didn't think it odd. A lot of people were coming to the event from out of the area. A few had stopped earlier at the restaurant where I waitressed. I was on the passenger side of the car, and he was talking across the console and bucket-seat, so I thought nothing of stepping closer."

Rage intensified the gold flecks in her eyes. Even after eight years, she was beating herself up over her decision for the thousandth time.

"The young boy was in the backseat. I remember he wore a green and yellow team shirt, 'The Falcons', and he held a soccer ball on his lap."

Nicole's pink tongue darted across her lips and again she stared out the window as if that was where her memories were stored. She wrapped her arms around her body as if she was protecting herself.

"Next thing I knew, I was grabbed from behind and then my neck felt like a lightning bolt zapped through it. My whole body shook and I peed myself. I would've hit the concrete if the guy hadn't held me up."

"They used a taser gun. You didn't see anyone walking along the street, following you before that?"

"No. No one."

"They had the spot picked out. The second man must've been hiding before you got there." He told her with his eyes he understood her anguish. No one would blame her for what happened. "Tell me every detail," he said knowing she needed to tell someone the whole story. She'd kept ordeal inside too long.

"He tossed me into the back of the SUV like a rag doll. I remember seeing white, fluffy clouds floating across the sky and thinking I might never see them again. Then he leaned over me and sneered. I'll never forget, his breath smelled like peppermint. To this day I can't stand the scent. Then he slammed the hatch closed."

Will stood motionless, giving her time and space. Behind him, the stove's digital clock clicked over twice.

When Nicole finally looked at him, tears made her brown eyes shimmer. "I could see what was happening and hear them, but I couldn't move. I don't think I even blinked, just watched the clouds disappear. Then I must've blacked out because that's the last thing I remember until I woke up in the back of one of those big delivery trucks, like they use to deliver mattresses." She made a large square in the air. "My hands and feet were bound with plastic straps and I had duct tape over my mouth."

Katrina—

No she wasn't Katrina. She was Nicole.

Cautiously he moved across the short distance and stood opposite her with the tiled counter separating them.

Nicole's fingers worked the hem of her tee shirt, twisting and untwisting the material. He gave her a second before he asked. "Were you alone, in the truck?"

"No." She placed her hands on the counter, clamping her fingers together. "There were two other girls. I'd never seen them before. They were huddled together." She swallowed. "I'll never forget their eyes. They looked as forlorn and scared as I felt."

"How long were you in the truck?"

"Days. They didn't drive all the time. Sometimes we just sat still. We tried making noise once, by kicking the sides of the walls, hoping someone would hear us, but they opened the door and one guy put a gun to one of the girl's head and told us if we tried that again they'd kill us. We could've screamed our lungs out and it wouldn't have done us any good. From what I saw, we were sitting in a deserted parking lot."

"Did they stop anywhere else?"

"Yeah, but always on a back road with nothing around but trees. They gave us water, a bite of food and allowed us to go to… You know." Her cheeks flushed. "I guess a few days went by when Becca was thrown into the van with us. She landed up against me and we sort of stuck together from then on, until they took her away." Nicole's words choked.

He could see how hard recalling all this was on her, but d oing so was important, and she was remembering. Many victims blocked the memories and years of therapy passed before they realized they were no longer in danger. Telling their stories was freeing. The littlest detail could help his case. "How long were you all in there?"

"I'm not sure. I think six days. I tried to keep track by counting the seconds ticking off and then the minutes, but after I fell asleep a few times, I gave up. Then I made note whether I saw dark or daylight every time they opened the door to check on us and give us water and food." She rocked back and forth, seemingly uncomfortable. "It seemed like they never stopped driving."

This all took place eight years ago. Their operation could've shut down or moved. "Do you know where they took you?"

"A warehouse. It was dark when we arrived. I didn't see any signs."

"Anything you can remember will help us pin-point the location. Anything."

"There were just buildings. No trees." Her eyes widened. "Wait. I did see a sign, a bill-board sign, for a bakery. Patter's bread. I remember the name because my history teacher was Mr. Patter."

Will's pulse kicked up. Patter's bread was not a national brand. "Good. Very good. Did you smell bread baking?"

"No."

"What about inside the warehouse?"

"There were people working. They just looked past us like we weren't even there, like we didn't exist."

Will's stomach rolled. How could any human being stand by and watch as children were herded by them, knowing what would happen to them? That answer was easy. Those who were slaves themselves, trained by those controlling them, would do nothing.

Will's temples throbbed, contemplating the size of the ring responsible for the loss of so many young lives. "What were the people doing?"

"They were packaging stuff. Tee shirts, sweatshirts."

Her eyes widened. “Sports gear, I think. You know NFL and MBL jerseys.”

“Black market knock offs.” Good lead. He could check with the FBI and see if they had any leads. “Can you tell me anything else? What about smell. Close your eyes.”

She did as he said and inhaled a slow deep breath, before her eyes popped open. “Diesel fumes and grapes,” she said as if asking a question and not making a statement.

“Odd combination.”

“Maybe I’m wrong. It was so long ago.”

“You’d be surprised how the strange turns out to be accurate.” He gave her a reassuring smile. “You feel okay continuing?”

“Yes.” She nodded.

“Okay. What happened next?”

“They put us into a small room. Like an old refrigerator locker,” she said. “They gave us water and a real meal. Becca was sick and she got worse as time went by. She was diabetic and hadn’t taken her insulin in several days by then.” Nicole brushed her finger tip across her eye. “I think we were there two days before we were taken to a hotel in New York.”

“A hotel? How do you know you were in New York?”

“I saw the skyline when we entered the room. I think we were on the twenty-third floor.” She crossed her arms, hugging her waist. “We were ordered to take showers. The bathroom was huge and the shower was tiled and open, like my school’s gym shower. The men, they watched us. Becca was so weak by then, I had to help her, hold her up. The men thought we were lovers and made lewd remarks. They were disgusting.”

Nicole rubbed her hands up and down her arms. He

could see by the way her neck muscles worked that she was fighting the urge to vomit.

"Afterwards, we were examined by a woman. She said she was a doctor. When she told the head guy…"

Nicole's eyes brightened.

"One of the men called him Travis. When the doctor told Travis Becca and I were virgins, you would've thought by his actions he'd won the lottery." Her nose crinkled. "He got this big shitty grin. His chest puffed out. He kept saying *Yes*. Then he started making phone calls."

"To who?"

"Buyers." She looked away, as blush crept into her cheeks. "A little later, the other two girls were told to get dressed and they were hustled out. Travis told his men to take them back to the meat locker. Becca and I remained in the hotel."

Then her brow crinkled with pain as she recalled another memory.

"Becca feared if they found out she was diabetic they would get rid of her. Not eating properly and without her insulin, it was only a matter of time before…" Nicole's words choked and she took a moment before she continued. "The next morning Becca felt worse and by the afternoon, she was acting funny. Like she was on something. Her words were slurred. She kept falling asleep. Soon I couldn't wake her.

"Travis called the doctor back. I told her Becca was diabetic thinking she would help Becca, but she didn't. She told Travis and he called his two men back. We held onto each other, well, more me than her. She tried. She really did. Her eyes were glassy with tears. I pleaded with them to let her stay with me. I fought for her, but they wouldn't listen to me. Travis and his one man held me down while the doctor gave me a shot. I never saw Becca again."

A tear rolled down Nicole's cheek.

"Later, another woman came. She washed and styled my hair. She put makeup on me and dressed me in a sheer gown."

She shivered and stood and walked into the living room area. Drawing a breath, she looked at him. "Then the men came. Six of them. One by one. Each took their time looking at me. Touching me."

"Was Gorgon one of them?"

"Yes." She nodded. "He was the last. He and the man had words. I think they were bickering over a price. He owed Gorgon money. The next thing I knew, Gorgon pulled a gun and shot the man in the face."

Her stare was detached. Was she recalling the shock she'd felt at that moment or had the number of violent acts she'd witnessed since made her cold-hearted? He'd guess a little of both.

Well, he could scratch the name Travis off the mental list he made of things to check out later. "What about Travis' men? Were they there?"

"Yes. They did nothing. I think Gorgon got to them before he even walked into the room."

"And then Gorgon took you." Even to himself, his words sounded like a cell door closing.

"Yes." Tears shimmered on her lids before falling to her cheeks.

Will rounded the counter. He now understood why she had refused to testify against Gorgon. She feared for her family's life, but he also knew if she didn't help him many more young lives would be lost. He couldn't let that happen. There had to be a way.

Chapter Sixteen

The empathy in Will's eyes held Nicole in place. What was he offering her, a handshake on the promise to keep her family safe? A shoulder to cry on?

Oh, how she needed a shoulder to cry on, and strong arms to hold her and make her feel safe.

Nicole didn't want Will to see her cry, so she wrapped her arms around her waist and turned away from his reach. She couldn't recall the last time she truly felt safe.

Yes, she could. When she was nine. While at the county fair, she had thought she was all grown up and lagged behind her family and had become separated from them.

The sting of the tears on her cheeks brought the emotions she'd buried to the surface and Nicole bit back the pain which threatened to constrict her chest. She remembered a crowd had surrounded her, staring at her. Suddenly, her father had pushed through the throng and snatched her up into his strong arms. Fear had etched deep across his face. His hard muscles wrapped her so close she had gasped for air. Nothing ever felt so good.

Nicole closed her eyes. The tears which rimmed her lids cascaded over them. Dad had smelled of spices and home and love. She had squeezed her eyes closed tight then too, so as to never ever forget him.

Over the past nine years, Dad holding her was one of the memories she'd kept close to her heart. She sniffled and clamped her lips tight, fearing Will would hear her pain. The floor boards under her foot creaked.

"You're a strong woman, Nicole," Will said behind her.

Her knees wobbled and she locked them while wiping the tears from her cheeks with her palms. Stiffening her spine, she turned back to Will. "I don't feel very strong."

Will's hands now hung by his side and part of her regretted not snapping up the opportunity to walk into his arms.

"You are. You survived. Most don't. You lived in hell with the devil himself and you escaped the nightmare. Not only that. You saved Susie, and your son. That took courage, lady."

Courage? She never thought of herself as being a brave person, but she guessed Will was right. She had guts to even plan her escape, to go to the post office and get a box, and to acquire Becca's birth certificate. She'd known Gorgon would kill her if he found any part out, and yet, she had moved forward with her plan.

Will smiled at her.

He liked what she had done. But what kind of person would Will think she was if he knew the truth about what she almost did? "I thought about escaping while Gorgon was busy with her."

"But you didn't." His brow arched. He shoved his hands into his jean pockets. "I have a feeling you were the reason Gorgon never got to Susie. Am I wrong?"

She dipped her head once. "She had a fever. Gorgon would've given her to his men without a thought, as if he'd changed his mind about what he wanted for dessert. I told him she'd be alright by the next day. He believed me."

"You're quick."

She couldn't stop the heat creeping up her neck or the smile that pulled on her lips. "You think so?"

"I know so." He stepped toward her.

Will's tender gaze caressed her face with such reverence her pulse quickened sending her heart into a flutter against her ribs. She wanted to move toward him and allow him to put his arms around her, but she couldn't. Not until she was sure he wanted to hold her for her and not for what she could do to help him with his case. She lowered her eyes. "So will you keep your promise concerning my family?"

Will's nostrils flared as he inhaled. "The best way to protect your family from Gorgon and his mafia connections is to put them away for good. If you testify, we can do that."

"Gorgon has an army. You can't put them all away." Hatred for Gorgon, frustration over her crappy situation, and rage with herself for not being as brave as she needed to be, churned her burning stomach. She laced her fingers together in front of her. "I want to help but don't you see, I can't testify?"

Will stepped toward her. His brows knitted together and his jaw line was set like he held back words he wasn't sure he could share. "Every day Gorgon is loose, many lives are lost. If you hadn't been there for Susie, where would she be now?"

"Goddamn it! Don't you think I know that?"

"Sorry. I know you know." Will raised his hand. "It's just for the past three years I've worked on this case, and in that time, I've had to tell hundreds of parents we had no answers for them. The anguish in their eyes rips my heart out every time."

"Hundreds?"

"Yes." He nodded.

The number of victims set Nicole back on her heels. Listening to Gorgon and his men, she knew there were many, but she didn't think hundreds.

"Over fifty-eight thousand children disappear each year in non-family abductions, Nicole. How many do think Gorgon's ring is directly involved in?"

She felt numb inside.

"Do you know what happens to them?"

Again she stared at him while iced panic ran through her veins.

"Some, like you, are sold to one owner and if they're lucky, they remain with that owner. Most are sold to pimps. They're drugged up and made to work the streets as prostitutes, until they die. Some are sent overseas as slaves."

"What? Overseas? How do they get them out of the country?"

"Trafficking is a twenty-eight billion dollar a year business. They have their ways."

Vomit tickled the back of Nicole's throat. She swallowed hard. Was her life and the lives of her family any more important than those of the thousands of children? No.

An image of Luka popped into her head and sorrow flooded her heart. They would never have a normal life together as long as Gorgon lived. There had to be a way to take him down for good.

Will's eyes followed her as she paced back and forth.

"I understand you're afraid, but we need your help. You're our best chance to stop…"

Will's plea drifted away as she thought back over the years she spent with Gorgon. She had seen acts that would haunt her the rest of her life.

She had learned to understand their language word by word. They thought she understood nothing, but she had understood much. And she knew Gorgon kept his records in the safe in their house.

Her heart leaped.

Would the records be enough to help Will?

Nicole's hands trembled as she faced him and cut off his speech. "Gorgon keeps records in a safe in our house."

Will stopped in mid word. The blue of his eyes deepened to almost gray, telling her he was very interested. "What kind of records?"

"Contacts, transactions, bank account information. I heard him speak of them to his brother, in case anything would happen to him. Could you use them against him?"

"Possibly. Do you know where the safe is?"

"Yes. And I know the combination. If I give you the numbers, you could get to the documents. With them, you wouldn't need me, right?" She was nearly standing on her toes with excitement.

Will shook his head and her heels fell to the floor, along with her spirits. "Why not?"

"It's not that easy. Unless you collaborate what you know to a judge, we'll never get a search warrant."

Her throat suddenly went dry. "Would Gorgon find out later that I was the one who told you about the records?"

"Yes. His lawyers would have the right to know."

"But what about the reporters who keep their sources hidden?"

"We're not talking about showing up at a place and at a time a crime was supposed to happen. Or, looking for evidence that is lying out in plain sight—if we were invited into the home." He sighed. "As much as I hate to say this, we would be violating the bastard's rights if we broke into his safe. The courts would consider our actions to be an illegal search and seizure. The evidence would be inadmissible as evidence. I'm sorry."

Nicole nodded. "Yeah."

She went to the door and stared down on the lush

grass of her landlord's yard. She knew where the safe was.

Nicole trapped her bottom lip between her teeth. Hell, she even knew the combination. She could slip into the house and get all the evidence Will needed, if she had the guts.

She spun around and said before she could change her mind, "What if I get his records?"

"What? No!"

"Listen to me." She paced while running the scenario out in her head. "I've heard garbage is public property. I could put everything out with the garbage."

She stopped in front of Will and knew by the glint in his eyes she had hit on a way to take Gorgon down.

"I can't let you go back there, even if Gorgon isn't there. I'm sure there are alarms and—"

"No. Gorgon would never have an alarm system installed. He doesn't trust them. He fears they're a way for the government to know his business. Besides, he said guarding his home was his men's job. If they failed, he'd have their heads."

Will stepped back from her excitement and shook his head. "Even so, I can't let you—"

"I'm right. Aren't I?" She dared him to lie with her eyes.

"Yes, but I'm not going to let you risk your life."

"Testifying against Gorgon is just as dangerous. Maybe more." She lifted her chin and folded her arms across her chest. "Besides, it's not your choice. It's mine."

Chapter Seventeen

Will switched on his sedan's lights.

Long shadows fell across the rolling green hills lined with white fences. Dozens of horses dotted the landscape, ignoring the looming dusk and continued to munch on the sweet grass. In the distance, golden glows popped on, filling window panes. Families were gathering together inside. This time of night always made Nicole homesick.

An eighteen-wheeler zoomed by them like they stood still in the middle of the interstate, drowning out the soft rock melody on Will's car radio.

"He's flying," Nicole said, tucking behind her ear the strand of hair blown loose from her ponytail by the warm breeze coming in her partially opened window.

"Sure is." Will eased up on the gas a bit and kept his attention on the truck changing lanes in front of them.

A spasm picked her lower back and Nicole arched her spine as far as the seat belt would allow without unsnapping strap.

"Are you okay?" Will's gaze held a hint of concern.

Since he'd learned her secret, there was a difference in him. He treated her like she was a fragile package. His thoughtfulness made her smile. "Yeah. Just a little stiff. I'm not used to sitting still. Luka keeps me on the run pretty much. How long until we get to Gary and—"

"His wife's name is Sharon. We should cross into Pennsylvania in about twenty minutes and then another couple of hours or so until we roll into Scranton. I'll stop at the next rest area. It's a few miles ahead. I could stretch my legs too. Or how about some dinner? Are you hungry?"

"Not really. I'm still full from that burger."

"Pretty big, wasn't it?"

"Yeah. Good too, but if you want something—"

"No. I'm good," he said, patting his belly. "Besides, if I know Sharon, she'll have something waiting for us."

"Sharon sounds nice."

"She is. Great mom too, so Luka was in good hands."

"Hmm. You said before she was a marshal too. Did she work with you and Gary?"

"No. Gary and Sharon met at a fundraiser for a local kid's club. Sharon outshot him at some water pistol game. It was love at first squirt." Will chuckled. "At least that is what Sharon says. I know she's right, because Gary never stopped hounding her until she agreed to marry him."

"How long have they been together?"

"Seven years."

"So how long have you and Gary been partners?"

"Going on eight."

"That's a long time. You must know each other pretty well."

"Sometimes that is not such a good thing." He winked.

No one knew her that well. Luka was the closest person to her, but he was a child. She protected him from the world. She couldn't share her fears with him or her wishes to be held by a man, like Will.

The thought of Will's strong hands moving over her body caused her abdomen to clench with want. The temperature in the car shot up. She rolled down her window a little further and turned her heated face into the breeze. She was not going to go there. Desiring Will was fruitless. She had enough problems on her plate and before she could even think of a starting a relationship with any man, she had to get her life back.

The digital clock read eight-thirty. A couple more hours. She wiggled in her seat. She missed Luka so much. Nicole snagged her purse off the floor and plopped the leather bag onto her lap.

"Anxious to see Luka?"

"Yeah." Her cheeks warmed again, knowing Will had picked up on her anticipation. "He sounded excited on the phone, knowing I'd be sleeping with him tonight."

"He missed you. Sharon said he asked if you called almost every hour. FYI. He didn't ask for his dad."

Nicole dropped her gaze to her lap where her fingers played with her purse's strap. How had she left her son behind? At the time the decision seemed like the best for him. Thank God Will had been the agent with them. Another officer would've undoubtedly followed the letter of the law and given Luka back to his father or Gorgon's parents. Will had stuck his neck out for her and Luka. How could she ever repay him? Nicole moistened her lips. "Thank you."

Will's brow ceased. "For?"

"For keeping Luka safe. And for coming to find me."

"Just doing my job."

She saw Will's lips purse for a second and the way his fingers had tightened on the steering wheel. He wasn't fooling her. Both Will and his partner had gambled with their careers, by not turning Luka over to child services. "Right. I hope you won't get into trouble doing what you did. You know, giving Luka to Sharon."

"Maybe a slap on the wrist. Nothing I can't handle."

When she first met Will, he had come off as this bad ass cop who didn't know the word empathy, but Will had more heart than anyone she'd ever known. "Can I ask you a question?"

"Depends on whether the subject has to do with

national security." He shot her a lopsided smile and she couldn't help but smile too.

"What made you become a U.S. Marshal?"

His smile disappeared like her question had wiped his jovial mood away.

"I'm sorry. You don't have to answer if it's too personal a question."

His shoulders straightened. "I wanted to do something that made a difference in the world."

"You were instructed to give that answer, weren't you?"

Will smiled. "Part of the U.S. Marshal public relations speech, but it's true." He stretched his neck and she knew there was more to his story.

Nicole yanked on her seat belt, loosening it, and shifted on her seat, in order to face him, trapping her one leg under the other. "You know all about my past. Tell me something about yours. Where did you grow up?"

"About forty miles south of Pittsburg in a little town called Sawville."

He'd given the information without thought, so she'd assume he was telling her the truth. "Does your family still live there?"

"My parents do. My brother moved to Pittsburgh after he graduated from college. More jobs."

"What does he do?"

"He works in marketing for a large mushroom company."

Her nose crinkled. "Mushrooms?"

He chuckled at her reaction. "What? You don't like mushrooms?"

"No. Are you sure there is a mushroom company in Pittsburgh?"

"Yes. Pittsburgh area is one of largest producers of mushrooms in the world. They grow well in the old coal mines."

"Humph. You learn something new every day." She snuggled into the seat, feeling very comfortable, talking to Will like they were old friends. "Did you like living in Sawville?"

"Yeah. It's a nice place. A small town of about a thousand people. Everyone knows everyone."

"Humph. Sawville sounds a lot like my home town." She pushed away the melancholy feeling before the mood settled on her shoulders. "So why did you leave?"

"I joined the army."

"Really?"

He glanced at her from the corner of his eye and then concentrated on passing a tractor-trailer. "Does that surprise you?"

"No. Where were you stationed?"

"Several bases here in the states and I served in Germany for two years."

"What did you do?"

"Classified."

"I should've guess." She sniggered. "How long were you in the army?"

"Just four years. I got out and applied for a position with the U.S. Marshals. Here I am."

"So, why the Marshals and not the FBI or CIA or Secret Service?"

"You're not going to give up, are you?"

She smiled. "I'd like to know. There's not much you don't know about me. It seems only fair."

The Beatles song 'Yesterday' filled the silence between them and Nicole thought how appropriate the song was to their conversation, and their lives.

Will's upper lip curled between his teeth. Lines edged the corners of his squinting eyes. Whatever Will would share was going to be very personal.

"I joined because of my best friend, Joe," Will said. "We knew each other our entire lives."

"He's a U.S. Marshal too?"

"No." His nod was almost nonexistent.

She had a bad feeling and was almost afraid to ask where Joe was, but since she'd pushed Will to open up, she had to listen. "So what does Joe do?"

"Nothing." Will's Adam's apple dipped low in his neck as he veered the car to the right side, taking the exit for the rest area and making her scrabble for the console to regain her balance and to keep her purse from falling off her lap. "He's dead."

"I'm so sorry." Her heart told her to reach out to him, but his glare kept her hands on the console and purse. "What happened?"

"Long story." Will steered into the first open parking spot, jammed the sedan into park and threw the door open. "I'm going to use the rest room. Lock the doors. If anyone comes near the car, lay on the horn."

Without giving her a chance to respond, he was gone.

Under the security lights, Nicole noticed Will's broad shoulders bowed. She had a feeling there was more to Will's story. Something that tormented him.

She wished there was something she could do to help him.

***

Metal tinged against metal as Will threw doors wide, searching the restroom stalls for anyone inside. Satisfied he was alone, he hit the sink and splashed handfuls of water onto his face. Cold droplets clung to his nose and whiskers. He was so goddamn mad he swore steam spiraled from the beads.

"What the fuck is wrong with you?" he growled at his refection. No one besides his family, Gary, and his ex-girlfriend, Laura, the woman he'd thought he'd spend his life with, knew the truth behind what drove him to walk into scum-hell and kill the sons-of-bitches that stole lives. And he regretted baring his soul to Laura. Yet, just now, he almost spilled his guts to Nicole because she asked. Why? Was it because she was a victim, like Joe's sister? Or did he because every damn time she looked at him with those big puppy-dog eyes his gut twisted and he wanted to pull her into his arms and keep her safe.

Damn, he was tired. He washed away his next thought with another handful of water and yanked a half-dozen paper towels from the dispenser and scrubbed his face dry. A few more hours and they'd be at Gary and Sharon's house, then he could get a decent amount of sleep. In the meantime, he had to keep his mouth shut and focused on doing his job which was to keep Nicole safe so she could help him take down the largest trafficking ring the northeast had seen in years. Right now, she sat alone in a car in a semi-dark parking lot visible to anyone. Damn. He was a stupid fuck.

***

Will had been exceptionally quiet since they'd left the rest area. Nicole smoothed her moist palms along her blue-jeans and then readjusted her purse's strap on her shoulder. She wondered if she had upset him in some way by asking about his past or had he called Gary while in the restroom and some new development had occurred. She was going find out soon enough if the latter had happened.

Nicole stayed a step behind Will as he led the way up the sidewalks leading to Gary and Sharon's home– a nice two story in a nice neighborhood. The lights dotting the property showed off the beautiful landscape of the maintained large yard. The house was the kind of home she was raised in. The kind of home Luka deserved. She would earn him that life by laying her own on the line.

Inside, she heard the squeal of children and the patter of fast moving feet climbing stairs, sending Nicole's heart thumping against her rib cage.

Will pressed the lit doorbell and a scale of chimes flowed through the air.

She ran her tongue across her parched lips.

"Relax," Will said, nudging her elbow. "There is nothing to be nervous about."

She nodded, unable to get a handle on the ball of nerves rolling in her stomach at meeting Gary's wife—the woman who cared for her son the last two weeks and in all likelihood knew her story.

The door opened and Nicole fought the urge to step behind Will.

"Hi, Will." Sharon's height surprised Nicole. The woman didn't have to stretch her neck to stare Will in the eye. "And this must be Nicole. I've heard so much about you from Luka I feel like I know you."

The woman's words smoothed Nicole's jangled nerves. She smiled and placed her hand in Sharon's firm grip. "Nice to meet you too."

"Come on in." Sharon pulled her across the threshold into a small tiled foyer. "You must be anxious to see Luka."

The door closed behind her. She didn't have to look over her shoulder to make sure Will was there. She felt the comfort of his body heat through her thin sweater.

"Yes. Yes. I am."

"Where's Gary?" Will's tone held a bit of business, making her wonder again if something was up and reminding her, this family had put their lives on the line to help her and Luka.

"Where else? In the study, on the phone." Sharon crossed to the stairs and called toward the second floor, "Luka, you have company."

"Is my mom here?"

At hearing Luka's voice, Nicole stepped forward. She clutched the banister in an attempt to not be rude and charge up the stairway, invading the Wayne's home without permission. "I'm here." Her words had come out choked. She glanced past Sharon's smile and met Will's twinkling eyes. How was she ever going to repay him?

"Mom."

Will nodded toward the upstairs landing. Never had she seen a more glorious sight than her son charging down the stairs, wearing a glow that would outshine a hundred birthday candles.

"Luka." Nicole dropped to her knees, her purse slipping from her shoulder to the floor, and clung to her son, breathing in his scent. Their hearts pounded together. She was such a fool. She'd never leave him behind again. Never.

Through bleary vision, Nicole looked up. Two boys, twins, about Luka's age knelt on the floor, peeking between the spindles and down at them. They favored their father more than their mother.

Placing a kiss at Luka's temple, she pulled back. "I'm here."

"Why are you crying, mom?"

Worry and fear darkened Luka's raven eyes. Her screw up had put him through hell too. Damn. She was an idiot. Nicole swiped the tears from her cheeks. But that was the past. They were moving beyond the past. "I'm just happy to see you, baby. Have you been a good boy for Mrs. Wayne?"

"He certainly was," Sharon said, ruffling Luka's hair. "I couldn't have asked for a more polite guest."

"I'm proud of you." Nicole smiled at Luka and then grabbed her purse and rose, pulling Luka close to her side. "Thank you for taking care of my son."

"You're welcome." Sharon clapped her hands and shot a glance at both Will and Nicole. "Now, you've had a long drive. I'm sure you'd like to wash-up. I made an apple pie today and I have coffee and tea just about ready. Will, why don't you head down to the study and let Gary know you're here and we're ready whenever he is."

"I can do that." Will headed down the hallway along another railing which Nicole assumed was a second set of stairs leading to the basement. Rounding the corner, he gave her a reassuring look before he disappeared down the stairs.

"They won't be long," Sharon said before turning her attention to her two sons. "Have you guys finished cleaning up those toys?"

"Ah, mom," a chorus of two whined.

Sharon took a super mom stance. "I've already let you stay up way beyond your bedtime because we have a special guest, but there will be no late night snack until everything is cleaned up."

"What's the snack?" The twin on the right clipped.

Sharon cocked her head to the side. "Does it matter?"

The twin on the left elbowed his brother. "No."

"Good. Luka is going to help too." Sharon pointed up the stairs to Luka. "When you're finished and everything is put away, meet us on the patio."

"Are we doing s'mores?" Excitement pitched the boys tone.

"Maybe."

"Yea, we're doing s'mores," Luka cheered as he

raced up the stairs and followed the scrambling twins.

Sharon laughed. “Your son catches on quick. He’s a smart kid.”

Luka had been in good hands. “Thank you. For everything you’ve done. I don’t know how I’ll ...” Nicole dropped her gaze to the floor, clutching her purse.

Sharon took her hand. “The words are enough. I’m just happy I could help you. You’re one strong lady, Nicole. I like a woman with guts.” A smile grew on Sharon’s lips. “Come on, I’ll show you to the powder room and then you help me carry the trays out to the patio.”

“Sure.” Nicole returned the smile, knowing she had a friend in Sharon.

Chapter Eighteen

"Are you fuckin' nuts?" With his fists planted on his desk, Mike Adams, Will's superior, scowled down on him. The man's face grew a deeper shade of red with each tic of the bold-faced clock hanging on the side wall above them.

Gary had used the same exact words just last night, after the kids were tucked in bed, when he and Nicole had laid out their plan to enter Gorgon's house and break into his safe. This morning, it took him an hour to convince his team there wasn't a better way for them to get to the Novokoffs and stop the madness now.

With Gary, Chase, and Aden watching their backs and Jolene and Kyle planted underground, Will felt their chances of pulling off Nicole's idea could work. He glanced over at Gary who shifted uncomfortably on the hardback chair. His friend's eyes were trained forward. Chase and Aden stood behind him. While his team supported his decision, apparently he was going to have to sell the captain the hair-brained scheme himself.

"I'm waiting, Haus. Are you nuts?" the senior officer spat.

Will met Adams' glare head on. "No, sir. I am not nuts."

"She's a victim, goddamn it." Adams pounded the desktop before stalking around the office. "We can't let her go back there, after she escaped. Her parents want her back."

"No one told them she's been found, have they?" The wooden armrests of the chair seemed to soften under

Will's clenched fingers. He promised Nicole no one would contact her family.

"No. Not yet."

Relief washed through him. "Don't."

Adams stopped alongside his desk and glared down at him. "Who are you to order me?"

Will lifted his chin. "I'm not ordering you."

"Sounded like an order to me. Didn't it, Gary?"

"A request, sir," Gary said.

"That's what I heard," Chase chirped.

Glancing over his shoulder, Will caught Aden's nod.

Adams chuckled between a sneer. "Your team's got your back."

"Yes, sir." Will relaxed against the chair's back. "Besides, Nicole is twenty-four. An adult, and able to make her own decisions."

Adams stopped. "If I okay this hair-brained scheme and anything happens to her, my ass will be dog meat."

"No one is taking a greater risk than Nicole," Will replied. "I respect her decision."

Standing in front of them again, the captain continued his rant for another minute before ending with, "The op is too dangerous. No. No way."

Fear had prickled Will's gut from the moment Nicole proposed her plan. The smoldering determination he'd seen in her charcoal eyes told him she would try to get to the evidence with or without his help. Thanks to him, she knew Gorgon's records were her bargaining chip for a new life for her and Luka.

Will shifted forward on the chair and stared up at Adams. "Do you have another solution to this scenario, because I don't?"

His captain shoved his burly hands into his pants pockets. "Talk some sense into her. Make her testify."

"She's not going to testify, and I understand why.

She fears for her family's lives. If the Novokoffs so much as hear a rumor she's surfaced and is willing to talk, they'll kill them, eventually. We can't stand guard on all of them twenty-four seven forever. I can't say I blame her for not testifying."

"And, I can't see how I can put her life and those of my men in danger."

"We put our lives on the line every day. As for Nicole, in her own words, it's her choice." Will stood so he'd be eye level with Mike. "I got a feeling if we don't help her, she'll go on her own. No. I know she will, and I wouldn't let her go by herself."

"And if I order you not to help her?"

"Then I guess I'll have to turn in my resignation."

Gary jumped up beside him. "Will."

"No. man." Will shook off Gary's hand on his shoulder, knowing Chase and Aden had stepped forward. "I promised Nicole I'd help her, and I will. One way or the other."

Adams leveled his gaze on him. "You'd give up your career to help this woman?"

"Yes, and to stop others from becoming Gorgon's victims."

"How do you know you can trust her?"

"She's a victim. You said it yourself."

"She's also been under the Novokoff's influence for eight years. She could've turned. She could be setting a trap for us."

"She tried to put Gorgon in the morgue. All this woman wants is her life back, to raise her child in peace and to keep her family safe."

The captain huffed and then set his jaw. The fire in his eyes dimmed.

Will sensed Mike was working the aspects of the operation out in his head.

"All we need is my team to run interference," Will said, trying to help cement the plan in Mike's mind. "I'll be the only one on the property with Nicole. She says she can be in and out within ten minutes."

"Ten minutes?" Mike's gray brow arched.

"Yes. In and out, and we've got all the evidence we need to take the Novokoffs down for good."

Silence, like sludge, hung in the air. Just the breathing of his men provided movement on anyone's part.

The captain dropped onto his chair, causing its cushion to exhale. He ran a hand over his thinning hair. "Okay. Set things up. But if things go down on the wrong side, internal will have your head."

Excitement and angst mixed in Will's veins. As long as Nicole's and her family remained safe, he was good with taking the fall.

Chapter Nineteen

Nicole's hot breath pressed against her lungs waiting for the moment she'd exhale and inhale fresh air, while she crawled under the ten foot high chain-linked fence near the lot's back corner. The ground was soft because that was where Max always buried his bones, and escaped on occasion, to visit his girlfriend—the golden retriever three houses down.

God, she hoped her scheme worked. August fifth was not the date she wanted engraved on her tombstone, or on Will's.

Once inside the fence, Nicole listened for any movement for a few seconds before she scurried in a crab-crawl to the stand of pine trees near the back of the house. She wiggled below the branches into the soft bed of needles. A foot away, a pair of mice scurried away, disturbed from their nest by her intrusion, and Nicole captured her cry by stuffing her fist into her mouth. Damn, she hated mice. The only thing she hated more was snakes and she prayed like hell she didn't see or feel any of them tonight.

A toenail moon hung low in the star studded sky to the west. The heavy scent of pine surrounding her did little to abate the turmoil occurring in her stomach while she stared at the two-story house that had been her prison for eight years. She'd heard the saying 'knees knocking', but had never felt the sensation with such power until this very moment. How did she ever think she'd have the nerve to pull this off?

A snap behind her pulled Nicole's attention. Every

nerve in her body tingled, waiting for the moment she'd be drug from her hiding place.

A second later, Will silently inched alongside her right side and she left out a low sigh of relief. She wished he had let her come on her own. If they were discovered, they'd both die. Will was a good man. He didn't deserve to die at Gorgon's hand.

"Are you okay?" His elbow nudged hers.

He sounded so calm. How could he be so cool? She felt like a jiggling Jello under her skin. Nicole nodded--afraid a whisper would alarm Gorgon's men who stood guard over the property a mere hundred yards away.

If she wasn't scared shitless, she might've laughed at his appearance, which mirrored her own. With every inch of exposed skin smudged with black soot and dressed in black from head to toe, Will was barely visible, except for the whites of his eyes and teeth. When he smiled that smile, her heart leaped in her chest.

A cool breeze carried the sweet perfume of her petunias bordering the house across the lawn, rattled her wind chimes and rustled the limbs over their heads.

Will leaned toward her, his shoulder pressing against hers and held her gaze. "You don't have to do this."

She worked moisture into her throat and whispered, "Yes. I do."

"What if the dog starts barking?"

"He won't. He'll pick up my scent before he sees me."

"We're a go," Gary's voice came through their ear plugs.

Will pulled his Glock from his shoulder harness. The light from the pole hanging over the garage doors cut across his face and she saw the concern in his blue eyes.

Nicole swallowed the fear clogging her throat and affirmed she too was ready, with a single nod.

Will nudged her shoulder and spoke into his mic. "We're a go."

In the distance, tires squealed and a moment later headlights appeared through the large iron entrance gate. The driver laid on his car's horn, breaking the silence of the night and sending the neighborhood dogs into an uproar. To cause more chaos, Will's man, Chase, acting out his part in the ruse, rolled down his window and yelled in the direction of Gorgon's men. "Goddamn controller isn't working again. Come on. Open the funkin' gate, Jill. I'm tired."

From inside the house, Nicole heard Max join in on the ruckus.

Nicole and Will watched as Gorgon's men scanned the house, pulled their guns and cautiously moved toward the gate. One guard punched the keypad positioned on the brick wall holding the gate. The smaller walk-through gate opened and the other guard approached the driver. "You have the wrong house, buddy."

"Who the hell are you?" Chase slurred his words and acted as if he was drunk.

"Go," Will instructed her while aiming his gun in the direction of the pandemonium ensuing at the front of the property.

Nicole's pulse throbbed in her temples. She squirmed out from under the tree, pushed off, and sprinted toward the back door. She dropped onto her knees and lifted the rubber covering of the doggie door and then slid the panel up. While holding the heavy rubber in place, she pulled her shoulders together and wiggled through the opening, letting the rubber mat fall back into place. Inside the mudroom, she waited a second, taking in her surroundings.

Max still barked at the front of the house. He probably stood up at the window's ledge in the living room.

She had to move. Will's man wouldn't be able to distract Gorgon's guards for long.

Not wasting another second, Nicole stood and made her way into the kitchen. As she rounded the corner, she was met with a low growl and in the shadows saw Max, who now stood with his teeth bared in the foyer. She dropped onto one knee and called to him, "Come here, boy."

The dog's tail thumped against the wall. He jogged to her side and lowered his head waiting to be rubbed down.

"Good boy." Nicole buried her face in his coat. "I missed you too."

Shouts from outside reminded her why she was there and without further hesitation she raced up the stairs, with Max on her heels. At the doorway to the bedroom where she'd spent nights crying for freedom under Gorgon's hand and where she'd taken a stand, she drew a breath and was assaulted with the slight scent of bleach. They'd cleaned up Gorgon's blood and other body fluids which had spilled onto the floor after her attack on him.

Gorgon wouldn't ever hurt her ever again. She pushed away her fear, steeled her nerves and headed to the wall where the safe was housed. Moving her fingers along the frame work, she found the switch and a moment later the bookcase moved to the side.

Her fingers trembled over the numbers on the keypad. One wrong number and she would be locked out for twenty minutes. She didn't have twenty minutes.

You're a strong woman. Will's words came back to her. She inhaled a deep breath. She had to believe in herself.

Tap, tap, tap, tap. Not second guessing her memory, Nicole entered the four digit code. "Yes!" She patted

Max's head as the locking mechanism released and the door clicked open.

She pulled the heavy duty garbage bag she'd brought from her pocket and pulled all the files and a flash drive from the safe and stuffed them inside the bag. A expandable folder remained in the back corner. Gorgon sashed cash in the packet. He would have no use for this money in jail. She, however, would be supporting Luka. Careful not to disturb the wire she carried, Nicole pulled up her shirt and tucked the pouch into her bra between her breasts. She closed the safe and moved the bookcase back into place.

A beam of light swept the room, causing Nicole's heart to leap into her throat. On tip toes, she moved to the window and drew the sheer curtain back a fiction of an inch. The car had pulled away from the front gate, and Gorgon's men were walking up the driveway toward the house.

She grabbed the garbage bag and ran down the stairs. This time Max led the way.

***

"Damn," Will cursed under his breath. Ten minutes had passed.

He watched Gorgon's goons stroll in his direction. His heart thumped against his arm tucked under him. They were heading in to do a sweep of the house. If so, they'd find Nicole. What the hell was he going to do?

Fuck. He should've never left her go in there.

"We have a problem," he whispered into his mic, knowing she could hear him too.

"What's going on?" Gary came across clearly.

"Bird is still in the nest and hawks are circling."

"Don't do anything stupid, eagle. Sit tight," Gary

ordered.

"Make your way to the front gate," Nicole broke into the conversation, sounding cooler than a summer cucumber just hanging on a vine.

"I'm not leaving without you," he growled into the mic, keeping his voice low. His fingers tightened around the hilt of his Glock.

"Do as I say," she ordered. "I have a plan, but you need to move before they open the door."

Bathed in the outside garage light, the men stopped in-line with the pines.

"Did you hear something?" One goon asked the other.

With his breath captured in his lungs, Will held his position and his finger on the trigger.

The men scanned the surrounding area, listening beyond the crickets chirping in the night.

A cloud moved across the moon and as if on cue the breeze rustled the wind chimes hanging off the patio roof.

"Nah. You're hearing things. Come on. I'll keep a watch on the gate while you check the house this time."

Both men walked toward the back door.

"Will, you need to move now. Go," Nicole whispered into his ear. "The smaller gate code is zero eight zero eight. Trust me."

She could see him. Will scanned the house and he saw a dark shape cross the kitchen window. She was walking right toward them. What the hell was she doing?

"Do what she says, Will," Gary ordered.

With his eyes trained on the men, Will reluctantly shimmied back and out from under the branches. Careful to remain in the shadows he made his way toward the front gate, glimpsing over his shoulder every few feet. When he neared the exit, he heard the wild barking of a dog and one of the men bellow, "Get him."

The dog ran around and under the pine tree, sniffing the spot he'd just vacated. He knew then Nicole had hoped that the dog would lead the men away from the house.

Will hit the keypad and slipped through the gate, holding the wrought iron ajar. He watched as the dog raced in circles around the yard sniffing, undoubtedly picking up his scent. He had to get out of there before the dog led Gorgon's men right to him, but how could leave Nicole behind?

He couldn't.

He stood pasted against the bricks like a fly on a wall and sent a prayer up that somehow they'd get out of this mess.

Meanwhile, Nicole watched from inside the back door, waiting and hoping. When Max headed toward the back yard where Will and she had entered the fence, she let out the breath she didn't realize she'd been holding. "That a boy, Max."

The moment Gorgon's men disappeared into the pines, Nicole slipped out the back door, tiptoed along the house and then sprinted across the front lawn, hoping her rubber legs could make the distance, and Gorgon's man didn't see her. Had Will waited for her?

As she approached, the gate swung wide. Her grin grew as she raced through the opening and she saw Will.

He grabbed her hand and together they raced across the street and disappeared into the night. She pumped her legs in double time, trying to keep up with his long strides.

Just when she thought her lungs would burst, a car swung around the corner ahead, flooding the street with its white beams. Will dove in between Cypress trees which edged a wall surrounding another home, yanking her with him.

They watched from the shadows as the car passed by them.

"Damn. That was close," she said while gulping the warm night air and pressing her free hand against her stomach. Ringlets of hair escaped her ponytail and lay pasted against her cheek.

"Too close for my comfort." Will's fingers tightened around hers in a reassuring tug. "Don't worry. We'll figure out another way to get Gorgon."

"What are you talking about?" She arched her brow. "I got the files. They're in a bag among the other garbage in the laundry room. I couldn't bring it with me. They'd have noticed a lone bag on the curb. First thing tomorrow morning, the cleaning lady and yard man will carry the bags to the curb and then you'll have everything you need. Gorgon will not know everything is gone until it's too late." She smiled. "I told you not to worry."

"That is easier said than done. I thought you were trapped and those goons would find you."

"You would've stopped them."

"Yeah, somehow." His throat muscles worked while he stared to the sky. When he looked at her again, his scowl had softened. He turned her wrist over and switched off the receiver and then did the same to his. Looking down at her, he said, "If anything would've happened to you, Nicole, I would've never forgiven myself."

He brushed his thumb over the back of her hand, sending tingles up her arm and down her spine.

"I'm okay, Will. Really."

He pulled her against the hard plane of his body without warning, causing Nicole to gasp. His strong arm wound around her waist and anchored her in place. Flames of desire flashed in his blue eyes.

Warmth pooled between Nicole's legs.

Will's gaze dropped to her lips.

Oh, my God. He was going kiss her. She lowered her eyes to his chest where his heart pounded against her palm, separated by only the thin fabric of his dark shirt. As much as she wanted him to kiss her, how could she be sure Nicole was who he wanted to kiss and not Katrina. Only forty-eight hours had passed since he'd learned the truth about who she was. Until that point she had been Katrina to him.

She was no longer that woman, the woman who pleased men because that is what they wanted. Until she knew for sure who he desired, she couldn't give any part of herself to him. She pushed away. "Please don't."

Will let her go. "I'm sorry. I thought—"

"You thought wrong." She smoothed her hands over her hips not knowing what to do with them. "I'm not that person. I'm not Katrina."

His spine stiffened as if she'd slap him. "What? No. I don't—"

A crackle behind them caused Will's attention to shoot over her shoulder. In a blink, his Glock appeared in his hand.

Nicole spun around, expecting to feel the punch of a bullet to her chest.

Out of nowhere, Max buzzed into the bushes and in a fit of joy jumped on her, knocking her back against Will's hard frame.

"Settle him down," Will whispered in her ear.

She grabbed the dog's collar and tried to calm him. "Yes. Good boy. You found us."

"If he found us, Gorgon's men can't be far behind. We need to move now." Cooler air surrounded her as Will side-stepped her and Max, and peeked out from their hiding place.

"We need to take him with us." Nicole latched onto

the dog's collar. "Luka and I have missed him so much."

"I don't have much of a choice, do I?" Will said, looking over his shoulder at her and then down at the dog wagging his tail wildly and rustling the tree beside them.

She couldn't help the smile forming on her lips. "I guess not. "He'll follow us."

Chapter Twenty

Papa's driver made the sharp turn into the driveway, slowly. The iron-gate protecting the six acre estate parted and the limo passed the armed men standing guard. Gorgon couldn't see their eyes through the sunglasses they wore, but he knew they watched for a glimpse of him.

His villa came into view and Gorgon's fingers tightened around the smooth handle of the cane he held. He closed his eyes and remembered the jostle of the gurney and how he fought to open his eyes only to see the flash of red and blue lights crossing the roof line and reflecting off the windows. The memory of his heart fighting to keep life flowing through his veins caused a chill to crawl up his spine now.

"Why do you have to come back here?" Mama scowled beside him. She gathered her thin sweater together over her chest as if they approached a frozen hell.

"Mama, please leave Gorgon be," Donnie said. "He's been through enough."

Gorgon opened his eyes and caught his brother's sympathetic wink. Donnie knew how much he missed his old life.

"Leave him. Umph. Gorgon needs to use his head," Mama scolded her youngest son and then turned back to him. "You should be going home to your wife. Not here. Eva waits for you."

The car came to a stop and his brother opened the door and exited first.

"As she should." Gorgon snapped, clenching his jaw at the thought of spending night after night sharing his bed with the woman who was as dry as the sands of Egypt, and not with his Katrina. How he longed to feel his kitten's soft hair wrapped around his fingers while she pleasured him with her full lips.

"Do not speak to your mother with such a tone," Papa reprimanded him before stepping out of the car.

Papa did not understand his feelings. He married for love and not to bring peace between two families as he had.

Uncomfortable sitting next to his mother, Gorgon slid along the limo seat, putting inches between them. "Forgive me, Mama," he responded loud enough so papa would hear and smooth the old man's ruffled feathers. "I just need to get a few things and then we will go."

"I will not cross the threshold of that brothel." Mama plopped her purse on her lap and stared out the front window.

He didn't care if mama came inside or not. She never had stepped foot in the house before when her own grandchild was inside. The only time his mama would acknowledge Luka was when Katrina was not present. "As you wish."

Feeling a twinge of pain, Gorgon slid to the edge of the limo's seat. His mother had never approved of his relationship with Katrina. She should've understood though. She'd said often enough over the years, the heart wants what the heart wants. Why would the adage not apply to him?

Gorgon took his time stepping from the car with the help of his father. Every minute stretch of his abdominal muscles sent a stabbing pain through his gut.

Clenching his jaw, he pulled himself to his full height, and stared down at his father. He nodded toward the car. "Why did you not leave her at home?"

"You are her son. There was no stopping her from coming to the hospital and seeing you home safely."

Papa followed Donnie up the stairs leading to the front door.

Gorgon turned his face to the bright sun. He drew in a breath of air that wasn't tinted with antiseptic, but with the fresh scent of newly mowed grass. He didn't expect anyone to understand his reasoning for coming back here to the house he had shared with Katrina. He didn't understand the need himself.

With a heavy heart, he made his way into the house.

Then against his father's protests, he climbed the stairs one at a time to the second floor. He needed a moment alone.

Gorgon stood at the corner of the bed. The bedding was gone, as was the carpet. Images of his blood soaking into both blurred his vision. He shook as the hard lines of Katrina's face replaced them. Why had she acted so? Their life had been perfect. He had treated her like his queen, spending more nights with her than with Eva.

The girl. He brought the girl home. Had Katrina been jealous over her?

The only reason he had was because the girl had been worth a half-million dollars. Because she was a virgin and was beautiful and played classical piano, the teen was made to order for one of Gorgon's richest clients. She had been targeted and he didn't want to take a chance of anything happening to her before he could make arrangements to have the girl exported out of the country.

Katrina should've trusted him. He would make her understand her mistake when he found her.

"Gorgon, are you alright?" His father's bellow from downstairs broke his muse.

"Ya. I will be there in a moment." He walked to the bookcase with a plan to find Katrina already forming in his mind. The bookcase moved to the side and he entered the code into the safe's keypad. Staring into the empty box, his mouth went as dry as Eva's cunt. "Son of a Bitch."

A cold bead of sweat trickled down Gorgon's spine. With his left hand trapped against the pain gnawing at his stomach, he rushed from the bedroom. His cane hammered against the hardwood floor like rapid gun fire. Donnie hadn't removed the contents of his safe. He would've said so.

God help them all.

The foyer below was empty. As quickly as he could, Gorgon made his descent down the staircase. The rush of despair made his mind swim and his vision blurred.

Fearing he'd fall the few steps remaining to the tiled landing, he clutched the banister and gulped in breaths of a warm breeze that rushed through the open front door. The sweet scent of the petunias Katrina had planted rode on the gust and caused Gorgon's stomach to roll.

"What are you doing climbing stairs?" His mother hurried through the threshold, shaking her finger at him. "The doctor gave you orders—no stairs. Already you do not listen."

"Where's Donnie? I need to talk to him." Gorgon straightened, ignoring the moisture blotting his brow. His hands trembled on the cane and the railing. "Donnie, where are you?" He yelled.

"Yegor." His mother ran up the stairs, grabbed his arm and helped him down the last few steps. "Yegor, come here. Gorgon needs you."

Out of the corner of his eye, his father and Donnie rushed into the foyer from the hallway leading to the kitchen.

"What in the hell is going on?" Yegor questioned.

Gorgon avoided his father's uneasy scrutiny and stared at his brother. "Donnie, did you take my things out of the safe?"

Donnie's brow furrowed. "No. Why?"

He shook off his mother's hand and took a step down. "Someone was."

"What? How can that be?"

"You tell me. The men were on guard, right?"

"Yes. 24/7. What is gone?"

"Everything."

Donnie's face paled. He knew of some of the records Gorgon kept locked in there.

"Shit." His brother shot up the stairs past him, apparently needing to see for himself that their operation and lives were in jeopardy.

"What is gone?" His father's bushy brows knitted over sharp eyes.

Gorgon's knees shook. He should sit down before he fell flat on his ass, but he wouldn't. Instead he balanced his weight on the cane, locked his joints and jutted his chin forward, knowing he had to face his father's rage. "All my records. My contracts. Bank information. Cash. Everything."

A crimson flush inched its way up Yegor's neck and past the man's jowls. "How could you let this happen?"

"I wasn't here. I was in the fuckin' hospital."

"Don't talk to your father like a hoodlum." His mother slapped his arm. "He is your father."

Papa grabbed mama's arm and directed her to the door. "Who knew where the safe was?"

"Donnie, the person who installed the unit, and…" he hesitated sharing the last name. "Katrina."

His mother spun and spat on the floor. "That whore was here? She should be buried in the bowels of hell for what she has done to you."

"Sophia, go to the car. We know how you feel about the woman. Go, now." The old man ushered the tiny woman out the door and then turned his hot glare to him. "How much information was in there?"

Gorgon clenched his jaw.

Apparently, seeing the downfall of the family in his eyes, Papa pointed toward the door. "We need to leave now. All of us."

Footsteps pounded the stairs behind him and his father's eyes lifted over his head.

"Donnie, call Gali and tell her to get ready," Papa ordered. "Until we know what happened to Gorgon's records, we all must leave the country." Then he turned back to Gorgon and poked his own head with his finger. "You have brought this evil upon us because you do not think."

The salty taste of his blood laced Gorgon's tongue. Maybe his father had been right. He should've killed Katrina after she had given him a son.

Chapter Twenty-one

The little bungalow with its slate roof and peeling window casings wasn't much but the house represented something Nicole hadn't felt in years, freedom. Even though she and Luka lived here a little over a month, Nicole's throat closed thick with emotion. She loved every inch of the little brick house including the rain gutters sprouting with spindly maple shoots and the sweet honeysuckle taking over the north side of the house.

What she loved most of all about this house was its location. Logan Summit was Will's hometown and knowing he was close by made her feel very safe.

People didn't know Will like she knew him. To the townspeople, he was a software engineer for a large communications company. The cover gave him a low profile and a valid reason for being out of town for days at a time, even weeks. Like this past week.

A bit of angst needled her, wondering if the reason he was gone was because of Gorgon, who had disappeared the same morning he'd been released from the hospital and the day the garbage containing his records had been picked up by the U. S. Marshal's Office. His whole family had gone underground.

Will had reassured her that the moment the Novokoffs resurfaced they'd be picked up and arrested. Gorgon's records were the nails needed for their coffins.

Nicole pulled back her sweater and blouse's sleeve and glanced at her watch. She was going to be late for work if they didn't hurry.

"Luka- Luke, let's go," she called and instantly

chided herself for the slip of tongue. She glanced around the quiet neighborhood and was relieved to see there was no one in sight. She had to think of him as Luke. Luke was doing better at not forgetting their new names.

"Coming. Max needed his treat and ball," he answered as he ran out of the house, pulling the door closed behind him.

Wearing a grin that stretched beyond his dimples, Luke bounded down the steps, struggling to loop his book bag over his shoulder while not dropping his lunch bag. He was in his third week of pre-kindergarten and still was as excited as he had been the first day. Gorgon never allowed him contact with any other children other than those of the family, and none of them had been Luke's age. He was like a little bird spreading its wings and enjoying new adventures every day.

One day the newness would wear off, she was sure, but for now he had not a care in the world.

She'd hoped and prayed for this life for so many years, but in all honesty, she never thought her dream would come true. She owed her good fortune to Will.

"Let me help you." She took Luka's lunch box.

"Can I go to Sam's after school?" Luka skipped and hitched his jeans up. "His mom said I could."

"We'll see."

Luca's smile faded like the shadows as the sun moved out from behind a cloud. "You always say that and then I can't."

"Sam's mom works too. I'm sure she's tired when she gets home."

"She is. That is why she said I can come over. I keep Sam busy. We keep each other busy." Hope sparked in his eyes.

Opening the back door of the 2000 sedan the government had given her, Nicole chuckled. Her son had a future in negotiating. "I understand that."

Luca scampered inside and settled onto the seat. His book bag hit the floor with a thud.

She caught the fresh scent of Luca's new laundered shirt while latching his seat belt. "Okay, tell you what. I'll think about it really hard this time, but right now I've got to get you to school, and I've got to get to work."

"Okay." Luca's feet wiggled with excitement.

Trying to make up time, Nicole hurried around the vehicle, sending her soft cotton skirt swirling around her calves.

A few minutes later, the memory of Luke's smile as he joined his friends in front of the school's double doors warmed her heart. Grinning, she drove under century old oaks which lined the residential streets and made her way into the business district.

Just before nine, she pulled into the back parking lot of Sara's Whimsical Gifts where the agency had obtained her a job. In the little mountain village known for its many outdoor activities, the little shop was the only one which carried unusual gifts and local artists' crafts. The job wasn't high paying. She probably could earn more as a waitress with tips, but she earned enough to support her and Luke's everyday needs and still managed to stash away some savings even though she didn't need to. Gorgon had had a hundred thousand dollars in the safe, which was hidden in her new home. She didn't have to worry about mortgages or car payments since the government had provided a home and car for her.

The tiny bell on the door tingled overhead announcing her arrival. Today's incense scent, spiced apple, tickled Nicole's nostrils.

"Good morning, Becca," her boss, Sara Brennan, called from the center of the store.

Nicole liked Sara the moment they'd met. Sara was a

small warm-hearted woman who often, out of the blue, recalled her days as a braless flower child bride. In fact, Sara still went braless because, as she stated more than once, she could, with her tiny bosom.

When those special memories rushed back at the older woman, Nicole envied the way Sara's peach and cream complexion glowed. One day she hoped to love a man as much as Sara loved her husband.

Why did Will's face always came to mind during that musing?

"Sorry, I'm late," Nicole said rushing through the aisle. "Luke needed a few extra minutes to say goodbye to Max. He just loves that dog."

"Pssh." Sara waved her off and then pushed her long blonde braid over her shoulder. "If the world was meant to run on a second hand, God would've installed wrist watches on our arms."

Nicole stored her purse under the counter and then pulled from a drawer an imprinted green and red apple apron that matched the one Sara wore.

"Thanks for being understanding. I'll get started on dusting the shelves in the back." She pulled the apron's strings tight around her waist and then grabbed the stepstool and headed to the rear of the store. Her flats padding the knotty pine flooring echoed among the store's many displays.

A short while later, the doorbell jangled and Nicole heard Sara call, "Hi, stranger. I haven't seen you around lately."

"Hi, Sara."

Will's deep tone grabbed Nicole's attention and almost caused her to lose her balance on the stepstool. She steadied herself with one hand and placed the smooth glass blown pumpkin she dusted back on the shelf with the others.

Will looked damn good sporting a shadow of a beard.

His intense gray gaze swept over her before returning to Sara.

"I was out of town on business, installing a new network system for a large hospital. How are you?"

Nicole focused on the display shelf in front of her. She swept her tongue across her lips and tasted the light berry tang of her lipstick. Her palms felt slick and she swiped them across her apron before picking up the next pumpkin. He was here to see her.

"You sure do travel a lot." Sara moved out from behind the central island hosting the registers.

"Believe me. The road is not all that great. I'm glad to be home."

"Well, what can I do for you today?"

Sara's thin frame blocked the aisle between her and Will.

"I need a get well card and gift for a friend." Will glanced over Sara's head and again met Nicole's eyes.

She smiled.

He didn't.

Her heart fell to her toes. Something was wrong. With a slight tremor, she guided the fragile orange globe between two others.

"Oh, I'm sorry to hear your friend is sick," Sara said pulling Will's attention back to her.

The phone next to the cash register buzzed.

"Oh, my. It was so quiet here this morning. Everything happens at once." Sara wavered between grabbing the phone and showing Will some of her wares. "I'm sorry, I need to get that. I've been waiting for a call from the artist scheduled to have a showing here this weekend. Could you wait a moment, or maybe Becca could help you choose something nice." Sara pointed in her direction.

"No problem. I'm in no hurry."

Nicole stepped down off the stool as Will approached. "I'd be happy to help you. So, is your friend a man or woman?" She asked loud enough for Sara to hear.

"Woman."

"Oh," Nicole wondered if Will was actually looking for a gift for another woman. Her heart dipped in sorrow at the thought. "We have a nice assortment of cards right over here."

Will glanced over his shoulder. Seeing Sara was busy on the phone, he took her by the elbow and propelled her further down the aisle to the back corner of the store. "I need to talk to you."

The hairs on the back of her neck prickled. "Is something wrong? Have you found Gorgon?"

"No. We learned Yegor, his wife, and their daughter-in-law have left the country by boat through the Florida Keys."

"When?"

"A few days after we broke into Gorgon's house."

"What about Donnie and Gorgon?"

"They're underground. I guess Gorgon wasn't in any shape for some rough traveling, yet. We're assuming his brother must've stayed behind with him."

Fear's icy finger tickled Nicole's spine, causing her to shiver. "Or he didn't leave on purpose."

Will's warm hands latched onto her arms and he gave her a reassuring squeeze. "Hey, you don't have to worry. He's not going to find you and Luka."

"Luke." She glimpsed in Sara's direction. Fortunately her boss was still busy with the caller and missed Will's slip of tongue.

"Right." Between them, Will's hands trailed down

her arms and captured hers. "Because of you, if Gorgon's nose so much as breaks the surface we'll nab him and lock him away for life."

She had to believe Will was right. Nicole inhaled and set her shoulders. "Okay. I'm going to trust you." She glanced at his fingers still encasing hers, and then smiled up at him. "So what did you need to talk to me about?"

"I was wondering if you're free tonight? I'd like to stop by the house. I have something to show you. Do you have anyone you can leave Luke with for an hour or two?"

She looked down at her chest, thinking Will would see the pound of her heart against her blouse. Was Will asking her out?

No. He said he had something to show her. Undoubtedly, whatever he had to share had to do with the case. That was why he didn't want Luka around.

"Well, his friend did ask him to come over today after school. I told him I would think about it. Maybe Sam's mother will keep Luke a little longer."

"Great. What time should I come over?"

They heard Sara end her conversation and the receiver drop into its cradle.

"I have to call her first, and I work until five-thirty. Maybe around six-thirty. Can I let you know?" Nicole said while glimpsing at Sara.

"Sure. You have my cell number." Glancing over his shoulder, he checked Sara's location before he plucked a stuffed puppy with a bandaged head off the shelf and said openly, "This is perfect, Becca. Gloria is a dog person. Thanks."

He went to turn when she reached out and touched his elbow stopping him. "Should I be worried?"

"No." He smiled. "Trust me."

Nicole returned his smile. "Okay."

Will walked to the middle of the store and paid Sara for the toy.

Switching her position and thus her line of sight a few times, Nicole admired Will's strong shoulders and hard backside as he walked away.

"That man likes you," Sara said after the door had closed behind Will.

She shrugged and climbed up on the step stool. "He seems nice."

"He is." Sara moved a figurine a little to the left on a shelf below. "You know what's odd about him?"

Nicole stopped dusting the shelf and looked down at Sara quizzically.

"I've had this store for more than ten years and I think Will Hanson has been in here maybe twice."

"So?"

"So, he's been in here three times in the past month."

"Maybe something in his life changed or he's found someone. You said he wasn't married, right?"

"I never said anything like that, but I do believe you're right. I think he's definitely found someone."

Warmth crept up Nicole's neck and flushed her cheeks.

Sara winked before she headed back to the front of the store.

How she wished what Sara thought were true, but Will was interested in her for only one reason. Gorgon and his family. Nicole chewed her lip. What did Will have to show her?

Chapter Twenty-two

Both anticipation at seeing Will again and angst over what he had to show her had Nicole wearing a path in her porch's cement pad. She stopped in front of the porch swing, back dropped by a veil of honeysuckle. Even her favorite spot didn't hold an appeal for her to sit and wait. Maybe she missed Will's call when she went to lock her car.

She rushed inside, leaving the screen door to bang behind her and checked her answering machine. No messages. Where could he be?

Did Will have a picture of Gorgon in handcuffs? Or, maybe one of him in the morgue? No. He wouldn't have made her wait to hear that good news.

Nicole crossed from the living room's side window to the larger windows overlooking the porch and drew back the thin linen drape and peeked out. To the west, the late summer sun sparkled among the leafy tops of the old maple trees lining Madison Street. Its dwindling rays spread murky finger shadows across her front lawn and cast tiny beams off her freshly washed car sitting in the driveway.

She looked down over her jeans and long tailed white shirt which were still damp from where water had splattered back at her while she'd rinsed her car. Should she run upstairs and change?

Who was she kidding? She frowned. Her appearance wasn't that important. Will's visit wasn't social. What he had to share had to do with the case.

Behind her, Max whimpered.

"Do you need to go out, boy? Okay, come on." She led the dog through the small dining room and kitchen to the back door, attached his security collar, and let him out into the back yard. Nicole glanced at the stove's clock as she passed by on her way back to the front of the house. Seven ten. Will was late. He had said he'd be here around six thirty.

Wringing her fingers together, she continued to pace the area carpet covering the living room's hardwood floor while disappointment overtook her excitement. Maybe Will had been called away on urgent business. No. He would've called her. Or would he? After all, what was she to him? Just someone he had to deal with because he was a U.S. Marshal and she was who she was.

Honesty kicked her in the ass. There was an undeniable connection between her and Will. She thought of him every day, wondering where he was, what he was doing, if he was safe, and longed to see his smile or hear his voice. Her nerves seemed to sense when he was close.

And Will, he seemed to stand a little taller when she watched him and his blue eyes glistened with lust.

Not to mention both of them seized every opportunity to touch the other in some way.

There was definitely attraction between them. But, could there ever be something more? She could hope all she wanted, but if she was going to be honest with herself, she knew differently. Again, Will was who he was and she was who she was.

Nicole spied the tail end of one of Luka's toy trucks sticking out from underneath the sofa's skirt and bent over to pick the metal eighteen wheeler up by the trailer.

Outside, Max barked a split-second before footsteps scuffed the front porch steps.

With her stomach doing somersaults, Nicole dropped the Matchbox into Luka's toy box tucked into the room's corner, smoothed her hands over her hair and headed to the front door.

Will was down on a knee giving a happy Max a rub down.

"Hi."

"He found me." He grinned, looking at her.

Watching Will, Nicole's chest tightened with happiness. "I see."

He gave Max a final pat before standing and peered down at her through the screen door. "Sorry I'm late. I hope I didn't hold you up."

The brown specks in his aqua eyes shimmered like rocks under an ocean's spray, and Nicole couldn't help grinning. "No. I hadn't planned anything tonight, other than seeing you." The ball of delight in the pit of her stomach seemed to lift Nicole's toes off the floor.

Will's sandy blonde hair, still damp from a shower, was combed back. Its ends curled over the collar of his red polo shirt. Like her, he was dressed casually in a long sleeved tee shirt, jeans and sneakers. Except for the jagged scar marking Will's jaw line and neck, he looked like an ordinary guy, not like a man who fought the filth of the underworld every day.

Max, bored from lack of attention, brushed against Will's legs one last time and trotted off the porch, leaving them alone.

Will's presence suddenly made Nicole nervous. "I didn't hear you drive up." Past his broad shoulders, she glanced at the driveway again. "Where's your car?"

"I walked." He poked his thumb over his shoulder. "I live a few blocks from here. Over on Jefferson Street."

"I didn't know that." Her heart skipped a beat thinking how close Will was to her, most of the time. A heartbeat later she chided herself. She was his job. The things he did for her and Luka weren't personal. Moving them here, to his hometown, to keep her close and safe, was the agency's decision, not Will's. Although, she suspected, he had a voice in the outcome.

Once Gorgon and his brother were behind bars, they'd find another home for her and Luka. The thought brought her feet back to the floor.

"Hmmm, I thought I told you," Will said, breaking her muse.

"No. You didn't." Will confided, on the side, at her debriefing, that Logan Summit was his hometown but not where he lived in the little town. She would've remembered that bit of info.

Will cleared his throat. "Can I come in?"

"Ah, sorry. Yes. Please." Her cheeks warmed as she swung the wooden-framed door wide.

"So how are you doing?" Will asked while stepping inside.

"Good."

He surveyed the room and peered up the stairs to the second floor. "Do you like the house?"

"It's perfect. Luka and I love living here. And Max," she added hearing the dog's woof.

"I'd thought you'd like the place."

"Did you pick it out?"

"I saw a realtor post a sign in the yard about a month ago. I just suggested it to the higher ups."

Spying the manila folder he carried under his arm, her arm hair stood on end. "What's that?"

"This?" He showed her the file. "One of the two reasons I wanted to see you. First one being, I wanted to see you and make sure you and Luka were happy."

"We are. Thank you. So are you going to tell me what's in there?" Curious, she reached for the file.

He switched his hands, trapping the file next to his hip. "Maybe we should sit down?"

Nicole's stomach knotted. The folder probably contained more pictures of men he wanted her to identify. Men who had dealings with Gorgon. Or, maybe something else altogether. Something that might send her to her knees.

"Sure." She led him to the couch. After she sat, he settled in next to her, leaving a space of about a foot in-between. Resisting the urge to fidget, Nicole laced her fingers together and dropped her hands to her lap.

Will slid the folder onto the coffee table. "Before we get to this—" He tapped the file. "I want to thank you, for helping us. What you did, going back into Gorgon's house, took courage."

"I didn't have much of a choice."

"Yes, you did. With the information we retrieved, we've been able to round up two dozen of Gorgon's contacts and charge them with human trafficking. This past week we found two missing children and returned them to their families."

Her throat clogged with a mixture of happiness and pride. "That's wonderful. But there is no need to thank me. Helping you was part of our deal, so Luka and I could be together, here." Realizing her palms were moist, she ran her hands over her jean clad thighs. "So what is in the folder?"

Will handed the file to her. "It's my way of saying thank you for helping us."

Confusion knitted her brow. She stared at the thin folder and then at him.

"Open it."

His smile reassured her and she flipped open the cover. Staring down at two faces from the past, her breath caught. "My parents."

The picture depicted them walking through an outside market. They held hands. They looked older.

They looked wonderful and so happy.

Nicole's heart swelled with love. Sadness tried to intrude in on the moment but she pushed the feeling away and enjoyed the feeling of total contentment settling over her heart. Eight years had slipped by since she'd seen them. She traced the outline of their faces with trembling fingertips.

"I thought you'd like to know what your family looks like now and what they've been up to since you—" Will's words broke off.

Will's kindhearted expression constricted Nicole's throat. Tears blurred her vision and fell to her cheeks. "It's okay, Will."

He leaned forward, pulled a handkerchief from his back pocket and handed the white linen to her. "Here. Wipe your tears away before you have me bawling." He chuckled.

She laughed along with Will, imagining the tough guy crying over her sentimental outbreak. "Right. Thanks." She patted her cheeks dry and again stared at the picture in her lap.

"They never stopped looking for you, Nicole," Will's comforting voice filled her ear. "Your mother now works for a local division of Amber Alerts. Your father calls the State Marshal's office every week without fail. He wants to make sure you haven't fallen through the cracks."

They hadn't stopped hoping and searching for her. The flood of emotion filling her chest made breathing hard. She sniffled and swiped her nose with a shaky hand.

"There's more." Will reached over and flipped her parents' picture to the side. "This is your brother Justin. He graduated early from Wilkes University with honors this past December. He's now a junior civil engineer for the city of Harrisburg. And your sister, Ashley, she's continuing her education as a clinical pharmacist, and she's getting married in a few weeks."

Nicole's heart stretched a little more. She loved her little brother and sister so much. They were thirteen the last time she saw them. Now they were all grown up. She was proud of them, knowing they had continued on with their lives and done well, but bitterness that she'd been robbed of the opportunity to make something of herself, made her slap the file closed and shove it at Will.

"What's wrong?" Perplexed his head snapped back as if she'd slapped him across the face. "I thought you'd be happy to see these."

"I am. Thank you." She stood, rounded the coffee table, and crossed to one of the two windows overlooking the side yard. Perhaps picking up the scent of the squirrel she'd seen earlier, Max sniffed in the flower bed which lined the garage's southern wall.

Out of the corner of her eye, she saw Will lay the file to the side and rise from the couch. A second later he stood behind her.

Nicole longed to lean back against his chest and feel his strong arms around her. She wanted to love and to be loved.

"What's wrong?" He asked softly.

"Nothing, and everything." While shaking her head she bit her lip, trapping in the resentment that had reared up inside her and snatched away her joy.

"What happened to you was no one's fault but the men who kidnapped you, Nicole. Not yours, and not your family's."

How could he understand the way she felt?

Keeping her back to him, she said, "I know that. It's just, I see what they've become and I'm what? Nothing."

Will hands landed on her shoulders and suddenly she found herself facing him. Through her thin shirt her skin warmed under his touch.

Will's brow lined with furrows while he studied her.

"You're not nothing. You're a strong, brave woman who has put her life on the line not only to save herself, but her son and Susie and hundreds of others. If your parents were here, they'd tell you how proud they are of you."

Her laughter sounded evil to her own ears. "Proud that I was made to be a whore."

Will's skin flushed with crimson anger and his fingers bit into her skin as he shook her. "You're not a whore. You never were. I don't want to hear you call yourself that again. Do you understand, Nicole?"

Staring into the depths of his rage, she swallowed. Will truly understood her torment. She looked down, blinked back the hot tears welling up inside her, and nodded.

Will's grip relaxed and his hands slid over her shoulders to her back. He held her in place and stepped closer. The feel of his body meeting hers, chest to chest, thigh to thigh, sent Nicole's pulse racing.

He was just comforting her she thought. Will didn't love her. She'd be a fool to think he ever could.

With her head against his chest, she closed her eyes and listened to the rhythm of his heart. She recorded the feel of his hard muscles and the way his breath felt against her hair. She inhaled the mixed floral scent of the fabric softener he used and his spicy cologne. A smile tucked at her lips.

Oh, how she wished there could be something more between them. A wild thought popped to mind. A night together? One she could remember and cherish in the years to come while she slept alone.

No. That had to be the worst idea she'd ever had. While her body would thank her a hundred times over, her heart couldn't take the rejection that unquestionably would happen in the moments after. Somewhere over the last two months, she had fallen for Will and loving him was a mistake.

She leaned into him. One more minute of bliss and then she'd let him go.

Will's massage replaced the tension in her back muscles with tender comfort and sent hopeful tingles up her spine, acknowledging that a bond had formed between them.

He sighed against her head. "You know, this isn't the best idea."

Nicole braced herself against the ache surrounding her heart. Either Will knew how she felt about him and didn't feel the same way or he also knew there was no future between them.

"You're probably right." Sighing, she pulled back and was captured by the storm in his eyes.

Will's gaze dropped to her lips and just like hers, his heartbeat went wild under her palm. Afraid she'd miss the moment, she didn't blink.

"Oh, hell." Will lowered his head and his tender lips brushed across hers.

A feverish wave cascaded through Nicole, and she melted against Will, soaking in every tiny detail of their joining; his hand wrapped in her hair, holding her head in place. The way his breath grew hotter against her cheek. The sweet taste of his tongue darting inside her mouth, promising her the passion she longed to share.

Seconds turned into minutes and just as she was about to resign to being totally lost, Will pulled back.

Nicole didn't care for cool air separating them and with her eyes still closed, moaned her objection. Her skin burned for his touch. Her hands slid up over the hard muscles of Will's chest, shoulders and around his neck and she pulled him down.

Under feverish kisses, Nicole's ability to reason slipped away and the sweet bliss of insanity took over. She never thought she'd ever need a man much less want one. But she both needed and wanted Will.

Will's warm lips moved along her jaw, to her ear and Nicole's eyes rolled back as she allowed herself to feel the sensations this man caused in her. For so long, she had put herself somewhere else during moments like this.

What was she thinking? She'd never experienced moments like this.

She laced her fingers through his soft hair, wanting Will to move and suckle her skin lower, but instead he pulled back again and rested his forehead against hers. Blazing passion stared back at her.

"I'm sorry. I shouldn't have done that." Will's tone was rough and breathless.

He smoothed her hair back and her scalp prickled. Then gently he massaged her shoulders and her heart beat decelerated from its feverish pace. "Please don't tell me you were just comforting me."

"What? Hell no." He straightened. "I've wanted to kiss you. For a while. Just now, seeing you upset put me over the edge."

"How long? Since the day you first saw me?" She refused to look away. His answer was important.

Will studied her a moment before responding.

"I wondered a lot about you then, for obvious reasons, but I don't think I actually wanted to kiss you until the amusement park, when you dropped your cotton candy and we both bent over to pick the bag up. Remember?"

Will's cheeks flushed and she thought how cute the reaction made him. She would never forget that moment. She had thought he might kiss her then and was disappointed when he hadn't. "Yes, I remember."

"Watching you that day with Luka, the way you laughed, I felt like I was watching you being happy for the very first time. I didn't know..." He rested his hand on his stomach. "Something just clinked inside me."

"But you tore into me that day. You were upset and we left the park in a hurry."

He shrugged. "Misguided self-defense mechanism. I was angry at the parents of a group of unsupervised teens. They were too young to run around not chaperoned. I took my frustration out on you."

"Because I was Gorgon's woman."

Will stopped tracing her lobe with his finger. "Yes, and I liked you, and I didn't want to." He sighed. "A name doesn't change who you are, Nicole. I've told you before you're one of the bravest women I've ever known. You're a great mom, and—" He tugged her closer. "I find you interesting, attractive and you make me smile."

Nicole closed her eyes. Her heart beat echoed in her ears. Did he realize what he was doing to her?

Will squeezed her. "What's wrong?"

She shook her head, relishing the happiness filling her soul. A tear slipped from her eye and she swiped the droplet away. "Nothing is wrong. I've never been this happy."

With his finger under her chin, he lifted her gaze to meet his. "Then why are you crying?"

"Because I know it's going to end."

She pulled away from him and he let her go, knowing she needed to feel free— to do whatever she wanted whenever she wanted.

"What will end?"

"This." She pointed between them.

"Us? I'm not sure I know what you mean."

"Where can a relationship between us go?" She stared at him accusingly. "Are you ever going to forget who I was? Who I was with? Who Luka's father is?"

"I know who you are."

"That's not the question. Can you forget who I was?" she asked again, accenting each syllable, one at a time.

In a room warmed by the late sun, Will saw Nicole shiver.

He wanted to gather her back into his arms and make her happy, but she was right. He wouldn't forget. Sharing a kiss or two wasn't a concerned, but her past would matter if a whole hell of a lot more happened between them. He couldn't answer her question right now.

Maybe the best decision would be to stop this thing between them right now and he walked away. "Remember earlier when I said I wanted to see you and make sure you and Luka were happy. That was true, but what I really wanted was to see you. I'm attracted to you."

The tiny spark in Nicole's eyes encouraged him to continue. "I didn't have to tell you that. You know. I can see in your eyes that you know. And I can see you feel the same way." He might be making a mess laying his guts out like this, but he didn't know any other way but to be honest with her. "You're asking me about a future for us. I don't know if that will happen and it's not because of me not forgetting your past. I'm the first guy you've met and kissed after escaping from Gorgon."

She dropped her arms to her sides and opened her mouth to say something, but he cut her off. "Hear me out before you say anything." He combed his hand through his hair, wondering if he was doing the right thing. He was for her, but for himself—he wasn't too sure. "I can't believe I'm going to say this, but... I think best thing for both of us is for you see other men."

The instant he said the words, he felt like a fucking heel. Nicole did deserve better than him.

The sound of gravel crushing turned both their heads towards the window. Max's barking told him the dog raced from the back yard to the front of the house.

"Luka is home," Nicole said. She leveled her shoulders and slipped on her strong façade, distancing herself from the situation.

"Nicole?" He touched her arm, hoping she'd respond to his statement before Luka entered the house. He needed some indication of what was running through her mind.

"Don't." She snapped her arm back as if his touch had burnt her skin. "Just don't." Her hand trembled before him.

There he had his answer. He'd hurt her. Damn. He didn't want to cause her more pain than he already had.

Footsteps pounded the steps and a second later Luka shot through the door, leaving the screen door to bang behind him.

"Uncle Will, when did you get here?"

The kid's sparkling eyes lifted Will's spirits, somewhat. He liked the kid a lot. But just like his mother, Will didn't want to hurt him further. A clean break was best.

"Just a few minutes ago." He ruffled the boy's hair. "What have you been up to? How's school going?"

"It's great. I was over at my new friend's house. His name is Johnny. He's two months younger than me, but he's still pretty cool. We're in the same class. Guess what, Uncle Will?"

Staring down at the kid, Will pasted a shit ass grin on his face even though his mind was focused on Nicole and their conversation which still hung in the air. "What, kid?"

"My birthday is coming up. I'll be five."

"Really? When?"

"Next month. October 14th and mom is going to throw a birthday party for me. All my friends from school are coming. I never had a birthday party before. Only ones with my mom and dad. One time, Uncle Donnie and Aunt Gali came for cake. I don't remember them, but mom says they did. You're going to come too, right?"

He didn't want to break the kid's bubble but after what just happened between him and Nicole, he'd doubt she wanted him around. "I don't know—"

Luka circled him and grasped his mother's hand. "Tell Uncle Will he has to come, mom."

Looking down at the desperation on her son's face, Nicole bit her lip while her fingers combed through the kid's brown hair, straightening the mess he had made of the thick strands. Will knew she was stuck in a hard place and wasn't sure how to respond to her son's plea.

"I'll tell you what, kid, if I'm in town I'll be here. And if I'm not, I'll make sure my present is here for you to open. Okay?"

"Yeah!" Luka jumped up and down, already excited that he would have presents at his party.

Nicole glanced at him before snagging Luka's chin between her fingers and forcing the boy to focus on her. "Why don't you go upstairs and get your book bag. You have some homework to finish before your bath."

"Ah, mom. I haven't seen Uncle Will in a long time."

He had nowhere to be, but he checked his watch anyway. "Do as your mom says. I've got to run anyway." He winked.

Will moved to the side and Nicole led Luka to the stairs and directed him up. Once Luka was out of hearing range, he said, "I guess I better get going."

Nicole's sad expression twisted his gut. Not saying a word, she nodded an affirmation.

He opened the door and stepped onto the porch. With the door still in his hand, he turned. "Nicole, I just—"

"Don't." Tears glistened in her brown eyes. She pushed him back away from the door. "Don't be in town."

Then she closed the inside door and Will heard the lock click into place. A sinking feeling that he'd just royalty screwed up his life gripped his heart.

Chapter Twenty-three

Gorgon stooped and picked up the section of newspaper he dropped, and winced. The fire in his belly had burned out but a prickling stab shot through his middle every time he bent over too fast or stretched.

He folded the paper back into its tri-fold delivery shape and tossed it aside on the table. Cupping his hands together, with his elbows placed on either side of his plate, he watched the sunshine shimmering through the large window pane before him and danced across the brocade carpet in heated waves. The sheer curtain edging the window billowed and fell as if the wail of the siren below had disturbed its rest. Twenty five stories down, the hordes continued on with their lives and here he sat, waiting for his strength to return. But would ever get stronger? Everything he loved was gone and without love, how could he continue on?

How had he not seen Katrina's unhappiness?

Gorgon's knuckles turned white while anger stirred in his gut. How had he not seen her strength? He thought he had controlled her.

Where had they disappeared to and how would he find them?

"What's wrong, my brother? Do you not feel well?"

While wallowing in his misery, Gorgon hadn't heard Donnie enter the sitting room of their suite.

With his chin nestled against his hands, Gorgon inhaled through his nostrils and looked up from studying the spiral shape the dollop of cream made in his now cold morning coffee.

A fluffy, white towel hugged his younger brother's athletic hips while another hung around Donnie's neck, covering a portion of his hairy chest. Comb marks etched through Donnie's jet black waves still wet from his shower. He shouldn't be jealous of his brother, but he was. Donnie had the perks of being a Novokoff without shouldering the weight of responsibility for the family and its business.

"I feel like a caged animal," Gorgon said before stabbing his spoon into the mug and pushing it away.

"Bozhe moi. You're in a five star hotel in the capital city of the world. You have everything you need at your fingertips." Donnie pointed to the table laden with huge plates of sausages and pancakes. Bowls of whipped cream and strawberries sat alongside.

Gorgon glanced at the man guarding the door and between clenched teeth said, "Everything but what a man holds most dear to his heart." He tapped a finger against his chest. Fighting the ache of loneliness welling up inside him, he clamped his jaw closed and looked out the window. Gorgon curled his fists tighter until his fingernails bit into his palms. He would not let his weakness show.

Donnie poured coffee from the silver carafe and took a sip before responding to his pain. "And what is it you long for?"

"My family."

"Your wife waits for you in Brazil."

Gorgon rolled his eyes. His brother knew how he felt about the old woman he'd been saddled with fifteen years ago when he was just a young man of twenty-two. He'd wed the then thirty year old Eva for one purpose—to make peace with his family's enemy. Theirs had never been a Shakespearian love story. Eva's barren body had not given him the heir he'd hoped for. "Do not act the fool. You know who truly holds my heart, as my wife. Katrina."

Both he and Donnie caught the eye of the guard.

Donnie nodded to the man to leave them, which he did without uttering a word. Once the door clicked closed and they were alone, Donnie pulled a chair out from the table and dropped onto the seat. Leaning towards Gorgon, he said, "Who is acting like a fool, brother? Katrina betrayed you. She tried to kill you and if not for our men finding you as quickly as they had, we… All of us would be mourning you."

Gorgon had relived the nightmare over and over, giving Katrina's actions much thought. He came up with one answer. "Katrina was threatened."

"What the hell are you talking about? No one would threaten her. Why would they?"

"I brought the girl home."

"So? She was to be transported to her new owner in a few days. She was worth a half-million dollars. You took her home to protect her from any mishaps."

"Katrina had to think I was replacing her with the girl. That is the only explanation." Gorgon chuckled. "The one who had to worry about being replaced was Eva."

"Eva's a good woman."

"Eva acts like my mother not my wife, and I don't say that because she has not given me a son. I do not blame her as she thinks I do. We never were one."

Gorgon played with the fork lying on the table, lining the hotel utensil up with the knife. He stretched his back, wishing the fire inside his gut would go away. He missed Katrina's soft hands massaging his muscles. "You know what I mean, brother. I see the love between you and Gali."

"Katrina will never be Gali."

"Not as long as I'm married to Eva."

Donnie frowned. His chair moaned under his weight as he leaned back and crossed his arms over his chest. "Papa will never allow a divorce."

"His permission will not be necessary."

Donnie's stare became intense through squinting eyes. "What are you saying?"

"Eva's family is no longer a threat to us."

"You wouldn't kill her?"

"Katrina is the wife of my heart. She will be the one who lies beside me through eternity."

"Katrina is gone."

"I will find her."

"How, brother? How will you find her? And why would you want too? You know as well as I do, as well as Papa does, that she is the one who stole into your house and took your files. She is the reason many of our contacts are now in prison. She is the reason our family has fled the country and she is the reason you will rot in jail if you're caught. She betrayed you not once but twice."

Anger flared in Gorgon. He thought if anyone would understand how he felt, his brother would. The carpet scratched beneath the legs of his chair as he shoved back from the table and stood. "She thought I betrayed her."

"And just like that you'll forgive her?"

"If we were speaking of Gila, would you?" He cut the air between them with his hand. "You don't have to answer. I know you would because you love her more than your own life."

Donnie lowered his eyes, and Gorgon knew his brother now got him. Gorgon stood straighter, hiding the pain in his side, and folded his arms across his chest. He must appear strong enough to take on the world. "Help me find her."

His brother's jaw worked for a moment before he looked at him. "Do you know why I didn't leave with the family?"

"Because you love me."

"Yes. You are my brother and until you're strong again you need my protection. All law agents are looking for us."

"I know. Will you help me find Katrina and my son?"

Donnie sighed. "Do you have a plan?"

Gorgon grinned while taking a seat and pushing aside his plate. He felt his strength returning. "Yes."

Chapter Twenty-four

Condensation gradually obstructed Will's view as the air inside his government issued sedan grew clammy. He cracked the window and zipped closed his U.S. Marshal issued jacket. It was only mid-October, but today's storm, which had swooped down on New York from Canada, brought a winter-like dampness that chilled the bones.

Freezing his toes off along with his balls while staking out a flea-bag hotel located in Brooklyn's seedier hood was not his idea of a fun-filled Saturday night. If Kyle hadn't called around five, reporting some of Gorgon's top men were guests of the establishment down the street and possibly Gorgon too, he'd be in bed right now. Maybe here was the most productive place to be because in bed all he'd do was toss and turn while thinking about Nicole, just like he'd done every night since he'd kissed her.

Will dug his hands into his coat pockets not because they were cold but because he longed to feel the softness of Nicole's hair passing through his fingers. He had to get her out of his mind and concentrate on his job which was to find Gorgon and take him down. Then the agency could place Nicole and Luka in a permanent new life.

Will's heart sank at the thought.

He peered through the windshield and studied the shadows, pushing Nicole from his thoughts and focusing on the job at hand.

After receiving the informant's call, Gary jumped into his car with him and they made the drive from Scranton to Brooklyn in under two hours. Just their luck the Novakoff's men had decided on dinner and a movie ten minutes before they'd arrived. Their misfortune continued when Gorgon's bodyguards lost the tag the local PD had put on them. Now, the only choice Gary and he had was to wait and hope for the Russian goons to return.

A light drizzle pinged against the car's roof and again hindered Will's view of the ill-lit Brooklyn street. Turning the wipers on wasn't an option.

Moisture hit the side of his face and Will slid the window back up. Watching a big-gulp plastic cup roll down the sidewalk and tumble into the gutter with other discarded garbage, he bit back his frustration, shifted on the seat, and huffed a sigh. The most interesting thing to happen in the last hour was a dog taking a piss on some guy's tire while the john was propositioned by a couple of hookers trying to hold onto their umbrellas as they settled on the terms of the transaction.

A sudden leg cramp made Will jump and he winced with pain. The car seat moaned as he pushed back.

"You okay?" Gary, resting against the passenger door, peered at him through a slit of an eye.

"Yeah. I just got a cramp." Will stretched and rubbed his leg.

"What time is it?"

Pulling his cell phone from his jean's pocket, Will pushed the app and checked the time. "Two-thirty seven."

"No sign of them?"

"Nuh. Nothing."

"The bars have last call at four here in New York, I think," Gary mumbled, pulling his leather jacket together as if intending to go back to sleep.

Will arched his neck as far back as the headrest allowed. "Yeah, right. I'm sure Gorgon's men hang out at the most reputable establishments."

"And the best. If I had their money, I know I would."

He arched his brow. "You think they get paid that well?"

"Hell, yes they do. Ask Kyle when this is over. He'll tell you."

"Too bad Gorgon's father demoted Kyle after Nicole stabbed his bastard of a son. We'd know where Gorgon was right now."

"Kyle's lucky the old man didn't put him and the other guard in the ground. Getting Gorgon to the hospital as fast as he did, is what saved Kyle's life. Granted, he'd hoped Gorgon had died on the way, but shit happens. He's getting cozy with old man Novokoff's men. He'll find out eventually where Gorgon and his brother are."

"Can't happen soon enough for me. Son-of-a-bitch." Will rubbed the charley horse still gripping the inside of his thigh. "This freakin' cold weather."

"Who are you trying to kid. I told you that you were pushing yourself too hard."

Gary referred to the workout he'd done today at the agency's gym. Work and working out had become his life over the past three weeks since he made the mistake and had given into his desire to kiss Nicole. But no matter how he tried to forget, the moment haunted him.

Gary shifted up on his seat and grabbed his thermos mug off the floor. His recoil after taking a swallow told Will the coffee was not much warmer than the cold rain slapping the window.

"So how is Nicole doing?" Gary asked, dropping his mug to the floor again.

Out of the corner of his eye, Will glanced at his partner. Maybe being partners for five years wasn't a good thing after all. The guy sensed his every thought. "I haven't seen her."

"Why not? I thought the whole purpose of settling

her into Logan's Summit was so you could keep an eye on her."

He ignored Gary's wiggle of brows. "I've checked in."

"When?"

Will stretched his arms out in front of him, pressing his knuckles against the chilly windshield.

"Will?"

"What?" He exhaled and rested his wrists on the steering wheel and casually looked at Gary.

"When's the last time you spoke to her?"

"I don't know. A few weeks ago, but I drive by the house every few days, and I've checked in with her boss. She and the kid are doing okay."

"I see."

Gary's choice of two words had a hidden agenda. "What do you see?"

"She's gotten to you."

"What? You don't know what you're talking about." Will shook his head and focused on the hotel's front entrance—a silent signal for Gary to drop the subject and do his job.

"Don't I? I've been there, my friend, in exactly the same place you are. When I met Sharon I fell hard. I couldn't believe a woman like her would want a man like me. Let me tell you, she scared the shit out of me. I stayed away, just like you're doing and almost lost her to some other guy."

"Nicole is not Sharon," Will said half-heartily, knowing Nicole had already gone out on several dates with Erin Dwitter, a local high school history teacher. Sara, Nicole's boss, had been all bubbly relating how Nicole and Erin had met right there in the store. He swallowed the hurt clogging his throat. Nicole hadn't taken long to move on like he'd suggested.

"Are you thinking she's not the girl you'd take home to meet mom?" Gary broke into his misery-coated muse.

"Hell no. I know her past is not her fault. It's just…"

A crack of thunder filled the void.

Gary folded his arms across his chest. "What?"

"I think Nicole needs to live her life before she settles down." He said the words, but in his mind, Will was aiming his Glock at Dwitter's knee. He'd already run a check on the guy and God himself wasn't as clean. "She doesn't know who she is yet. What she wants. I mean, I was the first guy to kiss her after Gorgon."

Gary slapped his knee. The car's interior echoed with Gary's howl. "I knew it. You kissed her." Wearing a huge grin, Gary wagged his finger at him.

Will regretted his slip of tongue immediately.

"Yeah." Will's heart beat matched the pounding rain on the roof while he remembered the softness of Nicole's lips against his and the way she fit perfectly into his arms. "It was a mistake. I shouldn't have taken advantage of her like that."

"What advantage? She's a grown woman. One who's been around the block more than most." Gary put up his hand as if preparing to be clocked. "I don't mean that in bad way. Believe me. You know what I mean. I like Nicole. She's been through hell and survived. I have the utmost respect for her."

"Yeah, I know."

"Sharon loves her. Hell, she thinks you two are a perfect match."

"She thought Laura was perfect too." Hell why did he bring up his ex-fiancée.

"Forget Laura. She's history, right?"

"Dead and buried. Now can we get back to work?" He pointed to the hotel.

"Sure. I'm just telling you what Sharon thinks."

Shifting on his seat to face Gary, Will's knee thudded against the console. "You two discuss my love life?"

"Hell, yes, all the time. Sharon thinks you need someone, so you stop hanging around our place so much." Gary chuckled. "Just kidding."

"Look." Will gripped the lower part of the steering wheel one finger at a time. "Can we just drop the subject and concentrate on our jobs?"

"Sure. No problem."

They both faced the hotel.

"I think the rain is slowing down." Grabbing his mug, Gary took another sip. "Yuck." He peered up and down the street. "Any place open where we can get a cup of coffee? I don't care if all I get is warm slush."

Will nodded over his shoulder. "I think there's a twenty-four hour shop around the block."

Gary's eyes lit up brighter than the street lights. "Great. You want some?" He asked with his hand already on the door's handle.

"Tell you what, you stay here. I'll go. I need to stretch my legs and get rid of this cramp."

"Okay. I don't mind staying dry." Gary handed him his cup. "Put mine in here."

"This isn't Mayberry. Now, if the Novokoffs come back, don't you jump the gun without me," he warned Gary. "You understand?"

Gary knew he was as anxious as a horn-dog to nail a bitch to snag Gorgon. "Hey, do I look stupid? I'm no freakin' psycho hero."

"What the hell was I thinking?" Will shoved the door open, climbed out and slammed it, cutting off Gary's rebuttal filling the interior.

He hustled to the sidewalk and with his shoulders pulled up, he stayed as close to the buildings as possible to protect himself from the storm's onslaught. In a little under ten minutes, he found the coffee shop, got their brew and head back to the car. As he neared the corner, gunshots rang through the air.

The carry-out cups exploded upon impact with the sidewalk and hot liquid spewed over his jeans. Will yanked his gun from his holster and hugged the building. Cautiously, he peeked around the corner and his pounding heart wedged in his throat. The rear windshield of his car was blown out. He couldn't see Gary.

Two men walked to the front of the vehicle as if on a Sunday stroll. The son-of-bitches had semi-automatic weapons. Armed with a Glock, his only hope to survive the assault and save Gary was to aim true, and there wasn't a second to waste.

"U.S. Marshal, drop your weapons," Will shouted, stepping out into the open, hoping they'd turn on him and give Gary a chance to react, if he could react.

The men spun in his direction.

Will shot off several rounds dropping one of the men to the street while bullets whizzed by him. He dove for cover behind thick walls of the Emerald Grocery. Along with raindrops, bits of concrete pelted his face. He fought to catch his breath. His heart felt huge and pounded against his ribs as fast as the rapid fire threatening him. Shit. Gary hadn't responded.

"You, sons-of-a-bitches. I said put down your weapons," he snarled before dropping to the wet sidewalk, peering around the corner and squeezing off another couple of rounds in the direction of the remaining attacker.

In the distance, sirens blared. He couldn't be sure because of the wind's howl and the echo of the return fire overhead, but he thought the responders drew closer. He hoped they drew closer. He didn't want to die in the

Brooklyn gutter. Oh, he could run but he wasn't going anywhere without his partner.

He lifted his chin. The rain stopped as if someone turned off the faucet overhead and the wind's rush faded away. He held his breath, listening for footsteps. He heard none.

He glimpsed around the corner. The guy was gone.

Will jumped to his feet and with his gun trained on the area he headed toward the bullet-rifled sedan. He still couldn't see Gary.

Reaching the back bumper, he lowered his weapon. The car leaned to the left on flatten tires. The headrest on the driver's side was blown apart, its cushion with its stuffing spilling out looked like one of those corkscrew hairy dogs.

He gulped a breath that wasn't easy to swallow. "Gary."

Will mentally prepared himself for the worst and opened the passenger door.

***

A soft knock made Gorgon look up from his Sunday morning paper.

Donnie jumped from the couch, drew his gun and after peeking through the peek hole, unlocked the door. Two of their men stood in the threshold. "Well?"

"We lost Marco," Rafe said, dropping his gaze to the floor.

Gorgon clamped his lips together, biting back his anger. Marco had been with the family for more than twenty years—since he was a young teen. He would miss Marco's humor.

Folding his paper, Gorgon placed the daily news on the coffee table. "We don't discuss our business in the hall. Get in here."

He took pleasure in the fear that widened both Rafe's and Drat's eyes. The men still saw him as the leader of the family.

Donnie nodded for them to enter and closed the door. "How the hell did that happen?"

Drat hung his head. Rafe on the other hand stood tall, lacing his fingers in front of him, and fixed his eyes on Donnie. "One of the cops wasn't in the car when Drat and Marco hit it. He came up behind them."

"Where were you?" Gorgon stood and Rafe's eyes shot in his direction.

Rafe's nostrils flared with an intake of air. "In the car, down the street."

Gorgon respected the man not to flinch under his scrutiny. "Someone tip him off?"

"I don't think so. Their man confessed he was alone in our ranks. Who else would tell them we would show our revenge?"

Kyle had guarded his home, his family. He was still alive because of Kyle's quick actions and getting him to the hospital. He was sickened thinking a man he trusted had betrayed him. "Where is Kyle now?"

"Dead."

There was no other choice. "What did you do with him?"

"He committed suicide. Jumped from the Brooklyn bridge, but missed the water by this much." Rafe smiled while extending his arms a yard's width. "His people will get the message that coming close will mean death."

Gorgon nodded. Rafe's act wasn't the death he would've chosen for the man. "What's done is done."

"The cop in the car, is he dead?" Donnie asked.

"He had to be," Drat spoke up. "We hit the car hard."

Gorgon raised his chin and looked down the nose at

the man. "But you don't know for sure?"

Drat shook his head. "No."

"It doesn't matter. We're leaving the city today," Gorgon said, frowning. "Pack your things and be ready to go in an hour."

Chapter Twenty-Five

Nicole scooted up on her bed, the comforter dropping to her lap. Darkness owned the room. Her hair fell over her shoulder and she whisked the long wisps back behind her ear. The tree, which she swore over and over she'd climb and rip its branch off, scraped its pointed nubs across the rain gutter above her bedroom window. No. That wasn't the same sound she'd grown use to. She'd heard something more. Or had she?

Was her mind playing tricks on her? After all, she'd read in the paper tonight about a man, now labeled "the midnight rapist", who, in a county west of Logan's Summit, lured his victims outside by turning on their outside water spigots. The women inside, his targets, thought they'd sprung a leak and went outside to investigate. He then forced them back into their homes and raped them. A recent newspaper article had laid out his latest victim's terrifying account explicitly and given Nicole the chills. So much so, she'd double-checked her windows and door locks before climbing the stairs, taking a quick shower and climbing into bed. Of course, memories of her own ordeals hadn't helped diminish her angst.

Nicole listened to the quiet beyond the branch's scrape and to the thump of her heartbeat. Maybe the midnight rapist had widened his zone of attack.

With that thought, she fumbled for the light on the nightstand. She hated guns, but sometimes she wished she had a big one. However, having a weapon was against her agreement with the agency. Will was supposed to be her protection, but she hadn't seen a glimpse of him in over a week.

Nicole jumped, fisting the covers. There was the sound again.

With her heart now lodged between her ribs, her thoughts flew to Luca. He wasn't tucked in his bed where she could ease her mind by peeking in on him. Since the schools were closed tomorrow for Columbus Day holiday, Luca had begged to go on his first sleep over at Tommy's house.

Her eyebrows pulled together as she listened harder. Was someone knocking on her front door? Maybe her baby had taken sick and Tommy's mom brought Luka home. But why wouldn't Ann just call her to come get him? Because she knows you're alone and she had a husband as a safety net.

Nicole threw back the covers and instantly the cool night air made its way under her cotton nightshirt, causing her to shiver. She shoved her feet into her fleece-lined slipper boots before snatching her terrycloth robe from the chair and slipped her arms through the soft material, on her way out the door.

The soft rapping grew louder as Nicole crept down the stairs and approached her front door. She'd seen a television show last week where a woman heard cries for help outside her house late at night and opened her door only to be raped and killed.

Damn. She had to stay away from the news. Whoever was knocking on her door wasn't howling for help. Man, she wished she had a gun, or that Will was here backing her up.

She tied her robe's belt snuggly around her waist before flipping on the porch lights. Tentatively, she drew back the lace curtain covering the small pane windows edging the door and peeked outside.

"Oh, my God. Will."

He blinked under the bright light and then raised his hand to shield his eyes. "Nicole, open up."

Will's movement billowed his jacket and exposed his white shirt underneath. Her eyes zeroed in on the red blotch marking his white shirt. Blood. "Are you alright?"

"I'm okay. Opening up."

"A weight settled in her chest, blocking her next breath from entering her lungs. Had something happened to Luka? Was that why Will was here at this hour? Would Will know something happened to Luka before she did?

Nicole's fingers seemed like two sets of thumbs as she fumbled to unlock the deadbolt. How had Gorgon found Luka?

Damn. She knew letting him do a sleep over was a mistake.

Damn. Shit. Fuck. Feeling safe in this sleepy town, she had let her guard down and look what had happened.

What about Tommy's family? What had happened to them? Her stomach rolled into a knot while she chided herself for only thinking of Luka.

Finally the lock clicked and she jumped back and swung the door wide. Leaves rustled in the corner of the porch and autumn's spicy scent tickled her nostrils as she stared up at Will. Under the bright light, his blue eyes lacked their usual sparkle. His strong shoulders, which normally carried the weight of the world with ease, were bowed, forming a perfect C.

Nicole's gaze flew to the red stains marking the exposed V of his white shirt and which she now saw also smeared across Will's coat front and arms. She reached out, her fingers hovering above the blood and swallowed hard, forcing calmness to her lips. "What's happened? Was it Gorgon?"

He nodded and panic ripped through the knot in her

stomach and gripped her throat in a choke hold. She brushed past Will. "I've got to get to Luka."

Will grabbed her robe by the sleeve, stopping her before she reached the porch steps. As she yanked back, he strengthened his hold by clamping onto her wrist. "Where are you going?"

"To get Luka. He slept at Tommy's house. Let me go." She twisted her arm, trying to free herself from his strong grasp, but Will had her anchored in place.

"No." He pulled her back toward the door and then stood between her and the stairs. "Luka's okay. You're safe."

"But you said-"

"Gary."

Her brow furrowed. "What do you mean? What happened to him?"

Will's gaze dropped from hers and her hopes went in the same direction.

Staring up at the pain etching Will's face, what moisture Nicole had in her mouth dried up like an Arizona drizzle on a blistering afternoon. Something terrible had happened to Gary, and Will had witnessed everything. He didn't have to say the words for her to know his thoughts. He had been the lucky one and wished for a way to turn back time.

She didn't want to hear the details. She could imagine the horror, but Will needed to talk to someone and he had come to her. Nicole put her hand on his forearm. "Is he okay?"

"He's in critical condition."

"Oh, my God." She covered her upper chest exposed by her nightgown, fending off a chill.

The fear of losing his partner had caused Will's complexion to ashen. He was in pain.

And Gary's family. They were probably devastated.

This happened because of her. Guilt twisted her insides. "Sharon?" She asked with a shaky voice. "How is she? Is she with him?"

"Yeah."

She laced her fingers with his. "How about the kids? They're not at the hospital, are they? They're too young to be facing—"

"No. Sharon's parents are with them."

"Yes. Of course." Sharon had family available to help her.

Will let go of her hand and pointed toward the house. "Can we go inside before your neighbors see us? They'll wonder what I'm doing here after midnight. The way I look… The less questions raised, is better for both of us."

If her neighbor, Mr. Ripkey, thought something was wrong, he might come over to investigate and then he'd see the state Will and his clothing were in. Not good. "Yes. You're right."

Will held the door open for her, allowing her to enter first and then followed her in her footsteps. Darkness surrounded them as he closed the inside door. The intimate space was alive with emotions they both held in check. Nicole wanted to pull Will into an embrace, share his sorrow and somehow comfort him, but she didn't have the guts. Besides, would he let her?

And, if she tried and he refused her, how would she stand the rejection? Did he come to her as a friend or had Will come to her because Gorgon was involved?

Man, she hated the Russian bastard. Now, she wished to turn back time. She would've been stronger. She should've picked up Gorgon's gun and blown his brains out while she had the chance. But she hadn't, fearing first she'd wake Luka and he'd witness the act, and second, alarming Gorgon's men. If only she'd known one of them had been Will's man undercover, they could've staged a break-in, made the scene look like Gorgon's enemy's work. Then she and Luka could've disappeared without fear because Yegor, Gorgon's father, would've never spent any man power to search for them.

If only she had known, Gary wouldn't be fighting for his life now, Will wouldn't be distressed, and she and Luka would be living…

Where would they be? Not here in Will's hometown. And she wouldn't be harboring notions that there was a possibility she and Will could have a long happy life here together.

She was a fool. Nicole turned her thoughts to Gary's wife and kids as she padded across the carpet and touched the base of a table lamp. Its soft glow popped on and brought the shadows lurking in the corners into the light.

Turning around, she saw Will still stood by the door with his full bottom lip trapped between his teeth. "You look chilled to the bone. Let's go into the kitchen. I'll make us some coffee and if you want, you can tell me what happened?"

Nicole didn't give him a chance to say no. She turned on her slipper clad heel and headed toward the kitchen. Without glancing over her shoulder, she knew Will followed.

She switched on the lights and turned to face him. "Take off your coat and shirt. I think I have an old sweatshirt that will fit you. I'll get it."

He looked down at his clothing and his face paled before looking up at her. "Damn. I didn't think. I should've changed before coming here. I needed to talk to you."

He said talk, not be with or need to hold you. He needed to talk to her. Why? While some real bad scenarios played out in the back of her mind, her gut tightened.

"I understand. I'll be just a second." Her feet were weights, heading into the small laundry room off the kitchen. She dug through the wash she'd done earlier in the day and found the old sweatshirt that was three times her size. Her twisting stomach told her Will had some more bad news to share with her.

When she entered the kitchen, Nicole stopped cold. Will's hard muscles bulged while he pulled the cotton tee-shirt over his head and her womb clenched with need.

He stretched and tugged free from the blood stained shirt.

Staring at the red cloth hanging limp from his hand, Nicole forgot about his body and how she would love to run her hands over the curls covering Will's chest, and remembered what had brought him here.

"Here, let me take that." She traded shirts with him, keeping her eyes focused on the shirts and not on Will's body."

"I'll put these in a paper bag, in case you need them. Take a seat."

"Thanks." Will slipped the sweatshirt over his head and worked the material down over his tightly packed torso.

Nicole quickly wrapped the garments.

"I promised you coffee." She felt Will's eyes on her as she moved around the small kitchen filling the coffee maker, grabbing mugs, spoons and a few items from the refrigerator. Placing the milk and the doughnuts she'd bought earlier in the day on her way home from Tommy's house on the table, she said, "I'll bet the last dollar I have in my new bank account that you haven't eaten for a while."

"You started a bank account?"

She smiled. "Yeah. I did."

"Good."

The corner of Will's mouth lifted and pride flowed through Nicole. She'd take his hint of a smile to mean he was proud of her.

God. She hoped Will wasn't going to tell her that she and Luka had to move.

Nicole flexed her fingers, willing them to remain steady while she poured the coffee into mugs. She avoided eye contact with Will as she lowered onto the seat next to him and slid his mug across the table. Steam coated her palm when she covered her mug.

"Are you cold?" Will asked.

"It's a little cool in here. Would you like something stronger than milk in your coffee? I have a small bottle of brandy. My neighbor, Mrs. Ripkey, gave me a welcome basket. She said she used a little when cooking. I don't think she meant in the food she cooked." She smiled.

Will forced a weak smile and the mood in the room lightened.

"No. This is fine. Thanks." He took a quick swallow before setting the mug down.

Nicole studied his hands. They remained curled around the warm ceramic mug. Apparently, Will had washed them, but a small amount of Gary's blood remained trapped along his cuticles. Her stomach churned and she lifted her eyes to Will's face where she noted his jaw muscles worked under the shadow of a day's worth of whiskers. It was obvious Will was recalling the moments before and during the battle. "Tell me what happened," she said softly.

Staring beyond the doughnuts, Will took a second before meeting her gaze. Sorrow cloaked his blue eyes with a barren sheen as if life had beaten him up and left him for dead alongside the road.

"Gary and I got a call right as we were leaving the office last night from Kyle. He said Gorgon and Donnie were possibly holed up in a hotel in Brooklyn. Their men were definitely there. We high-tailed up to New York right away, but when we arrived we were told by the hotel manager that they'd just left. Apparently they'd gone for dinner. The local cops put a tail on them, but I guess the Novokoffs pegged them and somehow lost them. Gary and I staked out the hotel, watching from down the street in the off chance they'd show."

He scrubbed his hands over his face and then combed his fingers through his dusty blonde hair, leaving a couple of strands protruding out at an odd angles. "The whole thing was a set up," he said on the tail of a frustrated gasp. "They hit the car with over a hundred rounds before I got back to him."

Tears stung her eyes watching the pain etching his face. She inhaled a breath tinted with rich coffee and the bile tickling the back of her throat. Her grip tightened around the mug and Nicole steeled her nerves to hear more. "Where were you?"

Before Will touched his mug to his lips, a strained chuckle erupted from him.

"Gary wanted a hot cup of coffee." Will's Adam's apple bobbed before he continued. "If only I had let him go for the coffee instead of me, he wouldn't be lying in the hospital, shot all to hell. Fuck. He has kids."

She winced at the thought of him exchanging places with Gary, having to fight for his life. The silent thank you she sent to God that Will hadn't been the one in the car wasn't right, but she couldn't help herself.

She grabbed his forearm. Beneath the coarse hair, his strong muscles trembled.

"Don't do this." Nicole scooted her chair closer toward him until her knees brushed against his leg. She squeezed his arm. "You can't blame yourself for what happened. This is Gorgon's fault, and mine. Not yours."

"Don't even put this on your shoulders, Nicole. It's not your fault." Will pounded his fist on the table and the dishes clattered in response. His eyes bore into hers with such a fire, Nicole snapped her hand away. "I'm the one Sharon, and Gary's kids, and his whole fuckin' family can blame for what happened to him. If I wasn't throwing a self-pity party for myself over the last three weeks, I would've been focused on our surroundings. I might've picked up on a clue, something, and been able to stop Novokoff's men from getting to Gary. Instead I was thinking about—"

Will's knuckles whitened as he gripped the table's edge. His gaze tore from hers and fell to the floor, seemingly embarrassed at what he'd almost let slip.

Nicole sat on the edge of the seat. What had Will been thinking about? What caused his guilt over his partner's condition? "Instead of what, Will?" she prompted him softly.

He snatched up the mug and took a chug of coffee like he would a few fingers of stiff whiskey before he looked at her again. "You."

"Me?" She pointed to her chest, surprise widening her eyes.

Before she could blink, Will sat the mug down with a thud and trapped her hand between his warm ones. "Yes. I was kicking my ass for telling you to go out with other men. Why did I when all I want is to keep you for myself."

The thunder of her blood racing through her veins made Nicole wondered if she'd heard him right. Her brow furrowed, while her heart was doing cartwheels. Will wanted her.

The rough pad of his thumb brushed across the backside of her hand, sending tingles up her arm.

"You were thinking about me," she said again, still

not believing what she'd heard.

"For the past three weeks, I did everything to keep my mind off of you, but nothing worked. Gary pointed out to me last night what an idiot I am."

"Gary said that? The two of you talked about us?" She pointed from herself to Will.

"Yes. He told me I was a fool to let you get away. He said I'd better get my act together before some other guy came along and snatched you up. He didn't know I'd already told you to date other men, and I didn't tell him about the teacher you've been seeing."

Her spine straightened. Did Will have someone else watching her while he was gone, or had he followed her and Erin himself? Had he seen Erin kiss her goodnight? Heat rose to her cheeks. "You know about Erin?"

"Yeah." His fingers tightened around hers. "This is a small town. Sara told me."

"Sara? Where did you see her?"

"I stopped by the shop. You weren't there. When I asked about you, she told me how happy you were—that you were seeing a teacher. I had to check him out."

She pulled her hand from his grasp. "For heaven's sakes why?"

"You're under my protection. My job is to make sure you're safe."

"Wait." She raised a finger while shaking the confusion from her head. "You told me to go out with other men, but you neglected to tell me you would need to check them out and spy on us."

"I—" His gaze jumped around the room like he was trying to decide which exit would be his best bet.

The veins in her temples throbbed. Will suddenly went from someone she pitied to someone she might kill. She stuffed her fists into her hips. "How could you forget to share that bit of information? Tell me, Will. Don't you have a memorized list of what you need to tell a person you're protecting? Some sort of Miranda type thing. I mean, it is your job."

"I—"

"Oh, stop mumbling." Her chair toppled as she jumped up. She reached down and Will grabbed her hand. Their faces were inches apart. Nicole's blood zinged through her veins. They were reliving the cotton candy scenario all over again and she had a feeling this scene was heading in a different direction.

"Don't see him again."

"What?" Her knees weakened under the desire she saw in Will's stare and she fumbled for the chair.

The chair Will sat upon scraped the vinyl flooring as he pushed back and stood. "You heard me. Please don't see him again."

Nicole's pulse kicked into overdrive as he pulled her to him and his strong arm slid around her waist. She clamped her lips closed. She'd broken off her short-lived relationship with Erin last weekend. Erin was nice, but when she was with him, all she did was compare him to the man holding her now. The one making her heart pound so hard it was a wonder he didn't hear the thump. Erin didn't measure up to Will, not one bit, but she wasn't going to tell Will any of this. She loved the way he was clinging to her, hoping for the same thing she'd wished for herself ever since he held her in his arms after she'd broken into Gorgon's house. "Well, we have a date next Friday night. He's taking Luka and I on the Halloween hayride."

"Break the date. I'll take you."

His thumb made tiny circles in the small of her back, sending heated charges to her womb. She licked the want from her lips before she asked, "What about going out with other men."

"No. No more." His voice grew huskier. "I was a stupid, stupid man. Please forgive me."

Before her happiness showed on Nicole's lips, Will lowered his head and his lips moved softly across hers in a sensual dance, whispering promises.

Chapter Twenty-six

Hospitals gave Will the willies. The air was thick with suffering. Sobs seemed relentless. Even the cushion under Will moaned as he leaned forward. He placed his elbows on his knees and dangled his bottle of water from his hands. He glanced out the large window and swore he saw a couple snow flurries dance by on the blustery October wind. Tonight was going to be cold.

That thought was followed by another. One that made him shift on the seat again as he imagined how Nicole would fit perfectly under his arm and cuddle up against him for warmth, while under a blanket. He checked the clock on the wall next to the door. A few minutes past noon. The hayride was tonight and he was to pick Nicole and Luka up at seven.

The crack of a bat brought his attention back to the game he watched with Gary. Will stared up at the small flat screen television as the ball flew over the second base man's head to the outfield, only to be caught by the center fielder at the wall. The baseball pennant race was in full swing and their team was in deep shit.

"Ahhh," Gary moaned between clenched teeth. His jaw was wired to minimized movement. The doctors who cared for Gary had stated more than a dozen times how he was damn lucky. Three inches higher and the bullet that had cracked his jawbone and exited through his right cheek, would've entered Gary's brain at his temple, killing him instantly.

Gary grumbled as he grabbed the side rail and with effort inched himself and the cast on his left leg further up on the bed. "Damn. Carlos always goes for the high balls." At least that was what Will thought he'd said. His friend's grumble sounded more like a foreigner's gibberish.

"He should've seen it coming." Will kept his eyes focused on Gary's eyes and not the bandages covering his right cheek. Will sat his bottle down on Gary's bedside table. "Relax, the game's not over."

In the bottom of the ninth, two men stood on first and third base with two outs and the Phillies pitcher was up to bat. They were down by two against the home team, The Yankees.

"Umph, relax he says," Gary mumbled, but Will got the meaning.

"We're coming to the top of the order. You want a sip of water?" Will slid Gary's styrofoam cup to the front of the lap table.

Gray waved the cup off. "Beer. I'd like. And—" He drew a breath and took a second to muster his strength. "To go to the john instead of a freakin' pan."

"Hey! The doctor told you not to overdo the talking," Sharon said as she walked into the room. She flashed a smile at Will, letting him know she was happy to hear her husband complain.

She dropped her purse and coat on the hardback chair in the corner and rounded the bed. Squinting, she waggled her finger between them. "I heard the two of you grumbling about the game the moment I entered the wing. You know, if you keep acting up, they're going to sedate you and throw Will out. Then, neither one of you will see the end of the game."

"Will." Gary tapped the bed railing and then wiggled his fingers. "Gun? I need protection." He coughed while splaying his hand over his chest.

"I mean it. Stop talking." Sharon bent over the rail

and planted a kiss on Gary's forehead, marked with cuts from the flying glass.

Will looked away, giving them a bit of privacy. He really never envied Gary, but he did now. If he was lying in the hospital bed, instead of Gary, who would be here to adjust his pillow like Sharon was doing right now for his partner? Who would take care of him when the time came to go home? Both questions brought Nicole's beautiful smile to mind.

Another crack of the bat resounded through the room followed by Gary's bellow. His partner's fist shot into the air while his face beamed with excitement. If Gary could get up, he'd be spinning Sharon around the room, but for the next two months he would be wearing that cast, until his femur mended.

Applauding their team's win, Will rose and high-fived his partner. "I told you. Didn't I tell you? Never doubt your team, buddy."

Gary winced, after a chuckle.

"Well, this is totally unexpected. What's all the cheering about in here?"

At the sound of her voice, Will's past fell on his shoulders with a thud. The floor seemed to open up and their camaraderie, which had brightened the room, slid into hell.

No. Not Laura. His hearing was playing tricks on him. She lived and worked in Virginia. As far as Will knew, Gary and Sharon hadn't spoken to her in years.

Staring at Gary's wide eyes, his grin disappeared and the hair on the back of his neck bristled. Why in the hell was Laura here?

Gary's eyes shifted several times between him and the woman who stood behind him. Finally, his partner shrugged with some effort, affirming he had no knowledge of Laura's visit.

Will shifted his eyes to Sharon who looked as guilty as anyone could with a smoking gun in their hand.

While ignoring Will's glare which asked the question, "What in the hell was his ex-fiancée doing here?", Sharon gave Gary one of those I-didn't-mean-for-this-to-happen looks. "I..."

Sharon's strained smile should've told Laura to run, but Will didn't hear steps of retreat.

"Laura heard what happened and called me last night," Sharon quickly explained, while stoking Gary's arm. "She wanted to stop by and see you."

Will snatched Sharon's gaze for a second as she looked from her husband to Laura. The second was all he needed to let her know that he was pissed beyond being pissed.

A quick dash of her tongue crossing her lips told him she clearly got his message.

"Come on in, Laura." Pasting a cordial smile on her face, Sharon waved. "These two were just celebrating. Their team just knocked the Yankees off."

"Go, Phillies," Laura cheered as if she was still part of the foursome who'd go out together whenever all their schedules allowed.

Will remained standing, much like a statue, with one hand curled into a fist and the other still pointing 'YEAH, MAN' at Gary. Feeling Laura's stare boring into the back of his skull, he dropped his hand to his side. They hadn't seen each other in three years — ever since she had walked out on him for a lousy career move. She hadn't thought the job was lousy. In reality, the opportunity had been a great career move, but it had been lousy in his book, since she had to decide between the job and him. His heart shattered into a million pieces when she had chosen her career.

Over the years, he heard bits and pieces about her or

her work. The most recent, being that she'd received another promotion and was now head of some task force for the Virginia senator's security detail. She was a big wig working closely with the Secret Service, since Virginia and D.C. shared so many faculties.

Her exotic scent wafted over his shoulder, tantalizing him. She still wore the perfume he'd purchased for her while they'd vacationed in the south of France.

Will stiffened his spine and pushed aside the flood of memories causing his pulse to dance— especially those of Laura's naked body silhouetted against a moonlight night. With every ounce of willpower, he focused on his plan of action to get the hell out of there.

Rumors and stories were easy to brush off and walk away from, but Laura in the flesh couldn't be ignored. He had no choice but to turn and face the woman he thought he'd love forever and who had stomped on his heart until it resembled chopped dog food.

"I need to get going. I have that thing tonight," he said, grabbing his ski jacket from the back of the chair and slipped into the sleeves.

"Don't be late. A good thing." Gary pulled his lip up in a lopsided smile and winced in the process.

Will smiled, thinking of the way Nicole looked up at him last Sunday night all starry-eyed while he held her in his arms and kissed her. He could've made love to her then, but he hadn't. He wanted more than sex. She needed to trust him. "Yeah, I think you're right. You rest, buddy. I'll call you tomorrow."

Will had intended to pin Sharon with a glare, but her expression filled with remorse changed his mind. How could he not pity her? He knew exactly what happened. Laurie called, insisted on seeing Gary for just a few minutes and hadn't taken no for answer.

Without a glance over his shoulder to check where

Laura stood, Will walked around the bed, nudged Sharon's upper arm with his fist and then planted a kiss on her cheek. "You make him behave. I'll talk to you tomorrow."

"Thanks, Will." She grabbed his hand and squeezed. "And have a great time tonight. You deserve the best."

With his best friends' approval of his and Nicole's budding relationship, Will's spirits rose. He inhaled, knowing he had to get past Laurie before he'd truly feel happy, however. "Okay, I'm off."

He turned and his heart flipped unexpectedly against his chest. Laura's jet black bangs fringed emerald eyes that challenged Cleopatra's. Eyes that had haunted every lonely moment he'd had over the past three years. Once upon a time, they had looked up at him, glistening with the afterglow of their love making. Now, Laura's eyes neither sparkled nor glistened. They simply reached out to him.

For what?

Her long fingers worked the belt of her trench coat while her full red lips pulled up into a tentative smile. "Hi, Will."

The breathless two words were filled with questions. Questions he didn't want to answer and didn't intend to give the time of day. "I'll get out of your way."

He wanted to run, but couldn't believe taking the first step was this hard. His sneaker's soles felt cemented to the floor. Pulling his eyes from hers, the trance between them broke. Will side-stepped his ex-girlfriend, ignoring the hand she offered and rushed out into the brightly lit hallway.

Why hadn't he just thrown the fact he had a date in her face and rejoiced in her reaction? Because his life and who he spent his nights with wasn't Laura's damn business, that's why.

Will shook his head. Unbelievable. Laura really thought he'd forgive her for dumping him and just pick up as pals? Fuck her.

Relieved to be away from her, Will stalked toward the wing's exit. In the short time it took him to reach the elevators, anger had beaten up his past and kicked the baggage to the darkest recesses of his mind. Now, he was mentally ready to move on with his life. He stabbed the down button.

"Will, wait."

Laura's cry caused frustration to flare in his gut and he inhaled through his nostrils, trying to calm his angst.

The elevator's bell binged above him and the doors slid open. The passengers inside shifted their positions and then frowned with impatience at his hesitation to enter. They wanted to be on their way. He wanted to be on his way, but again, his shoes were glued to the floor. If he got onto the elevator, he'd always wonder what would've happened if he'd stayed and faced her. He had enough what-ifs in his life.

He turned.

Their gazes locked and Laura's gait slowed to a halt. Her fingers clasped together in prayer fashion. "Please. I need to talk to you."

As if some power with more insight into what was good for him and his future had made the decision, the elevator doors swished closed, leaving the two of them alone in the small foyer.

Laura's heels clicked against the vinyl flooring much like the slow tick-tock of a bomb.

Outside the large paned windows, the world moved on. Will shifted his weight to his other foot as she closed the short distance left between them.

Stopping within a foot of his personal space, warily, Laura reached out and wrapped her soft hand around his fingers.

Tingles charged up Will's arm and spiraled around his heart, searching for a way inside. Suddenly he wasn't so sure the past was behind them. And that frightened him. "What do you want?"

Laura squeezed his hand. "I just wanted to say good to see you."

Noting the smile playing on her lips, Will denied the urge to pull back from her touch, and held his position. He was aware of the way her body leaned toward him, the planes of her heart-shaped face, and the unyielding steadiness of her stare. Laura wanted something from him and was willing to use their past and his heart to get it.

Well, whatever it was, in order to get it, she was going to have to take as good as she gave. "I wish I could say the same."

The brown specks in Laura's green eyes flashed and her irises darkened into huge drops of resentment.

Her reaction confirmed his suspicions. It wasn't a reconciliation she was after. What was her game?

Taking the verbal slap like a champ, she tilted her chin up a notch and stared into his eyes. Then she reached out and laced her fingers with his. "I thought after three years you'd be over me."

"Don't flatter yourself. I am over you." He chuckled, squeezing her fingers, maybe a tad harder than he should've. He saw Laura flinch before she pulled her hand back. Nicole's smile entered his mind. "I've moved on."

"You have?"

"You say that like you're surprised. You always told me I was a catch. Don't you remember?"

"I remember."

"Look, you don't have to fish, Laura, or pry me with compliments. What do you want?"

Her perfectly plucked brow arched under her bangs. "What makes you think I want something?"

"Come on. You haven't had any contact with Gary or Sharon since you moved on with your life." He'd said moved on with your life as if he'd scratched the space between them with air quote marks. "So it's a safe bet you didn't drive all the way up here from Virginia to see Gary, not without a reason. You knew I would be here. After three damn years, what could you possible want with me?"

"You're right. I knew you would be here."

Will clamped his jaw together and looked up at the dropped paneled ceiling. His anger seemed to tighten the collar of his Henley thermo shirt around his neck. He glared at Laura. "Sharon?"

"No. Sharon didn't say a word to me." Her long, black hair fell over her shoulder, cascading past the mounds of her breasts.

He quickly changed direction of his attention away from the area he had loved to nuzzle and where he had laid his head after a long, hard day. "You've been spying on me?"

She sighed. "I reasoned you'd be here. Gary's not only your partner, but your best friend. I know you were with him when this happened. Sharon told me that much. And I know you. You've undoubtedly been beating yourself up thinking what happened to him was your fault. Even though, it wasn't."

"How would you know whose fault this is?"

"I know you're the best."

He felt the wall he'd built between them wobble. He was such a fool. How did the old saying go? Fool him once…

Will stretched his arm and pulled the sleeve of his jacket back to look at his watch. He knew what the time was, but he wanted to impress on Laura that he had more important things to do with his life than share chit chat with her. In about six hours, he'd be keeping Nicole warm and having a hell of a great time. "What do you want? I have a date."

"A date?" She blinked.

"Yes. A date. Is that so hard to fathom?" He didn't bother holding back the irritation he felt from echoing in his tone. Will turned and stabbed the elevator button again. The lit numbers above the doors showed both elevators had climbed to the top floors. Taking the stairs would've been faster, but they also would've been the coward's way out. "If you're going to tell me what you want, you've better do it now."

Apparently catching the elevator's light signaling its descent, Laura slipped in between him and the stainless steel doors. She tilted her head slightly to the left, the green of her eyes catching the sunlight steaming in the window and reflecting back at him with sorrow. In that split second, the wall crumbled and he couldn't help but think how beautiful she was.

"I don't want anything, Will. Just the opposite. I have something for you. Here." In her palm, his grandmother's engagement diamond ring sparkled. The ring he had given her when he had confessed he'd love her forever and asked her to marry him. "I thought it was about time I gave this back to you."

His brows pulled together. "I thought—," he stammered.

Laura's shoulder's relaxed and the strong lines of her face took on a humble appearance. "I know. I deserve every thought. The way I ended things between us was bad. Real bad."

She was right there. His heart cringed recalling the pain she had inflected upon him.

"I should've been more honest with you about my feelings and where I stood as far as marriage. I never wanted to get married, Will, not to anyone. Ever." She ran her tongue across her lip and peeked up at him through her dark lashes. "But I want you to know, because of you, I came damn close to changing my mind."

The elevator dinged.

Glancing at the doors, she drew a breath leveling her shoulders again, and smiled up at him. "Here." Her warm hand caressed his and she gently pressed his family's heirloom into the soft bed of his palm.

The tenderness of her touch remained with him for a moment after she withdrew her hand. He trapped the diamond in his fist, the stainless steel doors slid open.

Ignoring the world, Laura reached up and drew him into a hug. She whispered into his ear, "It was good to see you, Will. I wish you the best."

She lingered a kiss on his cheek, breathing in his scent before she let him go. He knew she was taking a memory with her.

As Will watched her walked away, he realized Laura no longer felt right in his arms. Thanks to her visit here today, his past was finally in the past.

Chapter Twenty-seven

Gorgon dropped his arm from over his eyes, sat up on the hotel's sofa, and arched his back, stretching the stiffness from his spine. He hated this sitting around. The damn cold damp weather was seeping into his bones. Fuck. He should be on a Caribbean island, sunning himself on the beach. And he would as soon as he had his woman and child back. They would leave this country for good. Well, he'd come back for business matters, but Katrina would never see her homeland again.

His wait wouldn't be long now. His plan was in its final stage.

A knock at the door turned his head. What did his man want now? He'd told Drat not to disturb him unless it was important. His doctor said he needed to rest even though he felt stronger than he had in months.

Holding his arm across his stomach, Gorgon pushed off the cushions. His muscles had healed, but the memory of pain shooting through his adnominal muscles when he moved made the action a habit.

The knock echoed through the suite again.

Gorgon straightened and tucked his shirt in his pants as he crossed the room. Without checking the spy hole, he opened the door. "What is it?"

"Sorry, boss. Arnold's here."

Arnold. He didn't expect to see the man so soon. Gorgon peered down the hall to where his other guard held the tough kid at bay. Gorgon had found Arnold last summer hustling in Atlantic City. The kid had guts and dreams which put him instantly on Gorgon's good side because he'd always said, "What good were dreams without guts?"

Gorgon's jaw twitched. And the kid had a hellva of a good right hook.

The smug look Arnold wore told Gorgon he had good news. "Okay. But frisk him good and then bring him in. Rafe can guard the door."

Gorgon flipped on the lights over the bar. As he reached for two glasses, the door closed behind him. He sat the glasses down and turned. "Arnold, you look as if you've swallowed the proverbial carney."

"I think you'll be very happy." The young man's lips curved upward. He shoved his hands into his leather jacket's pockets and arched up on his toes. Another attribute Gorgon liked in Arnold was that he always was eager to please.

"That so?" Gorgon heard the emphasis Arnold had put on the word 'very'. He trapped his bottom lip, fighting the show of excitement wanting to curl his mouth into a smile, and nodded. "Have a seat."

He stepped to the bar and grabbed a bottle of vodka. Maybe things were turning around for him at last. He poured three fingers of vodka into the glasses, turned, and handed one to Arnold. "I drink to your health."

Arnold raised his glass. "And I to yours, boss."

"Thank you." Gorgon watched the man kick back the shot tumbler over the rim of his own. The liquor's heat flowed down his throat and into his gut, chasing the chill from him.

After setting his glass on the table, he pulled a chair out and took a seat across from Arnold. "So, what do you have to tell me?"

Smiling, Arnold sat his glass aside. "We made our first run without problems."

"Did you expect trouble?"

"I expected some, yes. Since that marshal was shot last week, seems like every cop is on our ass."

"That is what happens. So you got one."

"Three." Arnold's brown eyes twinkled with the glow from the small chandelier over the table. He held up three fingers one at a time.

"Three?" Gorgon raised a brow, surprised by the number. "Junkies?"

"No. Good girls." Arnold smile widened to a broad-tooth grin. "Two are twins."

"Twins?"

"Identical. Blond haired, blue eyed, blossoming beauties."

Gorgon pictured his off-shore account doubling in size. "How old are they?"

"Fourteen. Maybe fifteen. Hard to tell nowadays the way they dress."

"Where did you get them?"

"Upstate New York. Last night, after a high school football game they had walked away from the school grounds and stood on a corner. My guess is to get away from the traffic emptying out of the parking lot and make finding them easier for their parents. My partner waited down the street with the van while I walked up behind them. Zap, zap, they were on the ground and a minute later they were in the van. No one was around to see us. Easy."

Gorgon reached over and poured Arnold another shot while he continued to tell his story.

"The other is a cute little red-head. Freckles. Huge brown eyes. She says she's nine. We picked her up later, at a Hamburger Heaven. Her mother let her go to the bathroom by herself. Mistake. I carried her out the side door. We drove through the drive-thru and got our burgers, and then hit the interstate a quarter mile down the road. Easy target."

"Where are they now?"

"We took them to the house in Valance."

Valance was one of the four locations he and Donnie had set up for their men to take their captives to and hold them without suspicions until they could find buyers.

All of the realtors Donnie had worked with had run circles and jumped through fire rings to find exactly the types of places he wanted and they needed. The realtors had thought Donnie was a ghost writer for a renowned author, searching for seclusion in order to do his work in peace. Gorgon chuckled inside. The government wasn't the only one who could run co-op operations.

Arnold reached inside his jacket and pulled out a few pictures taken with an old Polaroid camera, so as not to be traced by anyone, and slid them across the table. "I thought you'd like to see them."

Gorgon tipped his glass, emptying the last drops, before he sat forward and picked up the two photos. His pulsed picked up staring down at the twins. They were mouth-watering in their belly shirts and jeans, cut near all the inappropriate spots, or appropriate, depending on the viewer. Arnold had done very well indeed. They would most definitely bring them a huge price. But the nine year old that made his heart flutter. Her red hair, her freckles, her features over all reminded him of his Katrina. "This one…"

"You like her?" Arnold's brow arched.

"She is special. Mark my words. She will bring a good price."

"So you're happy boss?"

"Yes." Gorgon supported his stomach and rose. "I'll get your down payment. Setting up the auction will take a few days, until then, make sure these girls are not harmed. I don't want them touched by your men, or you.

Understand?" He rounded the table and laid his hand on Arnold's shoulder, causing him to jump. "They haven't been mistreated, have they?"

Fear reflected in Arnold's eyes. "No, sir. And I understand."

Gorgon held onto his gaze, searching for the truth. After a full ten seconds, he was satisfied that Arnold told the truth. He patted Arnold's arm. "Good. I'll be just a minute."

As Gorgon removed the fifteen thousand dollars down payment from the hotel safe, he couldn't get the image of the little girl out of his head. She wasn't Katrina. But what if he didn't find Katrina?

Chapter Twenty-eight

Off in the distance, among the shadows of the forest, an agonizing scream cut the night, followed by a sinister crackle and then silence. A chill crawled up Will's spine as he peered over his shoulder.

The crowd surrounding him ignored the plea for help. Not one single person turned their heads in the direction of the scream. Everyone continued on with their conversations as if the bloody cries for help were normal.

They were.

However, the memories of the last few weekends were still fresh in Will's mind, especially after visiting Gary in the hospital this afternoon, and with each plea, an icy finger cut from his ear and across his cardiac artery.

A tractor backfired and Will jumped, reaching behind his back with his free hand for a gun that wasn't there. The group of teenagers standing behind him snickered while he straightened his jacket and his face warmed. If only they knew or had seen one of the scenes he dealt with on a daily bases, they'd be scrambling for cover.

Stretching his neck from side to side, he drew in a breath of cold air tinted with rotting leaves, French Fries and diesel fuel, and attempted to relax, but he couldn't. Nicole was taking a long time to grab a hot drink. A half-hour, if not more, had passed since she left his side.

After draping the blankets he held on the fence, he stepped from his spot in line for the haunted hayride and searched the crowd mingling in front of the refreshment stand. Where was Nicole?

Will's pulse kicked up as the crowd moved, blocking his view. He caught a glimpse of a gray knit hat resembling the one Nicole wore, near the front of the line. The crowd shifted again and Nicole's auburn hair confirmed the woman was indeed her. Under the neon lights indicating the small building was the place to grab food and hot drinks to ward off the autumn dampness, the tones of Nicole's long locks shimmered in long waves over her pea coat.

Relieved she was in his view, Will realized he was on his toes and lowered his heels to the ground. He had to chill. He'd taken a night off from saving the world to be with Nicole and Luka, and he wanted to enjoy the time.

Seeing Laura today confirmed even more so, that there had been something missing in his life, a void that Nicole seemed to fill to perfection. He wanted to be with her—not as his charge, but as a woman.

He was ready to get on with his life and he wanted Nicole and Luka in it.

Some of his friends and co-workers would say he was nuts, taking up a relationship with Nicole. After all, she was Gorgon's woman and has the Russian's kid in tow, but he didn't care. Both Nicole and Luka couldn't help their ties to Gorgon. All he knew was he couldn't get Nicole out of his mind and when he was with her, he felt like he was walking three feet off the ground. And Luka, regardless of who his father was, was a damn nice kid. There was no doubt in Will's mind that Nicole had everything to do with Luka's behavior.

Nicole turned from the counter and Will could almost hear the laughter escaping her lips by the smile she wore. The guy who'd waited on her was laughing too.

Will's heated glare honed in on the man. His leer followed Nicole as she walked away until the next person in line pounded their hand on the counter, gaining his attention. Jealousy was an emotion Will very seldom experienced, but emotion was fast becoming one he had to handle every few minutes while in Nicole's company.

He searched for Nicole and found her again, dodging kids. She hurried toward the jungle gym area where she stopped Luka in mid-chase of some of his friends and offered him one of the two cups she carried. Without taking a sip, Luka shook his head and skirted around her, racing after the gang of boys.

Nicole turned, smiled and shrugged before making her way through the maze of children toward him.

Will would describe himself as a man's man, but somewhere over the last three and a half months Nicole had managed to wrap his heart with fuzzy warmth and caused an inestimable hunger for her in him. He didn't give a damn one bit.

He studied her full lips. Their sweetness lingered in his memory. Last Sunday night, when things had grown pretty heated between the two of them, he could've laid Nicole right there on her kitchen table, but just having sex wasn't what he wanted from her. He wanted more. He wanted to make love to her for a thousand nights. Perhaps for the rest of his life.

That notion caused his stomach to flip-flop. His angst had nothing to do with her past. His hesitancy was all about him having the guts to give his heart to someone, again.

As she grew closer, he noticed the forty degree temperature brightened Nicole's cheeks like the crimson leaves falling to the ground. Her faded jeans, turtleneck and pea coat fit her much better than the heels, short skirt and top he had first seen her wearing. God, she was beautiful.

His heartbeat zoomed when she smiled up at him.

With a gloved hand, she held out a cup. "Here you

go."

The cords of his shoulders relaxed now that she was back at his side. He returned her smile and took the semi-steaming brew. "Thanks."

The warm plastic cup containing hot cider warmed his bare fingers. He had gloves in his pocket, but refused to wear them. He didn't want anything between him and the possibility of feeling Nicole's soft skin. Like now. A gust blew across the field and lifted a strand of hair across her face. He grabbed the opportunity before she could react and brushed the silky strands back, trailing his fingers along her smooth jaw line.

With her eyes closed, Nicole tilted her head up, letting him know she enjoyed his touch. Passion glimmered in her eyes when she opened them, and Will fought the urge to drop his cider to the ground, grab her by the hand and pull her into a dark shadow away from prying eyes where their dance could move to the next level.

Instead he took a sip of his cider and cleared the want from his throat. Adjusting his stance and lessening the pressure against his zipper, Will knew he needed to focus on something else other than the woman who was heating his blood. He turned his attention to the playground. "Luke's too busy for a drink, huh?" He nodded toward the boy, but on a quick glance, caught Nicole taking a quick swallow of her own cider. He smiled behind his cup.

"Running around like he is, he's not cold. I, on the other hand, am chilled to the bone." She pulled her coat together at the lapels and then stomped her feet on the packed gravel path. "I probably should've worn my thermal socks under these hiking boots. My toes are so cold."

His eyes darted toward the section of the parking lot

where his car was parked. He could warm her up there.

Nicole hunkered over her cup and Will watched with fascination as this time she'd pursed her full lips and blew across the hot liquid, before taking a sip.

Feeling his reaction to her actions growing larger, Will directed his eyes to the playground again and saw that Luka and his best friend, Tommy, now climbed the stairs on the sliding board. A few seconds later Luka followed by Tommy sailed down the board. Laughing over their collision, the pair scrambled to their feet and raced back to the ladder. Will couldn't recall the last time he felt as free and as joyous as the two boys.

"Thanks for letting Tommy come with us," Nicole said while watching the boys play.

"No problem. He's company for Luka. I'm sure we'd have bored him to death."

She brushed her hair back from her cheek with the back of her gloved hand and tilted her face up toward him. "You wouldn't. He likes you a lot, Will."

Her long hair cascaded over her shoulders in soft waves and Will couldn't stop the image of Laura from popping into his mind. It was like a psychology test for his heart. Laura pitted against Nicole. Laura's image faded and his heart warmed as he stared at the rosy cheeked vixen standing before him. "Thanks. I like him too. He's a good kid."

"Yes, he is, and loves living here." Her irises grew larger as her attention was pulled beyond his shoulder.

The hairs on the nape of Will's neck stood on end and his spine stiffened with an intake of air. Cautiously, Will glanced behind him and down the line of customers waiting for their turn on the hayride, checking each face for signs of interest in him and Nicole or in Luka. He saw nothing out of the ordinary. There were strangers mingled in with the local town's people, but no one stood out as being a threat. He turned back to Nicole. "Is something wrong? Did you see someone who looked familiar?"

"No." She shook her head. "Sorry. I didn't mean to put you on guard. "I was just checking if anyone is paying attention to us."

He leaned down and whispered into her ear, "You don't have to worry."

Nicole pulled back slightly, staying cheek to cheek with him. She looked deep into his eyes, causing his pulse to flutter. "I'm not worried. Not when you're with me. I was just going to ask something and I didn't want anyone to overhear."

The smile which had formed on his lips at her compliment faded. "What?"

"How is Gary?"

Will sighed as he pulled back, wishing she had wanted to ask him to kiss her, instead of reminding him of the troubles he wanted to leave behind for a few hours. But he appreciated her concern over his friend. "He's doing real well, for what had happened to him. Sharon said the doctors think he'll be there for another week and then they'll send him home. He'll have a few months of physical therapy after the cast comes off, but he should recover fully in about six months."

"He was lucky."

Will stuffed his free hand into his pocket. The image of Gary lying in the hospital bed, bandaged just about everywhere and his left leg in a cast, made Will's stomach sour. How only three bullets out of so many had hit home, cracking Gary's jaw, lodging in his shoulder and shattering his femur, was a miracle. "He was damn lucky."

"I'm glad he's doing well. I feel like—"

Will bowed his head next to hers, pulled his hand from his pocket and pointed his index finger at her nose.

"Don't say it. You know you had no part in what happened to him. Understand?"

Nicole's gaze dropped to her cup. Torment chewed away at her psyche much like she was doing to her bottom lip. Her dark lashes blinked several times against her smooth cheeks, and he knew without seeing them that tears threatened to fall from her eyes.

Will reached out and with his finger placed under her chin, gently forced her to look at him. "Don't do this to yourself. What happened wasn't your fault. Just like it wasn't my fault. If Gary was here, he'd tell you the same thing." He stared hard into Nicole's eyes until she pulled back from his touch and nodded. Hearing a child's cry, he checked Luke's whereabouts and made sure that the boy was fine before he took another swallow of his now lukewarm cider.

"I'd like to visit him, but I know that's out of the question." She sniffled and swiped her gloved finger along her lashes." So will you tell him I asked about him? When you see him again?"

"I already did."

A tiny smile turned the corner of her lips up. "Thanks." She inhaled and looked toward the playground.

To someone who wasn't trained to watch people, Nicole's brave front might've worked, but he noted her fingers tightened around the styrofoam cup.

Will downed the last gulp of his drink, wishing the cider was something a bit stronger. Nicole's past, his work, and Gorgon had somehow found their way into their date. He mentally slammed his fist against an imagery wall. Damn. They both deserved to have a good time. And he was going to do everything in his power to make sure they would.

"You know when I was a kid, I used to work our community's Halloween event."

"Really? Doing what?" Nicole's eyes sparkled with interest and he knew he'd hit on the key to turning the night around. First dates were all about learning about each other, sharing memories, and likes and dislikes. If he wanted her to open up to him, he had to share something of himself.

"Yeah. We had a haunted hayride too. I played a lot of parts, but I think my favorite was Dracula." He swooped his arm in the air and then draped hand over her shoulder, pulling her close to his side."

Her chuckle chased the chill from his toes. He leaned in and gazed deep into her eyes. Then in his best Count Dracula tone, he said, "Deep within the woods, where the sun dares not enter, I would lie, waiting for my next vic—I mean wife to come to me."

"Isn't that a little lazy or sexist to assume they would come to you?" Nicole nudged him with her elbow.

"Oww." He played injured, stared down his nose at her and wiggled his brows. "I was the count. They always came to me."

The chug, chug, chug of a tractor grew louder and louder, becoming deafening as John Deere pulled up to the loading dock which was about twenty feet from them. At a snail's pace, the waiting line they stood in moved forward. The feel of her body moving against his, sent erotic thoughts to his brain and a second later every vein in his body burned with the rush of hot blood. Especially those to the south of his belt.

He stopped the path his mind was headed onto and concentrated on his story. "Some came by foot, but most arrived on a wagon just like this one." With a crooked finger, he pointed to the dark, dank forest beyond the wagon and then drifted his digit to the people climbing the straw bales and taking a seat in the wagon.

Tiny bits of humor flared in her cynical eyes. "There

are many women on the wagons, and many wagons. How would you know which woman was to be your next vic—" Nicole coughed into her shoulder. "—type?"

Staring into her shimmering pupils, which darted on occasion to those around them, Will knew he acted carefree and a bit crazy. But damn if he cared. He cared little of what others thought of him. The only one he was trying to impress was the beautiful woman standing beside him, and she seemed to enjoy his antics.

He trailed his hand across her back, brushing the nape of her neck with his thumb pad, and then down her arm, lingering at her wrist a moment, before he snatched the cup dangling from her grip. He tossed both cups into the nearby trash can and then took her gloved hand in his. "I just knew."

Open fervor widened her eyes as he slipped her glove from her hand and raised her warm fingers to his lips.

"Mom," Luka screamed.

Nicole jumped, pulling her hand from his grasp. The same moment she turned, Luka dashed up to them and crashed into her. He wrapped his thin arms tightly around her waist and hung on as if someone or something would pry him away forever.

"What's wrong? Where's Tommy?" Nicole asked.

Over Nicole's bent head, Will scanned the area searching for Tommy and saw the boy running towards them.

"He's after me," Luka squealed, scooting behind Nicole.

Will heard Nicole's sigh of relief.

Tommy slid to a stop. "Chicken."

"Don't call me that," Luka whined, peeking around Nicole's hip.

"Chicken, chicken. Luke is a chicken."

"I am not. Mom, make him stop."

"Tommy. That is not nice."

"He started it. He called me a girl lover."

Will chuckled, glancing at Nicole before bending over and looking at Tommy at his level. "A what?"

Tommy blushed while he twisted his sneaker's toe into the gravel. "A girl lover."

"He kissed Brittani Wort." Luca, showing his bravery came out from behind Nicole. "Under the sliding board."

Nicole tried hard to hide her amusement. "Is that true, Tommy?"

"She kissed me. She chased me and I couldn't get away."

Tears edged the boy's lower lids.

Will rubbed Tommy's shoulders. "It's okay, buddy. I understand completely."

"You do?" Nicole stared down at him.

"Yeah. Us boys need to stick together." Will turned to Tommy. "So why were you calling Luke chicken."

"Because he wouldn't help me get away from her."

"I didn't want to get kissed. Not by no girl."

"I see." Will stood. A second later, Nicole and he both broke out in laughter while the boys stared at them.

"Okay, guys. I tell you what. Why don't you both stay right here with us—where Ms. Wort can't get to either one of you. Besides, here comes the next wagon. Are you ready to get really scared?" He reached down and tickled first Tommy and then Luca.

Both boys shouted with glee.

A few minutes later, they were loaded onto the wagon and took their seats.

The ride on the hay wagon wasn't going to be as he expected. Will looked over Tommy and Luca's heads at Nicole and sighed.

Chapter Twenty-nine

The old steps creaked under Will's weight.

Through her pea coat, Nicole swore she felt the heat of his body as he followed her up the stairs to the second floor. Maybe the warmth making her want to shed her clothing was caused by the delectable images which slid into her mind as they climbed higher toward her bedroom.

She'd dreamt a hundred times over about this trek. However, in her dreams, their climb upstairs had been a whole lot different. Their hands had been all over each other, fumbling to remove the clothing separating hot skin from hot skin. Her shirt had lay crumpled on the floor at the base of the steps while Will's had been tossed haphazardly across the polished railing. The same smooth railing her hand slid across now.

As her fingertips had relished in the feel of Will's coarse chest hairs, he had removed her bra with a snap and zip and flung the scrap of lace wayward. His warm lips had then suckled her already taunt nipples and before her eyes had drifted closed with delight, she'd catch a glimpse of the lacy material twirling on the living room's ceiling fan by its thin strap.

Yes, her dreams had been totally different. She sighed, pushing her pulse kicking musings away, and concentrated on the here and now, and said over her shoulder, "You shouldn't have troubled yourself. I could've carried Luka up to bed."

Will shifted the sleeping boy higher on his shoulder and smiled up at her. "No problem. I'm in no rush."

Nicole's pulse kicked up. Did he mean he intended to stay for a while? She hoped so.

Reaching around the door jamb and hitting the light switch, she entered Luka's bedroom. She hurried across the carpet designed to look like a city block and dimmed the superhero desk lamp to its nightlight mode. She pulled back the fresh laundered bed comforter and sheets and the scent of a sunny autumn day wafted into the air.

While a frost-promising wind rattled the window, Nicole's heart warmed watching Will cradle Luka's head and gently lay him on the bed. Will was a good man and Luka worshipped the ground on which he stood.

Her gaze trailed over Will's strong shoulders and back. She laced her fingers together so as not to reach out and touch him, disturbing the picture. She wished Will was her son's father.

Nicole trapped her bottom lip between her teeth. This wasn't the first time she wished Luka had different blood running through his veins, but it was the first time she allowed herself to wish Will was the man with whom she shared the bond. The only reason she had entertained the notion was because of Will's actions last Sunday night, when he came to her and pleaded for her not to see any other men.

She knew what had caused Will's change of heart. It was because of what Gary had told him and because of the attack which had almost taken his friend's life.

"After all the running around he and Tommy did tonight, I think he'll sleep until noon tomorrow," Will said, glancing over his shoulder.

The dim light reflected the amusement dancing in Will's hazel eyes and Nicole wondered if he was recalling a similar good time from his own past. She'd lay odds he had been a handful growing up, questioning and investigating everything. Or maybe he was the boy who stood guard over those who needed help.

"I think you're right." She smiled, imaging Will as that boy.

Will tapped Luka's chin just like he always did before he stepped back from the bed and allowed her to take over.

While she removed Luka's shoes and coat, she remained conscious that Will lingered at the foot of the bed watching her every move. Did he contemplate what life would be like to be a family?

She quietly placed Luka's shoes under the bed and handed his coat to Will. Their fingers brushed and tingles shot up her arm, but Will, seemingly unaffected, just turned and hung the jacket on the peg behind the door.

Nicole quickly turned back to Luka. What the hell was she doing to herself? Of course Will didn't think about them as family. He cared about her and Luka—that was a given. And the attraction between them was undeniable, but men didn't think about a long term commitment the way women did. Girls started to plan their weddings, homes, and families the moment their first love looked at them. Guys, they planned what kind of car or bike they'd drive in high school, college and after they landed a great job. Something that made them look cool. A chick magnet.

Maybe Will wasn't the marrying kind of guy and never would be. Did it matter? She'd given up on the dream of true love, marriage and a happily ever after life a long time ago. She was happy here in Logan's Summit. She was happy to see Will and be with him.

As she unbuttoned Luka's shirt, she realized the stir of want she'd felt a few minutes ago was gone.

Luka moaned and his eyes fluttered open while she pulled his sweatshirt over his head. She brushed his soft hair to the side and hummed his favorite tune, lulling him back to sleep.

"Should I hang it up on the peg too?" Will whispered while reaching for Luka's shirt.

In the dim light, their gazes locked and something about the way he looked at her made Nicole's heart skip. What was he thinking? "Yes, please."

Luka's zipper sang as she undid his jeans. Careful not to wake him again, Nicole wiggled his jeans down over his trim hips inch by inch and pulled them off. Leaving him dressed in his thermal underwear, she tucked the covers around her son and placed a kiss on his head before she stood and faced Will.

A smile pulled the corners of his mouth upward. "You're a good mom."

What a nice thing to say. "Thanks," she clipped softly, more out of embarrassment than out of fear of waking Luka. In the dim light, she was sure Will couldn't see her blush, but she certainly felt the fire in her cheeks, and lowered her head.

Will's warm hand enveloped hers, sending her pulse racing. He led her from the room. "Come on. Our turn to get comfortable and warm."

His voice was soft and deep, and sexy as all hell. Its tone sent her pulse rushing.

Maybe she was just wishing. "I'll make us some hot cocoa." She closed the door behind them and turned to find Will stood so close she had to tilt her head back to look at him.

He stared down at her with hungry eyes. "I don't want cocoa, Nicole."

She wasn't wishing or dreaming or fantasizing. A list of things she wanted this man to do to her since she'd she first seen him whirled through her mind. The images sent her blood flooding south, sensitizing every nerve in its quake. Her nipples hardened against the soft material of her blouse, aching for his touch. "What is it you—" Her tongue darted out, swiping her dry lips. "you want?"

His hands trailed up her arms, massaging her skin through the thick layers of her sweater and blouse. "I think you know."

He backed her against the wall, trapping her with his body.

Nicole swallowed hard. His male scent mixed with fresh air and a hint of straw swirled around her. His hard rise pressed against her stomach causing her to gush with need.

In the depths of his eyes, she saw he wanted her as much as she needed him, here and now. But what about tomorrow, and the day after that, and next month? And a year from now? Would he still want her as much? And would she be happy being the woman to share Will's bed whenever he wanted someone without further commitment?

Yes. The answer came to her without reservations.

Nicole traced her fingers along his jawline. She liked his shadow of a beard and wondered what delicious sensations the stubble would cause for both of them if he ran its roughness against her extended nipples and lower.

"We need to talk." His tone suggested there would be little talking between them.

Nicole pushed inside his jacket and skimmed her hands over his hard chest, longing to feel his skin against her palms. Through his sweater, Will's nipples grew hard as she swirled her palms over them. Smiling, Nicole threaded her hands around his neck. "I think you're right."

He bowed his head and she rose up on her toes to meet him. His lips made love to hers, first brushing them lightly and then deepening the kiss until the fever inside them became too much and they broke apart breathlessly.

Will's forehead pressed against hers. "I'm dying here." His eyes drifted closed. She felt the flutter of his pulse in his neck against her wrist. He opened his eyes and stared into hers. "I want to make love to you, but the decision is yours, Nicole."

Her decision. Nicole trembled inside with joy. Will was letting her make the decision to take their relationship to the next level. Her decision. There was no doubt in her mind that if she said, "No. Stop." he'd back away.

His soft hair bristled through her fingers. Over the past several months she had fallen in love with Will, and if being his mistress is what her life was to be, making love to the man she loved without commitment, she'd take it.

Her heart rejoiced with her decision.

"Come with me." She grasped his hand and led him across the hall to her bedroom. Stepping inside, the street light pouring through the tiny panes of the two half-moon stained glass panels above her windows caused a dreamlike glow to dance about the room. Her bed, covered with a pale blue country quilt and an assortment of a half dozen pillows, shimmered in the luminosity.

The door's lock clicked behind her. She heard a swish and thud and knew Will had removed his coat and tossed it on the rattan chair in the corner of the room. A moment later, he was behind her, peeling her coat from her shoulders and sliding the weighty garment slowly over her arms.

In the dim light, she waited for his next move. Her heart thumped wildly with anticipation.

His arm circled her waist, drawing her against the solid plane of his chest. She leaned into him, swayed her hips a bit and was rewarded with the feel of his shaft nestled between in the valley of her ass cheeks.

Will's groan feathered her ear.

Her knees weakened as his free hand lifted aside her hair and his warm lips nibbled at the sensitive skin at the nape of her neck. Under his wet, delicious assault, her eyes rolled back and closed. Thank goodness he supported her, if not, she'd be at his feet.

His urging rock against her backside had her wanting more of him. She twisted in his grasp, wound her arms around his neck, and stood on tip-toes to press her lips to his. Their tongues mingled and danced, probing and fueling the fire building in them.

She pressed her aching breasts against his hard chest seeking relief while Will cupped her rear-end and lifted her up against his hard cock, grinding against her mound. She moaned and behind closed eyes she saw the white plain of a climax on the horizon. Her blood surged through her veins in a free-fall. She sent a quick prayer to the heavens not to have a heart attack before she knew what having Will inside of her was like.

Needing to feel his skin against hers, she yanked his tee-shirt from his jeans, skated her hands up under the soft material and over compact muscles covering. His rough chest hair tickled the inside of her fingers as she combed and moved her palms over his tight pecs. His nipples peaked under her touch. He muttered into her mouth, "I need you."

She wanted to drive him out of his mind with want the way he was driving her insane and reached down and cup his balls.

"Nicole." He kissed her temple, her cheeks, her eyelids. "If you keep that up, I might not make it to the bed."

"We don't want that."

They fumbled and nipped while Nicole pulled Will across the room. She wanted to stand in the light where he'd be able to see her while she undressed, and, more importantly, she'd be able to see every inch of him.

She kissed him deeply, trailing her hands over his strong biceps, before she arched her back and broke their full body contact.

"You sure about this?" His fingers brushed the sides of her breasts, causing them to tighten.

Nicole's soul cried out in joy. Gorgon had never asked her permission. As quick as her past had popped into her thoughts, she shoved them away and focused on her future. "I've had sex a few times, Will. I'm not a virgin. But, I've never wanted to have sex." She brushed her fingertips across his lower lip and stared longing into his eyes. "I want to make love to you. I want to feel the passion of sex."

His eyes darkened.

She shook her head. "Don't… Don't think about my past. I'm putting it behind me. We're starting here, now. Please, Will, make love to me."

His smile made her sex clench.

He gathered her close and kissed her deeply before pulling back, again. The fever in Will's wild eyes matched the zeal making every nerve in her body hum with need.

At the same moment, each grabbed the other's sweater hems.

"I guess we both had the same idea." She laughed and the mood turned playful.

His eyebrows rose devilishly. "I guess, but I'm willing to remove all of your clothing with my teeth."

He tipped his teeth with his tongue and her panties moistened at the thought Will's mouth licking every inch of her heated flesh.

She placed her hands on her hips and took a step back, smoothing her hand up under shirt, exposing her skin to him. “I’ll let you, but only if you’re nude.”

“Anything you want.” Will stripped his sweater and tee shirt off like he was on fire, exposing strong abs covered with a triangle of sandy colored hair. His back muscles moved under his tan skin while he fumbled to unlace his boots. Racing to strip off his jeans, he toppled onto the bed.

Afraid he’d wake Luka with his curses and scuffling, she crossed to him. The thought of the strong U.S. Marshal needing help to get out of his pants brought an amused smirk to her lips.

“Okay, go ahead, laugh. Your time is coming.” Will looked up at her with a devilish glare.

Sex had never been this much fun. She yanked him free of his jeans. “I hope so and you better be good too.”

“Lady, you will not be disappointed.” In a fluid move, Will pushed off the bed, causing her to jump back. He quickly peeled his shorts away.

Nicole’s eyes widened at the sight of his thick cock. She longed to feel the length of him in her hand, against her stomach, filling and stretching her until she cried out in ecstasy. “I’m not disappointed yet.”

“And you won’t be.” Will closed the gap between them and before she blinked. “It’s your turn.” He bent at the waist and took the hem of her sweater in his teeth.

She fought to contain her laughter while he struggled to wiggle the garment up over her ribs, rubbing his whiskers against her belly. After a short minute, he let go of her top and stood. “Okay, not as easy as in the movies.”

She raised her brow. “Oh, you watch those kind of movies, do you?”

“Have to. Part of the job.”

“Right. I hear you.” She giggled.

He pointed a finger at her. “Laughing at me is not

good."

She couldn't help her happiness. He looked so damn sexy standing there with his manhood jugged toward her. "What are you going to do about it?"

"This." Will hulled her sweater over her head and threw it over his shoulder. It missed the chair, landed against the closet door and slid to the floor. "Ooops." Her shirt quickly followed.

His gaze dipped to her breasts covered by the flimsy, black lace bra and his tongue darted across his lips. "Wow!"

Nicole lifted his chin with her finger until he looked directly into her eyes. "That was my favorite sweater. I thought you had a better aim."

"I do. I'll prove it to you." The corner of his lips turned upward. He scooped her into his strong arms and dropped her onto the bed.

The mattress moaned as she bounced and settled among the pillows on the soft comforter. She looped her arm behind her head, supporting herself so that she'd have a better view of what he intended to do to her. "I'm waiting."

"I thought we discussed this before. Patience is a virtue."

"So is timeliness. I'm so hot. I need to cool off," she purred, while flashing a wicked grin and trailing her hands over her stomach, alongside her breasts and up through her hair.

Cole's chest expanded. Her actions had had the right effect on him.

"I think I can help you with that problem."

"Please."

He took her hands and raised them above her head again. "Keep them there. No touching until I say so."

His order made her hot. Tingles danced along the

trail Will's fingers made moving slowly along the tender under side of her arm, over her collar bone, down the strap of her bra and over the thin material covering her taunt nipples. "I like this. I like you in it, but…" He undid the front clasp and pushed the bra from her breasts. "Mmm, yes. That's much better."

His intake of air made her heart race faster.

"Don't you feel better?" His knuckles the underside of her breasts

"Definitely!"

He cupped each breast and worked her nipples into hardened peaks of pleasure. When she thought she couldn't stand anymore, he leaned over and swirled her inflamed points with his tongue, first the right and then the left. Nicole arched up into his mouth, wanting more of his hot breath. She moaned her disapproval when he let her go.

His eyes slanted up to meet hers. "I take it you like that."

She nodded, panting, anxious for Will to pay the same attention to every inch of her body.

"Good, because there's more." He grabbed her boots and removed them, dropping them over his shoulder to the floor with a clunk.

"You're going to wake Luka."

"Right." He removed one sock and then the other, caressing her toes. "And your moaning won't."

"I was quiet."

"I'm not done." His experienced fingers opened the clasp of her jeans and slid the zipper down, one tooth at a time. "You must be really quiet when I do..." He pulled her jeans down around her knees.

Her stomach muscles clenched as she raised her head. "Do what?" she asked, teasing him.

His look was deliciously wicked as he leaned over

her. "Do you trust me?"

"Do I have a choice?"

He raised his head. "Yes."

"Then yes, I trust you," she answered quickly. It was true. She'd trust Will with her life.

"Good."

His warm mouth tickled the skin just below her belly button while his hand trailed up the inside of her leg from her knee to her mound. A moment later, he pushed below the lace of her panties and he parted her slick folds. She gasped with delight as blew on her sensitive slit and he pushed two fingers inside her sex. Her muscles tightened around them and she moved her hips in rhythm with his hand, relishing the heat building inside her, but at the same time wanting more attention on her clit.

Nicole peeked through hooded eyes and saw the swollen head of his manhood against her leg. She wanted him to feel as wonderful as he was making her feel. She grasped his shaft and slid her hand up the length of him, and down. His moistened tip called to her and she grazed her thumb across the swollen head. Watching Will's jaw tighten as he fought to bite back his cry of gratification filled her with intense pleasure.

"You're so wet," he said between nibbles.

He pushed his fingers deeper into her and she arched her hips up to give him better access. With each pump of his hand, she drew nearer to the edge. Toppling over wouldn't be long. She bit her lip, fighting off her climax. She wanted Will to come with her.

She jolted up, making him withdraw his fingers. "I need you in me and you need to be in me, now."

In a quick frenzy, he removed her jeans and panties. His burning gaze made her throb with desire.

She squeezed her breasts together and thumbed her taut nipples before smoothing her hands over her stomach to her mound.

Will moved away from her side.

Had her brazen action changed his mind? Her heart fell in her chest as she pushed up on her elbows. "Where are you going?"

"Condom." He snatched his pants from the floor, pulled a foil package from the pocket and showed her.

Relief spiraled through her. "You carry those with you everywhere?" Her hands itched, watching him roll the sheath over his cock.

"Only since I watched you eating cotton candy." He winked. "You nearly made me cum right there in the park." He massaged the inside of her thighs, urging them apart and moved between them.

"That won't have been good." She reached between them and stroked his cock.

"Lucky I'm a man with a lot of control." His weight settled on her. His shaft rested against her folds, teasing her, kindling the burn to a roaring inferno inside her.

"You can lose control now, and…" She ran her hands over his strong shoulders and laced them around his neck. "If you need more, and I hope you do, they're in the top drawer of the nightstand," she whispered in his ear.

"What?" His gaze shot to the nightstand and then latched onto hers.

Her cheeks warmed remembering how embarrassed she was buying them. "I bought some, in case my dream came true."

He combed his fingers through her long hair, letting her locks fall onto the pillowcase. "You dreamt about me."

"Yes."

"That's good."

"Why is that good?"

"Because I've dreamt about being with you every single night since I've first seen you."

"You have?" Her heart throbbed so hard, she didn't know how he couldn't feel the pounding.

"Yes. I like you and I want you so fucking bad." He pushed inside of her, stretching her, filling her.

Nicole trapped her bottom lip between her teeth to prevent her cry of pleasure from waking her son, and the neighbors. Liking wasn't love, but, for now, she'd take it. She wanted this man more than anything. "I like you too," she moaned, wiggling her hips to take him in further.

Will pressed his grin against her lips and together they rocked, heading for the apex of bliss.

***

Will fought to keep his breathing shallow and even, afraid to move. He didn't want to wake Nicole and say goodbye just yet. He longed to hold her all day, but couldn't. His cell phone had buzzed more than once in the last hour. The outside world was waiting for him to respond.

He sighed, pressed his jaw against her head and breathed in the floral scent of her shampoo. Her soft skin pressed against the length of his side and he caught the moan rising up in his throat and stifled the cry behind clenched lips.

Without moving his head, he glanced over Nicole's head at the clock on the nightstand. He could hold her for another five minutes and then he should leave.

Dawn was pushing the night to the sidelines. The pale sky grew bluer with each second ticking off. Today was going to be a perfect autumn day and he wished he could spend it here with Nicole and Luka. The house needed a few repairs done before winter set in and all but a few leaves still clung to the oaks and maples in the yard. Nicole needed a little help and he didn't want another man offering his duties.

Maybe the call was nothing more than a check-in, but doubt prickled his conscious. His gut had a way of telling him when trouble was brewing.

He shoved the world away and focused on the woman in his arms. Picking up a lock of Nicole's hair, Will rubbed the strand in-between his fingers, enjoying its silky feel. Slowly he let each shimmering wisp fall to her bare shoulder and sighed again with contentment.

Nicole nestled closer into the crook of his arm, and Will froze, fearing she'd wake. His breath caught in his throat, noting her angelic face appeared to come alive with a yawn, but, a second later, she smacked her lips together and fell back into a peaceful state.

Will let out the trapped breath, closed his eyes, and relaxed onto the pillow. His heart felt safe nestled under her palm and he covered her hand with his.

Life was funny. Five months ago, he was a pathetic, walking, workaholic zombie, still trying to forget Laura. Four months ago, he'd seen Nicole for the first time and thought her a low-life who was part of the mafia unit trafficking children to be used as sex slaves. Three months ago he learned her true identity and with her help secured evidence that had taken down a large portion of the Novokoffs' business.

He had been attracted to Nicole almost from the start, but until he found her in Virginia and learned her true back story did he allow his true feelings to surface. Restrained, but there. When she had put her life on the line to take out Gorgon once and for all, and they stood under the cypress trees after breaking into Gorgon's house and escaping his men, holding each other, that was the moment things had changed between them. He wanted to be with her, not just this way, having sex, but, spending time with her and getting to know the real Nicole.

Something in his gut said he loved her, but his gut didn't handle that department. His heart was charge of that area. The heart she lovingly cradled below her palm.

His cell buzzed again. What if the caller was trying to reach him to share the news that Gorgon and his brother Donnie were history? How would his and Nicole's lives change? Once this thing was over, would she go back to her family and forget him? He couldn't ask her to stay here under an assumed name. She belonged with them.

A picture of Laura walking out the door popped into his mind. He'd be left behind again.

"Are you awake?" Nicole peered up at him. the morning light reflected the shimmering golden specks of her still sleepy brown eyes.

Will jumped. "Yeah."

She stretched and looked over her shoulder, sliding the sheet to just above the rosy nipple he'd suckled only hours ago. "It's almost six."

Her left cheek was red from lying against his ribs. "I know. I should leave before Luka wakes up."

Nicole's hand skimmed over his stomach and brushed against the grain of his chest hair, causing sparks to skip along his nerves and send a get-ready-for–action direction to his groin.

"He won't wake for a while. He is not an early riser." She circled his navel with her pinky and grazed the head of his penis. "Not like you," she said with a husky tone that made him want to roll on top of her and for the third time make her his.

At the second pinky poke, he swallowed a moan.

"How about the neighbors?"

"You moved your car around the block last night."

The less people talked about Nicole, the less chance of someone, meaning Gorgon, would find her. That is why he drove the extra twenty miles to an out of town haunted hayride on the excuse that particular hayride was a much better event. He grabbed her hand and laid it on his chest, stopping her torment. "You don't think they'll see me duck out the back door?"

She sighed before a pout pushed her full bottom lip out and he fought the urge to kiss her.

"I guess you're right. We don't want the neighbors to talk."

"Not yet." He flicked her nipple—a payback for the things she was doing to him.

"Hey. If I can't—"

His phone buzzed again and both of them turned their attention to the cell. He looked at the display. "The office."

"Hmmm. Do you need to answer?"

He should answer. "Whatever they want, can wait a few minutes." He'll call back in a minute.

Nicole pulled the sheets and comforter a little higher and the aroma of their love making wafted around them. She skimmed her silky leg over his and snuggled closer. "Good. Since you wouldn't let me touch you below the belt, we can talk?"

"About?"

She tilted her face up to him, looking very serious. "Just now, you looked so sad. Why? You're not sorry we slept together are you?"

"What? Hell no!"

She moved to shift away, but he tightened his grip on her and kept Nicole tucked securely against him. She didn't believe him, but telling her what he actually thought would put her on the spot. She couldn't commit to anyone until all the chips fell and her life was hers. And to be honest, he didn't what to jump into the fire only to back out. Nicole deserved better. "I was just thinking how damn much I didn't want to leave you. It's going to be nice today and I noticed some things around here that need to be taken care of. Man things. How about, I go and catch a few hours of sleep and then I'll come back around eleven. I'll bring my tool box and a ladder. Do you have leaf rakes?"

"No. I've been meaning to buy one."

"I'll grab mine-I have two or three."

Trapping the sheet against her chest, Nicole rose up on her elbow and she swiped her long, silky hair back over her shoulder. "You want to help around here?"

"Yeah. You sound surprised. Why?"

"I don't know." She shrugged. "You're not feeling guilty because we slept together?"

"Okay, now you asked for it." He rolled her onto her back and climbed on top of her. His heart flipped, listening to her giggle. He trapped her with his weight, enjoying the feel of his cock pressing against her soft folds.

"What are you doing?" She brushed her hair from her face and her round eyes reminded him of chocolate drops.

"I want to get one thing straight I never have to hear that question again. I would not take back last night for anything. I made love to you because I wanted to. And you have my permission to jump me anytime you want."

"Really?" Her eyes took on a sly slant while her soft hands drifted over his back and cupped his ass. She wiggled her hips against him and Will felt all of his blood flow south. "I say when?"

"Yes." He moaned.

"Okay. Now."

Will grinned and gave into her wish.

***

A half-hour later, while Nicole was in the bathroom, Will dressed and then grabbed his cell phone and called the office.

"Where the hell have you been?" Aden barked. "I've been trying to reach you for the last few hours."

"I forgot to charge my battery." The excuse was the first thing that popped into his head and he went with it. "Died last night while I was sleeping, I guess. I'm plugged into the wall now. What's up?"

"We got word old man Yegor turned up in upstate New York, yesterday. He was seen exiting a gas station restroom."

"By who?"

"An off duty cop. He thought he recognized Yegor and when he went on duty last night, he checked the wanted postings."

"Damn. Why didn't he check right away?" Will's jaw locked.

"He was off duty and coaches his son's football pee-wee team. He was on the way to a game."

Will couldn't blame the cop for having a life. Didn't he just not answer his phone because he was busy building his own? "Where was Yegor headed?"

"The cop followed him a bit. He said he got onto the NY expressway and headed south."

At least the guy had followed his gut and got some worthwhile information. "Gorgon and Donnie are still in New York then."

"I'd bet my paycheck."

"Something is up if the old man came back." The

hair on the nape of Will's neck pickled. "Something big."

"Yeah, that is what we were thinking. So what do you want to do?"

"Let the guys in New York know. Circulate Yegor, Donnie and Gorgon's picture again in New York, New Jersey and Pennsylvania. Include Maryland and Virginia too, just in case they moved south a bit. We can't do much more until one of them is sighted again."

"Okay. Anything else?"

"Yeah. Request a twenty-four guard on Gary's room and his family."

"You think they'd go after them?"

"Like I said, something big is stirring and they might assume Gary knows where we've stashed Nicole and Luka. If the commander gives you a hassle about man hours, tell him I don't give a fuck and if he doesn't want me leaning over his desk, he better do approve the guards."

Aden chuckled. "I'll tell him that first."

"In the meantime, I think I'm going to stay here in Logan's Summit and keep an eye on Nicole and Luka."

"Need help. I mean I wouldn't mind watching over her."

Will rolled his shoulder at the wince of jealousy stabbing him in the back. "You just stay where you are, kid. I've got this end covered."

"Nice end."

Will's hold on the phone tightened. "Hey, show some respect." He disconnected without another word. He couldn't wait until Gary was back and sent a prayer to heaven he won't nail Aden for his off-color comments beforehand. He knew the kid didn't mean anything by them. Just man talk, but they still rubbed him the wrong way.

The bathroom door opened and he studied Nicole's

face, searching for how much of his conversation with Aden did she hear?

"Do you have to go in?"

"What?"

"To the office. Has something happened?"

He shook his head. There was no reason to get her upset when he didn't know what was going on. "No. Aden was just checking in. He's fairly new to the team and just got nervous when I didn't answer."

"Oh, so nothing new on Gorgon?"

"No. All is quiet. Maybe Gorgon decided to take a hike."

Her chuckle was filled with resentment. "Yeah, right. You don't know Gorgon."

"Look, let's not go there." He laced his arms around her waist and pulled her close. "I just had the most amazing night of my life and I don't want to think about anything else."

She melted against him. "Yeah, it was pretty nice."

"Just pretty?"

She titled her head side to side as if weighing her thoughts before saying, "Okay, nice."

He squeezed her. "Just nice?"

"Amazing." She smiled. "Let's do it again."

"Tonight. After we get the work done around here."

Her brow arched. "You're staying?"

"No. I'm coming back." He kissed her nose. "One question though."

"What?"

He let her go, knowing he could get punched. "What's for dinner?"

She stood straighter and crossed her arms over her chest. "Depends what you're cooking?"

"Huh." He splayed his hand over his heart. "I've got to do all the repairs and still make dinner."

"Okay, I'll help, but later, after Luka is in bed…" She walked up to him and wound her arms around his neck.

His scalp tingled as she combed her fingertips through his hair. "Yeah."

"I get to do to you what I want." She said each word between carefully placed kisses.

"Hmmm. You got it, babe."

Chapter Thirty

The doors to the bedroom suite opened and crashed against the wall, startling Gorgon from a sound sleep. He scrambled and dropped off the bed's edge, still in a stupor. A moving target was much harder to hit.

His guard's name edged his tongue, but Gorgon didn't call out. If the intruder was here, in his bedroom, his man was already dead. Instead, he huddled against the mattress for protection and skimmed the bed beneath the hotel's plump pillow for his Glock while feverishly blinking away the sleep from his eyes. His movements felt sluggish. He shouldn't have taken the sleeping pill last night, but memories of his Katrina had haunted him.

His fingers found the gun and swiftly he took aim and squeezed the trigger a fraction before Donnie cried out. "Gorgon, stop. It's us."

Gorgon eased off the trigger and focused past the barrel of his gun. His father stood in the center of the double door threshold with his own Glock pointed at him. The coldness of Papa's stare left no doubt in Gorgon's mind that his father, if given no choice, would've killed him out of self-preservation and for the good of the family. Everything Papa did was for the good of the family.

Gorgon released the breath lodged behind the lump in his throat and lowered his gun. His knees shook—not from fear, he didn't fear death. They wobbled on the high of adrenaline while he stood to his full height.

Papa's nose wrinkled.

Gorgon followed the line of Papa's stare to the long

red scar which ran from his breast bone into the hairs of his manhood and the scars which marked his side where drainage hoses had been inserted. Apparently his father was appalled at the state of his body. Fuck him.

Gorgon squared his shoulders and met his father's scowl. "What are you doing here?"

The old man nodded toward the gun hanging at his side.

Gorgon tossed the weapon on the bed.

Papa slipped his gun into his belt holster. "I came to take you and Donnie home."

"Donnie can go, but I'm staying."

Concern tightened Donnie's features and Gorgon wondered if his brother had called their father.

"Leave us," Yegor said to Donnie and Donnie left the room without a glance in his direction.

He was to stand alone against the old man. Gorgon snatched up his sweat pants he'd thrown across the chair the night before and stepped into them.

"I have given you the time you asked for," Yegor said in an even tone. "It's done. You will return home with us."

Gorgon yanked the strings at his waist band and tied them off. "I am not a child, Papa, that you can order me." He grabbed and slipped his tee shirt on.

"No. You are a man who is crazy." Yegor thumped his head with the heel of his palm. "Katrina has disappeared. Three months have gone by since you're out of the hospital and started your hunt, and still you have not found her."

"I will find her. It took time to set things up. The ads have been out for only two weeks."

"Ads," Yegor chided and frowned. "No one looks at those things and in the meantime, you hide. Look at you. You are as pale as a babe's behind. You can't walk down the street and feel the sun on your face for fear you'll be spotted by the Marshals who hunt you. The woman is not worth your life."

"And my son?" Gorgon's hands curled into fists. The pressure on his neck veins caused his temples to throb. "What about his life? My blood. Your blood. Your father's blood runs through Luka's veins. He is my son and I want him with me." He pounded his fist against his chest.

"I know your pain."

"Do you? How could you? Donnie and I, we are here." Tasting the bitterness of his father's betrayal lacing his tongue, Gorgon turned his back on the old man and walked to the window. The sun was a sliver of yellow breaking through the murky, gray sky above the Atlantic Ocean. Somewhere out there, Katrina and Luka slept soundly. She thought she was safe. She thought she had seen the last of him. She was wrong.

He inhaled deeply and turned to face his father. "Take Donnie and go. I'm staying and when I have Luka back, then maybe, I will come home."

"You're being a fool, my son."

"I am your son."

Yegor's jaw tightened. He turned on his heel.

"Tell mama…"

The old man stopped but did not turn to face him.

"Tell her I love her and to expect us for the Christmas holiday."

Before the sun hovered above the lowest of rooftops in lower Manhattan, his father and Donnie left the suite and then from his twentieth floor window, Gorgon watched while his father's limo pulled out and disappeared around the corner.

Chapter Thirty-one

Will gasped for air and fell to the mattress next to Nicole. For three weeks, they'd tumbled into bed at every opportunity when he was in town, and that they could steal while Luka was out of the house or fast asleep. Today, Luka was at a friend's birthday party for a couple of hours. At first, the sneaking around had been part of the thrill of being with Nicole. Now, doing so was a pain in the ass. "You're going to kill me," he managed to say between dragged breaths.

Nicole's breasts rose and fell in unison with his chest. In the afternoon sun, her dusty rose areolas called to him and even though he just spent himself, he felt his groin tighten.

She darted her tongue across her lips, causing his pulse race.

"Killing you wasn't in my plan."

Will wished they could be open about their relationship. He wanted every guy in town to know she belonged to him. He brushed a lone strand of hair off of her cheek. "What is your plan for me?"

Her finger latched onto his. "I just want to make you so happy you won't even think of looking at another woman."

"There are no worries there, sweetheart. I don't want anyone but you."

"Seriously?"

He shifted on his side and stared into her gorgeous eyes. "Have I ever lied to you?"

She pulled the sheet over her breasts and wearing a

smirk said, "Not today—that I know of."

Through the sheet, he pinched her nipple a little. "Never."

"Ouch." She laughed. "Okay, never."

He rolled over and sat up.

"Where are you going?"

"The john." He pointed to the condom sheathing his penis. "Want to come with me?"

"Sorry. No. I like my privacy. I'll give you yours."

"You want to go first?"

"No. I'm fine." She snuggled under the comforter. "I'll keep the bed warm. Hurry back."

Will crossed the room.

"Nice ass," she called after him.

He looked over his shoulder. "It's all yours." And so was his heart. The thought smacked him across the head. And, either the comment hit Nicole too or she saw his reaction to realizing he was totally in love with her because her smile faded from her lips and a mixture of joy and fear sparked in her eyes.

"Be out in a minute." He closed the bathroom door behind him and then flipped the water on, and with his hands on the counter stared into the mirror. He was in love with Nicole. He loved Luka like a son. He didn't ever want to give them up. Ever.

How could he ask her to stay with him without giving her the opportunity to experience life first? He couldn't. That decision had to be hers and by the startled look she'd just given him, he had just scared the hell out of her.

What was he going to do? He asked himself as he washed up. He had to be cool, as if they were just having fun. He couldn't push her, and somehow he had to make her love him.

***

A whirlwind of emotions spun through Nicole. She pressed her hands over her eyes and then combed them back through her hair. She trapped the joy threatening to escape her. Had she heard Will right? Did he really mean his ass belonged to her? Did he mean he was hers to keep forever?

She closed her eyes and relaxed onto the pillow and allowed herself the dream of Will, Luka and her becoming a real family. Maybe, one day, they'd have a baby together.

Her hands curled into fists over the comforter's edge. Why was she setting herself up for heartache? Will hadn't meant anything but that she could have sex with him anytime she wanted. Yes, he was attracted to her. He'd said as much. And yes, he said he didn't want her to see other men, but that was a guy thing. He didn't want to share what he had going on here.

She stared at the bathroom door. She wished he'd hurry. Every second Will was in there, doubts piled on top of her heart.

The bed groaned while Nicole pushed up on the mattress and repositioned herself, fluffing the pillows. She couldn't just come out and ask him if he was serious about her—if he was falling in love with her, could she?

She slid out from under the comforter. She needed to get dressed. If they were going discuss this, she wanted the conversation to be face to face and them on their feet.

Nicole slipped on her clothing before the door opened. Facing Will, she said, "We need to talk."

Chapter Thirty-two

The mid-sized sedan issued to her by the agency was nothing shiny and new. The car had a slight dent in its rear passenger panel and the metallic gray paint was sun-blasted to a flat shale color, but it was clean inside the heater blasted like a furnace, and ran like a charm. The vehicle fit her persona perfectly—a single mom with more lint in her pockets than money.

Over the past four months, she'd become a faceless single mother who made ends meet working as a clerk in a gift shop. With the exception of tumbling into bed with Will, her days were filled with normal activities like heading into a grocery store and arguing with Luka about sleepovers at his friend's house.

Pulling into a parking spot at Rex's Grocery, Nicole jammed the vehicle into park and climbed out. She hurried around the front of the van and opened the rear door just as Luka unsnapped his seat belt and his toes touched the floorboard.

"Put your game under the front seat please. Out of sight." Will had given the DS to Luka as a birthday present and the device immediately became an extension of her son's hand.

She entwined her fingers with Luka's the moment he jumped from the van and they turned into the scent of fresh baked goods wafting in the crisp autumn air. "Let's hurry. I have a million things to do today."

"Is Thanksgiving tomorrow?"

"No. Tomorrow is Wednesday. Thanksgiving is always on a Thursday and that is the day after. But, I have to work tomorrow afternoon, so I need to get a few things done if we're going to have a feast. You do want a feast, don't you?"

"Yeah."

A frosty gust swept across the grocery store's parking lot, making pre-thanksgiving shoppers scurry, load their bags into their cars, and then take shelter in their cabs.

"Hi, Becca and Luke," Margie Ballietson, the nice woman from the church they started attending, called out before slamming her car door closed and waving a gloved greeting from inside.

Nicole waved back with her free hand before pulling her parka's collar closer to prevent the wind from sending another chill through her. Becca Smith wasn't her name, but it was the one she went by now. And Logan's Summit wasn't her hometown, but the sleepy village nestled in the Appalachian Mountains of Northeast Pennsylvania was where the government had chosen to place her and Luka, near Will.

She hated deceiving the people who were becoming her friends and wondered would she ever be Nicole again? As much as she longed to see her family and friends from the past, she didn't want to leave Will. If her secret was ever revealed, she hoped her new friends wouldn't hold her past against her.

No. They could never know her past.

Pulling a grocery cart from the cart return, Nicole took a double take toward the highway where a car resembling Will's passed by. She'd seen him several times over the past week, at a distance watching her, and every time her heart had jumped and then plummeted as he smiled, waved and then disappeared into the shadows. They couldn't expose their relationship. Not yet. Maybe never.

Nicole stared at the car now sitting at the stop sign, waiting for the man driving to turn and smile, but he didn't. The car surged forward and disappeared from view.

"I'm cold." Luka broke her train of thought. With his arms huddled close to his sides and his hands shoved deep into his coat's pockets, Luka's bottom lip quivered. She needed to buy him a pair of gloves too. A couple pairs, because he'd lose one within forty-eight hours.

"Sure, babe." Throwing a glance over her shoulder one more time at the highway and the surrounding area, she yanked the shopping cart free from another cart. "I was just running my list of things I need through my head, so I don't forget anything and have to come back again. We want Thanksgiving to be special, don't we?"

"Is dad coming?"

Cold dread ran its finger up her spine. Luka hadn't mentioned his father in weeks. She'd hoped maybe he'd begun to forget Gorgon. God. She prayed he would. "No. He's still on his business trip."

"Will he be home for Christmas?"

"I don't think so. He said it would be a very long time until he can come back." She had to change the subject before anyone overheard this conversation. Nicole tossed her purse onto the cart's upper shelf and headed toward the automatic doors. "Let's pick up some cherries and we'll put them into the brownies. What do you think?"

"Yeah." Luka skipped ahead of her, surprisingly happy.

Inside the store, they fell into their new routine. She turned and dropped a box of oatmeal into the cart. "Luke, I'm not going to repeat myself a second time. I said no. Now put that back on the shelf."

"Come on." His foot hit the vinyl flooring. "Tommy

says it's really cool-- I mean good."

"Good, huh. I think you want this cereal because of the cheap toy inside." She pointed to the grocery shelf lined with more types of breakfast meals than the world needed. "I have eighty dollars to spend on the groceries. I need things for the Thanksgiving dinner and all of next week. I'm going to buy something you or the dog wouldn't eat. Put the box back."

"This sucks," he whined.

Mrs. Owens, the reverend's elderly wife, shot a perturbed glare at her and Luka before pushing her cart past them.

Nicole snatched the box out of Luka's grasp and shoved it onto an empty space on the shelf. Nicole steered her cart with one hand, while she latched onto Luka's elbow and hustled him further down the aisle. Outside of Mrs. Owen's ear shot, Nicole trapped Luka's jaw between her thumb and forefinger and tilted his pout up toward her. "What is going on, Luka? The last few days you've been acting like a real horse's butt."

"You mean ass."

The boy's use of words set her back on her heels. "Where did you hear that word?"

"Billy."

Another new friend Luka made in school recently. One that seemed to be influencing Luka more and more in ways she didn't like. "Well, I'll have to talk to Billy's mom."

His eyes widened. "Don't. He'll be mad at me."

"What you said was a bad word. Don't use it again."

Luka's chin hit his chest. "Okay."

"I have a feeling something else is going on. What? You can tell me."

"Nothing."

"I think there is. Spill."

Luka stuffed his hands into the front pockets of his jeans.

She folded her arms across her chest. "I'm waiting."

"The guys called me mama whipped."

Nicole couldn't help the chuckle that escaped her.

Luka's expression told her he didn't think what his friends had called him was funny at all, or her laughter. "I'm sorry. Why would they say that?"

He shrugged. "Billy said I do everything you tell me to, and Tommy and Pat agreed."

The threesome that Luka had fallen into company with were right. She'd trained him from an early age to do exactly as she said. Doing so was the only way she could keep their identities safe when the time came for them to escape Gorgon.

Nicole sighed. Maybe the time had come to loosen the apron strings, a little, and give him a little independence and teach him responsibility. She brushed his dark bangs off his forehead. "Doing what is right isn't a bad thing. I hope you understand that."

Looking down at his feet, Luka nodded.

No matter what she said, her words wouldn't erase the hurt his friends had caused. She glanced at her watch–nearly five. "I'll tell you what. After you help me carry the groceries into the house, you can call Tommy to come over and play."

His eyes lit up. "Can we play down in the basement?"

The place was an empty basement, except for the furnace and a few old boxes. She didn't see the attraction, but Tommy and Luka seemed to enjoy being down there, looking for spiders, playing in the old boxes as if they were cars or spaceships, or drawing chalk roads for their matchbox cars on the concrete floor. And it was warm. "Yes, as long as you keep the spiders downstairs. No begging for a jar to put them in."

"Okay. Can Tommy stay overnight?"

Will wasn't in town so there was no chance of him visiting and Tommy would keep Luka busy so she could get a jump start on the holiday dinner. "I'll ask. Let's get the rest of the stuff I need and we can head home." Nicole glanced at her list lying on top of the fresh vegetables and fruits she'd placed in the cart's top rack. "I need a dozen eggs, butter and a gallon of milk. Let's head over to the last aisle."

"Can I push the cart?"

"Sure."

A few minutes later their items rolled along the belt toward the scanner and Nicole struggled to open a plastic bag.

"Hi, Ms. Smith. Luke," Tory, the bag boy said stepping up to the counter. He grabbed and flipped open the sack like a pro. The store was busy and he worked hard to cover two checkouts.

"Hi, Tory. How's your dad doing?" Tory's father, she'd learned while helping out at a church fundraiser, had fallen off a house roof while working. He was a self-employed roofer. The fund raiser was held to help the family out, who had fallen in hard times. The boy was working this job after school in an effort to help his family out.

"Good. He gets the cast off next week. He can't wait to get back to work."

"I bet. Six months is a long time to be off. And your mom?" Tory's mother had just started cancer treatments.

"So far so good." He carefully placed her eggs, the last item, on the top shelf of the cart. "Thanks for asking."

"Tell them we hope you all have a nice Thanksgiving."

"I will. You too. Bye, Luke."

Luka waved and grabbed the cart intending to be 'the man' and show Tory he could push the cart.

Nicole fell instep behind Luka and didn't see Tory's cheery smile fade away when he picked up the milk carton they'd left behind.

***

Tory stared at the missing girl's picture. He studied Becca Smith's profile while she zippered up her son's coat and then while crossing the parking lot, pushing her cart.

He needed to be sure.

"I'll be right back. Ms. Smith forgot her milk," he said to the cashier and rushed out the door. "Ms. Smith, wait."

She turned from lifting a bag into the trunk. "Oh, my. Thanks. You saved me a trip back here. I'm just about out." She took the carton and tucked it inside a bag.

"No problem," Tory said, studying her. Her eyes were the same and her nose.

She looked at him quizzically. "Is something wrong?"

It couldn't be her. Ms. Smith was much older than the picture. "No. Again, have a nice Thanksgiving."

"Thanks."

Tory watched as she pulled out of the parking space and headed east on Main Street. What if he was wrong and it was her? The ad offered a quarter of a million dollars for any information that would lead to her rescue.

Rescue from whom? As far as he knew, Becca Smith lived with her son and no one else.

He shook his head. He had to be wrong.

Disappointment edged in on Tory's dreams as he

headed back inside. He sure didn't want to work here, bagging groceries for the rest of his life.

His family sure could use the money and going to college would be in his future again, if he was right. It was a phone call. That's all.

Chapter Thirty-three

Damn. With everything on her mind, she'd forgotten to stop for gas. Just one more thing she'd have to do tomorrow. Nicole shifted the bag in her arm and fished for her keys.

She barely had the back door open before Luka and Billy raced under her arm and through the kitchen. "Hey, I thought you two were going to help carry in the groceries?"

"We will. I want to show Tommy the new truck Will bought me. We'll be right back."

And there went her help she thought, watching the boys tear through the living room and rounding the steps with Max barking on their heels.

She grabbed the milk from the bag and placed the carton in the refrigerator. "Bring the truck downstairs, Luke. You're going to play in the basement and not in that bedroom," she called after them.

"Okay," Luka yelled.

She closed the refrigerator and glimpsed at the clock. It was five forty-five. Hot dogs would be dinner tonight, and then she was going to attempt to make her stuffing and bake her first apple pie. Damn. She wished she'd helped her mother in the kitchen more. She really wanted to impress Will.

While walking to the car for the rest of the groceries, her heart grew heavy. She missed her family. She missed the traditions and festivities of the holidays they always participated in. She'd give anything to be with them again and to have Luka experience the love they would surely shower over him.

Maybe next year they would be together.

Chapter Thirty-four

At six-thirty, the special ring for Gorgon's mock hotline number blurred. A grin bloomed on his face. He'd dropped the thirty-pound weights he curled to the floor, swiped the sweat from his brow with the towel that hung around his neck, and snatched the cell off the coffee table. Clutching the phone next to his ear, he cleared his throat, dispelling the angst coating his tongue and said in a professionally calm tone, "MP hotline. Gregory speaking. How can I help you?"

"Hi. My name is Tory Fisher. I'm calling about a picture I saw on a milk carton. Is this the right number?" The caller's voice cracked the way guys' voices did when they were becoming men.

His knees suddenly weak, Gorgon lowered to the couch, knowing in his heart that this was the call he'd prayed for every night. His Katrina and Luka would be found. His family would be one again. He swallowed the excitement rising in him. "Yes, sir. This is the missing person's hotline. What MP are you identifying?"

"MP?"

"Sorry. Missing person."

"Oh, right. I saw her on a milk carton. The name is Nicole, but I know her as Becca Smith. She's a lot older than the picture though. And she has a kid. Maybe it isn't her."

Gorgon's pulse drummed against his temples. He heard the indecision in the kid's tone and bit down on his lip to keep the desperation churning inside his gut from expelling in a cry. He couldn't lose this guy until he found out where in the hell Katrina and Luka were. "Really! A son?"

"Yeah," the kid responded, fortunately not catching Gorgon's slip of tongue. The teen had never mentioned the child's sex.

He had to earn the kid's confidence. "Son of a bitch," he bellowed between clenched teeth.

"What?"

He'd hooked the young man. Now to pull him in. "Look. Can I be honest? This job makes me sick. Too often these runaways get mixed up with the wrong people. They don't realize who they're dealing with until it's too late. Before they know what is happening they're doing things, drugs or acts-something they would've never done before. Their lives become a living hell. They're pimped out. They have no choice but to do as they're told and sometimes the girls, they get pregnant. Makes me sick when we find them and it's too late."

"Ms. Smith doesn't seem like that. She seems really okay. She's always happy, smiling."

Katrina was happy. He remembered the way his kitten smiled and laughed while playing with Luka. Gorgon's molars ground together. How could she be happy without him? "Somehow she must've gotten out."

"On second thought, I think I'm wrong. She can't be the same person. I'm sorry for taking up your time."

"Wait." Gorgon shot off the couch, clenching the phone like a life line. "Nicole's parents have been looking for her for years. If this woman you call Becca is her, don't you think they deserve to know she is okay? Think about your own parents. I'm sure they'd walk through fire to learn what happened to you if you'd disappeared. Nicole's parents have been in hell for a long time."

Silence filled the phone. Gorgon held his breath

waiting for the dial tone to start up. Had he lost the kid?

Finally, a sigh filled his ear and relief washed through him.

"I guess you're right. What do you need? Will this take long? I'm at work and on my break."

"Not long at all." Gorgon switched ears, expelling the breath he'd held and stretched the tension from his fingers. "You're doing the right thing." He grabbed a pen and pad. "Okay, for my records and so we can issue the reward money, if she turns out to be Nicole, I need to know your name and address and where we can find this girl. Um, woman."

While writing down the information, Gorgon's grin grew. He'd found his kitten and his son. They'd be home for Christmas just as he had said. He couldn't wait to see his father's face.

Chapter Thirty-five

Baked apples and cinnamon scented the kitchen. Nicole smiled. The pie looked perfect, if she did say so herself. Just like Sharon's—maybe prettier. She hoped it tasted as good as it looked. She wanted Will to enjoy every bite, if he did stop by. She hoped he would.

The phone rang.

Nicole glanced at the stove's digital clock. Darn. Nine twenty. She'd told Tommy's mom she'd bring him home at nine. She grabbed the phone. "Sue, I'm so sorry."

A deep chuckle filled her ear.

"Sorry. I'm not, Sue. I can call back later, if you're waiting for a call."

Warm bubbles floated through Nicole at hearing Will's voice. "No. It's okay. I picked up Tommy on the way home. Luka wanted someone to play with, and I promised Sue I'd bring Tommy home at nine. I've been so busy and just noticed the time."

"Oh. What were you doing?"

He sounded tired and she wondered what was going on that she hadn't seen him in days. He'd tell her, if anything had to do with her and Luka. Otherwise, his work was none of her business. Will had other cases. Like the teenaged twins on the news that had disappeared in New York a few weeks ago. While not directly his case, she was sure Will was in contact with whoever was in charge.

And that poor little nine year old who also disappeared around the same time. Both sets of parents must be going nuts. Especially with the holidays upon them. Her heart broke for them.

"Nicole, are you there?"

"Yes, sorry I was just thinking."

"About?"

"Nothing really."

"So what have you been doing tonight that you forgot about the time?"

"Making stuffing for the turkey and I baked an apple pie."

"You did. Yum. I love apple pie."

"Well, if you come over, I'll serve you a warm piece."

"That sounds too good an invitation to turn down." He exhaled. "But I'm just leaving work and need to be back here very early tomorrow. I think it would be in my employer's best interest if I just head home to bed. I wanted to check in with you and make sure you're okay."

She couldn't hide the disappointment she felt when she responded. "Is that the only reason you called?"

"No. I miss you."

Warmth threaded through her. "You've seen me."

"From a distance. Not the same as holding you. And not for a few days."

"Luka will be fast asleep by the time you get here," she said seductively.

He sighed. "You're killing me, you know that?"

"Does that mean you'll change your mind?"

"I can't." He yawned. "But I'll see you Thursday."

Joy lifted Nicole to her toes. "You're definitely coming for dinner. What about your family?"

"I told them I had to work and wouldn't be able to make the drive in time for dinner. It's a good four to five hour drive so they understand. They know I'm having dinner at a friend's house though."

"Gary and Sharon's?"

"No. They know about Gary. I told them I was seeing someone and I was having dinner with her."

Her eyes widened, along with her grin. "You did?"

"Sure. And I can't wait."

Her entire being was like warm butter. She could just pour herself through the phone line and wrap herself in Will's strong arms. "Me neither."

"You better get Tommy home. I'll see you soon."

"Okay."

"Nicole."

"Yes." The phone beeped in Nicole's ear signaling another call was waiting. "Damn, that must be Sue."

"It's okay. I've got to get going anyway. See you Thursday." Will hung-up without giving her a chance to say something more, which was probably for the best, because with the energy she had flowing through her right now, she could talk all night.

She hit the flash button and said in response to Sue's greeting, "I'm so sorry. I was so busy and then I got a phone call and lost track of time. We'll be there in a few minutes."

A few minutes later, Nicole rushed the boys and Max out the door and headed to the car to take Tommy home.

Chapter Thirty-six

The sky's deep velvet folds looked like they'd been dotted by an overzealous God. A half-moon positioned near the canvas's center was surrounded by a trillion twinkling stars. Nicole's lungs hiccupped with her deep drag of the crisp, late fall air.

Max rustled leaves as he sniffed the backyard like a dog on a search and rescue mission, crossing back and forth between lawn's edge and the dry mums bordering the back of the house.

Luka ran up the back steps and yanked the screen door open. "Can I have a cookie?"

"You and Tommy had a snack." Nicole jiggled her keys, searching under the dim light for the right one to unlock the back door.

"I'm still hungry." Luka turned the knob and the back door opened. "Can I? Please. I'll brush my teeth right afterwards. I promise."

The hairs on Nicole's arms stood on end. She could've sworn she'd pulled the door tight. "Luka, stop."

He slid to a stop next to the counter. "What?"

Cautiously she stepped inside. She held her finger up, signaling for him to remain quiet and looked around. "I thought I had locked the door."

"The house is falling apart. All the doors and windows need work."

Nicole stifled the chuckle in her throat at Luka's mimicking Will's words. Everything was in its place. If someone was in here, Max would be too, hopefully tearing whomever apart. She was just being paranoid.

"Go get ready for bed."

"You're being mean." Luka stamped his foot.

"Hey. You don't talk to your mother that way, young man." The voice came from behind Nicole, causing her to jump.

The floor squeaked beneath her sneaker's heel at her quick turn and she exhaled the breath caught in her throat. "What are you doing here, Sharon?"

"I'm sorry." Through the screen door, Sharon's brow knitted, looking at Nicole's fist. "I didn't mean to scare you."

Nicole shook her fingers out and slid her purse from her shoulder and dropped the leather bag on the counter top. "It's alright. Come on in. Luka, now. Upstairs. Get your teeth brushed and PJs on. I'll be up in a few minutes."

Luka glanced Sharon's way before dashing from the room.

"Good boy," Sharon called after him as she opened the door. "Ooops."

Max brushed along side of her and trotted to his water bowl and began lapping.

Sharon's brow furrowed looking at Nicole. "Is something wrong?"

She shook her head. "I'm jumpy. I thought I'd locked the back door and yet it was open."

Sharon ran her hand over the door's frame. "This looks okay. I'll check the house?"

"That's not necessary. I was in a rush to get Tommy home and thought I locked the door and didn't." She pointed through the archway, toward Max who'd found his corner of the couch and prepared to settle in. "Besides, if anyone was in here, Max would have him backed into a corner. So, why are you here?"

"I was over in Littleton and thought I'd swing by and

drop off the roasting pan you'd asked to borrow. That way, you wouldn't have to make the trip tomorrow. It's in the SUV."

"Oh, thanks. I forgot all about using it. Luka wanted a big turkey." She opened the refrigerator and pointed to the bird taking up most of the bottom shelf. "Well, he's getting one."

"That's a big bird for the two of you."

Smiling, Nicole closed the door. "Will's coming."

"He is? I had a feeling he would." Sharon's grin brightened the room.

"I'm glad you did."

"You didn't?" Sharon's right brow disappeared under her bangs. "Girl, you've got that man so tied up his nickname could be cornflake."

Joy threaded through Nicole listening to Sharon, making her want to dance around the room, but she kept her feet planted and just hosted a bit of a smile. "I don't think so."

"I know so." Sharon winked.

Nicole wished everything Sharon said was written in stone, but truth be told, she didn't know where her and Will's relationship would end up. Until her life was hers, there was no future for them. She picked up the tea kettle from the stove. "Do you want some tea? Or, I can make a pot of coffee?"

"I'd love to sit and chat, but my sitter is waiting for me and I'm sure Gary is ready for his sponge bath." Sharon smiled.

"I don't know how you do it all. Taking care of Gary and the kids and still find time to volunteer your time. You're one amazing lady."

"Stop. You're making me blush and I don't like to do that." Sharon backed toward the door. "I'll just go get the roaster and be back in a jiff."

"Okay, I'm just going to run upstairs and check on Luka. I'll be right back."

Max's big brown eyes looked up at her as she entered the room. Without moving his head, he watched her climb the stairs.

Nicole found Luka, sitting on his bed, reading. "Did you brush your teeth?"

"Yup." He displayed his white teeth to her.

"Good job on washing your face too and combing your hair." She nuzzled his neck, breathing in his youthful scent.

Luka laughed and tried his best to tickle her back.

"Okay, enough. Time for bed." She pulled back the covers and the book Luka had been reading fell to the floor. She picked it up and glanced at the cover and her hands trembled. "Luka, where did you get this book?"

Her son's eyes glistened as they danced beyond her to the darkest corner of the room. Her blood turned to ice. She didn't need to turn to know Gorgon had found them.

Chapter Thirty-Seven

Just inside Luka's room, soft footsteps padded the floor behind her.

"I've missed you, my kitten." Gorgon's warm, minty breath tickled her ear.

Nicole froze.

His hand skimmed along her spine, threaded under her hair, and seized her neck, squeezing just enough to let her know he was in control of her life.

Her held breath burned in her chest, a sign she should twist away from his hold and run for her life, but she wouldn't—not without her son.

Drawing courage from deep within, she met Gorgon's dark gaze. She expected to see a weakened, shadow of a man after the damage she had inflicted on him, but this man oozed strength that the monster that had enslaved her never had. His chest was broader and the flecks shining in his eyes held a wisdom she'd not seen before.

A smile ballooned on his face. He'd felt the shaking of her bones. Good. Let him believe she feared him.

"We have a good boy. He plays the game of secrets very well."

She had sworn if he ever touched her again, she'd kill him. Nicole stalled the impulse to lash out. Deep inside, she'd known this day would come. She'd prepared herself mentally. She had to buy her time.

Downstairs the screen door banged against its frame, causing Nicole's heart to stop in mid-beat. Oh, my God, Sharon.

Gorgon's eyes shifted toward the door, his grip tightening slightly on her neck cords. "Who is the woman?"

Sharon had been a cop a number of years ago, but unarmed, she'd be defenseless against Gorgon. Nicole shrugged. "Just a friend, dropping off a baking dish I needed to make Thanksgiving dinner."

"How nice." His hand dropped to her shoulder and he tugged her closer, planting his hip solidly against hers. "Too bad you will not need it."

His plans for her were evident in the way his gaze dropped and lingered on her lips before shifting back to the door.

Sharon stood in his way. Nicole knew she had to get rid of her friend before Gorgon did.

"I want Aunt Sharon to meet daddy." Luka's bedsprings squealed an off-key tune as he bounced on his knees. "Aunt—"

"No," Nicole snapped and broke from Gorgon's hold, putting her hand over Luka's mouth. "Aunt Sharon will meet daddy another time. She's late getting home. The twins are waiting for her." Nicole's hands trembled as she pushed Luka back onto his pillow and pulled the covers over his belly.

"But I--"

"No buts." She had to think of some way to first save Sharon and then both Luka and herself. She kissed his forehead, like she did every other night. "You go to sleep. Daddy and I need to talk."

"I don't want to go to bed," Luka pleaded. "Daddy said we're going to see Mama and Papa."

"We are leaving, Katrina," Gorgon said behind her, in a tone that told her there wouldn't be a discussion of any kind.

Nicole spun on her heel with her hand extended.

"Nicole, I've got to run?" Sharon called from the bottom of the stairs.

Gorgon took a step toward the door.

"No." Nicole grabbed his hand, the one that reached inside his coat where she knew he holstered his gun. "You will not hurt her," she ordered with a low growl between clenched teeth. "If you do, I swear I'll—"

He gasped her wrist with a bone crushing force. The angles of his face hardened. "You'll what? Kill me," he said soft enough for her ears only. "You will never try that again, if you want to see our son grow into a man. In fact, the day you fail to make me the happiest man on the face of this earth, that day will be your last."

Nicole fought the years of training the monster had instilled in her and refused to look away. "And you will have to go through me to get to her." She flicked a glance toward Luka. "Do you really want your son see you kill his mother and her friend? I think not." She jutted her chin out, waiting for Gorgon to give her any excuse to strike out.

"Nicole, are you okay?" Sharon's voice sounded closer. She was climbing the stairs.

"I'll be right there," Nicole called out, holding Gorgon's angry stare. After hearing Sharon's retreating footsteps fade, she whispered. "You stay with Luka and I'll get rid of her."

Nicole pulled away, but Gorgon held onto her wrist, twisting her arm just enough to be uncomfortable.

"If you do anything—"

She fought to keep her knees from bowing as she looked into his eyes which promised death. "I won't, and I will not go anywhere without Luka."

The seconds that passed seemed like minutes until Gorgon finally released her and nodded toward the door.

Looking at Luka, she forced a smile to her lips

before heading downstairs. How in the hell was she going to get away again? Her heart cried out for Will. She'd kiss the devil to have him here, holding her safe in his arms.

Nicole hesitated at the bottom of the steps where a notepad and pen laid on the sofa's end table. She sensed movement behind her. No. She couldn't take the chance of jotting and passing a quick note to Sharon. Gorgon might see her. She wouldn't jeopardize Sharon's life. She'd never forgive herself if anything happened to her friend.

Instead, Nicole scowled at Max for not warning her of Gorgon's presence. She drew a deep breath and exhaled before entering the kitchen where Sharon waited. "I'm sorry. I know you're in a hurry. Sometimes that kid has an agenda he needs to cover before saying goodnight."

"You don't have to tell me about boys." Sharon tilted her head to the side and squinted at her. "Are you alright?"

"Yeah, sure. Why?" Nicole glanced away and then mentally slapped herself for doing so.

"You're holding onto the roasting pan like a life jacket in a stormy sea."

She let go of the pan and smoothed her moist palms along her sides. "I'm just nervous about cooking. I never made Thanksgiving dinner and Will called earlier. He's coming."

"There's nothing to be worried about." Sharon chuckled and reached out and took her hand. "You could serve Will a burnt peanut butter and jelly sandwich and he wouldn't notice the difference. You'll do just fine."

Knowing Gorgon could be listening, she said, "Thanks. You better go. I've held you up enough."

With a wink, Sharon let her hand go and turned

toward the door, glancing toward the stove top. "The apple pie you baked looks fabulous by the way and smells delicious."

Unable to speak or smile, Nicole simply nodded.

"Don't worry about a thing." Sharon patted her arm. "Call me if you need anything else."

Nicole followed her friend as far as the door. Tears welled up in her eyes, knowing she'd never see Will again, or Sharon and Gary and their twins, or any of the many friends she'd made in the last few months. And her hopes of seeing her family again disappeared like a puff of smoke in a hurricane. She blinked the moisture from her eyes while Sharon crossed the porch and jogged down the steps. "Sharon."

"Yes." Standing on the fringe of light cast by the back porch light, Sharon smiled up at her and Nicole bit back the emotions clawing at her heart, wanting to be made vocal.

She clamped her fingers together, so as not to reach out. "Thank you for everything you've done for me. Tell Gary the same."

"No problem."

"And Will…"

Sharon's brows arched. "What about Will?"

Nicole pasted a smile on her face and chuckled. "Nothing. I'll tell him myself."

"Remember to call me if you need anything." Sharon jiggled her keys in hand and headed for her car.

Nicole switched off the porch light and stepped outside. Holding the screen door open with her right hand, she watched her friend back out of view. As Sharon's headlights swayed away from the garage and moonlight took over the back yard, Nicole saw what she should've noted before-a motorcycle parked in the darkest corner of the yard, beyond the huge oak tree whose empty fingers candled the pale moon.

She was so stupid. And Gorgon was smart. No cop would look for him to ride a motorcycle.

A shiver ran through her. The bike was no big hog. How could all three of them ride on it? The cool night air assaulted her lungs. Had Gorgon planned to leave her behind and take Luka?

Behind her, the kitchen lights went out. Dipping her head, she listened. A soft, long scrape like a blade raking across a sharpening stone filled the silence. Her heartbeat drummed in her ears. She could try to make a run for her life, but she wasn't going anywhere without Luka.

Her mind tumbled over itself as she recalled every possible weapon her kitchen housed. None within easy reach.

With fists clenched, she turned, ready to face whatever the monster had planned for her. In the dim shadows, Gorgon stood next to the stove. The butcher knife in his hand glistened red with the stove top's red digital time.

She let the screen door close softly behind her, thinking, the clock ticked away. Her time here was short.

"Who is Will?" Gorgon's tone sent a shot of fear rushing through her veins with every rapid beat of her heart.

The man I love. She swallowed. "Just a guy who has been very nice to Luka and I."

As long as Gorgon thought she fled and had made a life for them all on her own, without the aid of federal agents, he might relax his guard and give her a chance to finish him off herself. Was she strong enough? She set her shoulders. Yes. Damn it. She'd done taken him out before. With her hands behind her back, she inched along the counter. "He's sort of a handyman."

"Is that so? Just a handyman." Gorgon shook his

head. "You're a beautiful woman, Katrina. No man could look at you and not want you for his own."

"Not every man is like you."

"True." His chuckle sent a chill shimmering down her spine. "Did you make this for him?"

He sliced the pie she'd baked for the man she loved. She wanted to take that knife and drive it through the Russian bastard, but she had to be smart. By her time for the right moment. "No. For Luka and I. For Thanksgiving."

"Ah, yes Thanksgiving. The day Americans give thanks for their blessings. We should count our blessings each and every day, for we know not what tomorrow holds. Don't you agree?" His gaze locked onto hers as he brought the slice to his lips. He didn't trust her.

"Yes. Yes, I do." She relaxed against the counter and out of the corner of her eye scanned the items for anything she could use as a weapon.

The sight and sound of Gorgon lapping and licking his lips and fingers slammed her with memories of him eating away at a part of her soul. She wasn't going to let him steal away another moment of her life. "What do you want, Gorgon?"

With the knife still in hand, he crossed the distance between them before she'd had time to blink and trapped her against the counter. He pressed his weight against her. His breath was laced with the remnants of her pie. "I think that is obvious. I want my family back."

He dipped his head and nuzzled her neck, causing her skin to crawl.

"We are not a family," she spat into his ear, pushing against his chest, fully aware that fighting him was not the smartest move. She'd seen the results of Gorgon's anger when he lashed out. He still held the knife, but her hatred for him was too hard to subdue. "Luka is your son, but I'm just the woman who you raped."

Gorgon pulled back. Instability flashed in his raven eyes. "Rape?" He shook his head. "No. I loved you. I loved you from the moment you were first shown to me."

"You know nothing about love."

He tilted his head and looked at her mockingly. "And you do? Perhaps this Will, who you told your friend was coming to Thanksgiving dinner, has taught you about love."

Gorgon grabbed her face, pinching her skin together with vice grip pressure and forced her to look at him. His pupils widened as his face darkened. He had seen her love for Will.

Nicole thrashed to the right and shoved him with all her might, throwing him off balance. Gorgon stumbled back a step and she searched for anything within her reach to use against him.

The knife's blade skimmed across her forearm. "Owww." Immediately, warmth streamed down her arm.

Gorgon grabbed her by the hair and slammed her against the counter face first. Stars splintered her vision while pain ripped the breath from her lungs.

A second later, his arousal pushed into her backside. Her lungs said breathe, but the tip of the blade poked at her jugular. If she moved just a fraction of an inch, she'd be dead.

"Let me assure you, the cut of a knife doesn't hurt as much as the breaking of one's heart," he snarled and snatched the tea-towel from her grip and forced the terrycloth into her mouth.

Nicole's eyes widened. He was going to kill her.

Well, she wasn't going to make it easy. The second he moved the blade away she grabbed the counter with both hands and pushed against him.

Her arm wrenched with pain as he swung her around

to face him. Gorgon's evil laugh echoed in the small kitchen. He slapped her across the face, causing her to go dizzy and then threw her to the floor.

She squirmed away on her hands and knees, then rolled over and kicked out, intending to ring his tonsils with his balls, but Gorgon jumped away from her strike, grabbed and twisted her foot. She didn't know whether she'd heard the crack of her bones first or felt the horrific pain shooting up her leg. Stars popped in front of her closed eyelids as her limped foot hit the floor with a bang.

"Daddy, stop!" Luka stood next to the counter. His eyes reflected her pain and fear.

All those years she protected Luka from the knowledge of what a monster his father was, only to fail. When Gorgon was done with her, would Luka have to bear his wrath? She couldn't let that happen.

Nicole trembled as she struggled up on her elbows.

"Go back to your room," Gorgon snapped. "Now." His wild glare sent Luka bolting.

A tear trailed down Nicole's cheek. How was she going to protect Luka if she couldn't lift herself off the floor?

The air swooshed from her lungs when Gorgon settled onto her chest. One at a time, he trapped her arms at her sides. While he fumbled inside his coat pocket for something, she buckled under him.

She thrashed her head from side to side, trying to get the cloth free so that she could cry for help. She knew Luka would be the only one to hear her.

Max slinked into the kitchen and growled.

"Quiet," Gorgon snarled at the dog.

Nicole's heart sunk to her spine when Max also did as he was ordered and scampered out of the room with his tail between his legs.

Above her, Gorgon produced a length of rope and one at a time, grabbed her hands and secured them together. Then he rose and using her bound arms, drug her into the laundry room.

Nicole's nostrils rose and fell rapidly as she struggled to breathe hard through her nose. The side of her face felt like a balloon where his fist had met her face and her foot throbbed like a son-of-a-bitch. The chill from the floor seeped into her bones along with the realization she might've seen Luka for the last time.

Wearing a smirk, Gorgon stood and removed his belt. Was he going to rape her?

A tear leaked from her eye and trickled down the side of her cheek toward her ear. No. She wasn't going to let him take her. Nicole bit down on the towel threatening to clog her windpipe, arched her back, and kicked up and out with her good foot.

Gorgon bellowed and dropped to his knees like the sac of shit he was.

"You bitch," he snarled between ragged gulps of air. "I was going to play nice and kill you swiftly, but now…"

His cold glare sent a shiver down Nicole's spine.

He reached behind her and she heard the latch of the dog cage. Gorgon whistled and a few seconds later Max appeared at the door. "In." Gorgon pointed to the cage.

Max's muzzle hugged the floor. Beside her, he hesitated in his path, sniffing the pool of blood next to her arm. His forlorn eyes swept up to meet hers. She knew how the animal felt.

Once the dog was settled in his cage, Gorgon's attention returned to her. He flipped her over with surprising ease and using his belt secured the towel in her mouth so tight the edges of his belt cut into her lips. Any moisture she'd had in her mouth was absorbed by the terry cloth. Breathing instantly turned into an art form. Inhaling deeply made the cotton fibers tickle her throat, choking her. Too little and…

Gorgon grabbed her jean's waistband. His fingernails dug into her back and she winced. He yanked her up onto her knees and shoved her toward Max's cage. "Get in."

He wasn't going to kill her? Her pulse raced. Maybe she'd still have a chance to escape and save Luka.

Inside, Nicole huddled, her knees close, not to disturb Max and turned in the cramped space, flinching while bumping her foot. Gorgon reached in, grabbed her hands and in one swift motion slashed the blade across her wrist.

Her scream locked in her throat. Her wrist pulsed with searing pain while her stomach rolled with hot acid. She leaned against the cage. "Why?" she mumbled, trying to position her arms so she could press the gaping wound against her jeans, but doing so wasn't possible with her hands tied.

"All I wanted was my family back." Gorgon's expression softened as he smoothed her hair back from her face and traced a finger along her ear. "I loved you." He dropped his hand from her. "But you betrayed me. You whored yourself out to another man. No one betrays me. You know that, kitten. Now you'll die with the dog. If Max is lucky, someone will find him before he runs out of food."

Nicole shot a glance at the dog. She'd seen him lick his paws before. The action had a whole new meaning now. She scrambled for the door but Gorgon slammed the gate shut against her nose and slid the lock in place. And then he reached in his pocket and pulled out a plastic tie and secured it around the latch. Even if she did get her hands free, she wouldn't be able to get out of the cage without cutting the tie.

Gorgon peered at her through the bars. "Goodbye, my kitten."

In disbelief, she watched Gorgon as he rose to his feet, adjusted his pants and exited the washroom. The door closing behind him sounded like a death cell door slamming shut.

Nicole met Max's soulful stare again. She was his master only as long as she had control. She pressed her wrists together as hard as she could, but the flow of blood continued. Soon she'd slip into unconsciousness from blood loss and then how long would it be before he started to munch. Tomorrow?

Using her arms, she tried to slide Gorgon's belt off her head, so that she could spit out the cloth and cry for help. She doubted anyone would hear her—there were no windows in the laundry room and citizens of this small town rolled up the sidewalks at ten, but maybe...

She couldn't give up hope. Warm blood smeared along her face and into her hair. She wouldn't.

Max jumped up. She knew his wild eyes matched her own. He sensed her desperation.

She began to cough and fought to keep from choking. Tears blurred her vision. What would become of Luka?

She slammed against the door again and again, rattling the cage. The dog scurried from side to side, brushing against her back. She was not going to give up until she drew her last breath.

Chapter Thirty-eight

An uneasy feeling poked at Sharon while she backed her SUV out of Nicole's driveway. Was someone watching her from the front of the house? Maybe Luka, but her prickling hair at the nape of her neck told her peered outside was definitely someone else.

If she had to bet, and she wasn't a betting woman, she'd wager her entire Christmas club fund that Nicole and Luka were in trouble. That is why Nicole had said what sounded like her final farewells at the door.

Sharon slumped down in her bucket seat while keeping an eye on the house from a distance and punched Will's number into her cell. If Gorgon or his men were in the house, she was going to need a hell of a lot more help than the local cops.

Damn. The call went to voice mail. She redialed and again, voice mail.

She didn't want to upset her husband but she had no choice. Thankfully Gary picked up on the second ring. "Gary, have you heard from Will tonight?"

"No why?"

Fearing her husband's reaction and the strain on his well-being, Sharon wet her dry lips. "You know how you always say I have a sixth sense about things."

"What's going on?"

She heard the leeriness in Gary's voice. She hated to make Gary worry. He still needed help getting out of bed, so coming to her rescue was something out of his capabilities right now. She was a smart girl and knew what and who she could handle. Right now, she didn't know what was up. "I think we might have a problem."

"You're not leaving me for Will, are you?"

"What the hell. No." A smile bloomed on her face. Man, she loved the big dope. She shook her head and refocused on the trouble she felt brewing. "I just left Nicole and she was acting kind of funny."

"Funny how?"

"Funny like she's in serious deep shit trouble."

Gary's grunt filled her ear.

"Hon, don't you try to get off that bed without help. You promised me you wouldn't."

"That was before you called and told me this. Damn."

Sharon heard dishes crash and saw in her mind the mess she'd have to clean up when she arrived home. That was the least of her problems right now. "Damn, yourself. You stay put," she ordered, reaching to unlock the glove-compartment where she had a pistol stored. "Do you hear me? If you try to stand, your ass will be mine. I need you to use your head and not go off half-cocked. Now send me Chase and Aden's cell phone numbers. I'll contact them. Oh, wait." Her eyes widened at the sight of Nicole's sedan backing out of the driveway. Sharon slid down in her seat and peered through the space between her steering wheel and dash. "We have movement."

"What do you see?"

"Hard to tell, but…" The car's brake lights dimmed as the vehicle moved away from her. As the car rounded the corner, under the street light, Sharon saw no one sitting in the passenger seat. "Someone just left the house in Nicole's car."

"Was it Nicole?"

"I don't think so. Whoever was driving was much bigger."

"How about Luka?"

"He could be in the back seat. I don't know."

The second the sedan disappeared from her view, Sharon started her car, jammed it into gear and pulled away from the curb. She kept her lights off until she reached the corner and made sure she wasn't being baited. "I'm going to follow them. Get a hold of Chase or Aden and have them call me. And keep trying to get ahold of Will."

"Wait. Will had a tracking device installed on the car, just in case Nicole got cold feet and took off on her own again. I'll call the team and have them coordinate an interception. I want you to check the house. Make sure she and Luka are not there. That way we'll know who or what we're dealing with."

She rounded the block and pulled over. "I can do that."

"Do you have your gun?"

"I'm loading now," she said, reaching under her seat where Velcro held a loaded clip in place.

"Don't do anything stupid, sweetheart."

Suddenly the quiet streets took on a leery feel. The family portrait she and Gary and the boys had recently had taken for their holiday cards popped to the forefront of her mind. What the hell was she doing? She was as rusty as hell. Sharon stretched her neck. But she wasn't an idiot. "Don't worry. You're not going to ever get rid of me that easy," she said, keeping her tone light. She jumped from the car. "Now get a hold of your team. I'm going in. And Gary, I love you."

"Back at ya, babe."

Chapter Thirty-Nine

While strolling across the parking lot with his hands deep in his jean pockets, an exceptionally brilliant diamond in the black sky caught Will's attention, causing his groin to tighten. A rush of memories from a few weeks ago, featuring Nicole cradled in his arms under a similar sky, dimmed his view of the radiantly lit grocery store in front of him and made walking uncomfortable.

Will adjusted his stride, tugged his ski-jacket down over his hips and concentrated on the increased grumbling in his stomach and what he'd buy to satisfy his hunger and not the need of his balls. How his cock had energy was beyond him. Since the attempt on his and Gary's life, he and his team had worked overtime following up on tips, hoping to nail the Novokoffs, but the sons-of-bitches had disappeared without a trace.

The entrance doors slid open and the Christmas song, 'I'll Be Home For Christmas' surrounded Will, dampening his mood even more. If only Jolene had been able to stay undercover within the Novokoffs' folds. But, the situation just got too dicey. Especially, after the deaths of Kyle and the mafia gangster who had protected Jolene like she was his sister.

He'd hoped to make Nicole's holidays special by first handing her Gorgon's head and then reuniting her with her family, but it didn't look like that was going to happen.

If he wasn't so damn tired, he'd stop by her place, but there was no doubt in his mind if he did, they'd fall into bed together and he would get absolutely no sleep.

No, it was better if he just grabbed something to eat from the grocery's deli and go home. Maybe tomorrow they'd catch a break.

Will nodded to a few locals also doing a late night munchie run as he made his way to the back of the store where he grabbed a pre-made sub and a small container of potato salad. Remembering he hadn't bought milk in more than three weeks, he snatched a fresh carton of milk off the shelf and headed to check-out. He hated lumpy milk.

"Hi, Mr. Haus," both Jill, the checkout girl, and Tory, the bagboy, said in unison.

"Hey. You two look happy. Shift almost over, huh?" Will placed his items on the belt and fished in his back pocket for his wallet.

"Soon. Paper right?" Tory, the bag boy, flipped a paper bag open. "How are you doing tonight?"

"Doing okay. How about you?"

"He's doing great." The scanner beeped as Jill ran his potato salad over the glass. She flashed a huge grin between him and Tory.

Will knew from an earlier conversation with Tory that his family had a tough year. He pulled a twenty from his wallet. "Oh, yeah? What's the good news?"

"Looks like I'm going to get to go college next year." The kid was nearly jumping with excitement.

"That's great, man. Did you land a scholarship?"

"No. He found this woman, a run-away, right here in town and is going to collect the huge reward."

Jill held the milk carton up and Will's heart hit the brick wall of muscles in his chest. His snatched the carton from her. Staring down at a younger Nicole, his hands trembled.

"I was the first one to report her, so I get the reward," Tory said. "I haven't told anyone yet, just Jill here and my parents. The guy said I should keep quiet until she's checked out."

"What guy?"

"The federal agent. I called that number right there." Tory pointed to the carton. "Ms. Smith seems like such a nice lady. Who'd thought she—"

"When?" Will snapped.

"What?" Tory blinked.

"When did you call him?" Will opened his wallet and flashed his badge. Keeping his identity a secret from the town's people was no longer important. Nicole and Luka were his priority now. He pushed the urgency from his voice, held Tory's frightened stare and asked again, "It's very important you tell me when you called this guy?"

"Is Ms. Smith in trouble?" Jill interrupted. "I can have the manager call 911."

Will held up his hand, stopping her from reaching for the phone alongside her register.

The paper bag in Tory's grasp crumbled. "He's not a federal agent, is he?"

"No."

The blood drained from the kid's cheeks, leaving him as white as cream under the florescent lights. "I'm sorry. I didn't know. I was just trying—"

"I understand, Tory. Just tell me when."

"Around seven or seven-thirty. I was on my break."

Fuck. Going on three hours. If Gorgon was still hiding in New York or New Jersey, he could in the area an hour ago. Will reached for his cell. Fuck. He forgot he'd shut the phone down while trying to catch ten minutes of shut eye before Chase walked into his office and convinced him to go home. "Okay. You didn't give him your address did you?"

"Yes. He said he needed it in order to send me my

money."

Will's mind whirled with scenarios while his stomach wound into a fuckin' boulder. If Gorgon hadn't already gotten to Nicole, he might come looking for Tory. "Does he know where you work?"

"No."

It didn't matter. If Gorgon needed the information, he'd kill to get it. "You stay here. Don't go home."

Will headed toward the door, while dialing the local authorities. They had to watch over Tory's family while he got to Nicole and Luka. He prayed he wasn't too late.

***

Gorgon checked the rearview mirror. The road behind them disappeared into a black void. There hadn't been a street light or house for miles, just trees. His son, his heir, was strapped into his car seat. In a few hours, they would be in upstate New York. From there they would board a twin engine plane his family kept at a tiny airport and, in a hop, they'd land in Canada. Leaving Canada wouldn't present a problem. He had the proper documents waiting for them.

He sighed. Documents for three.

He shrugged and relaxed against the seat. Katrina had made her choice.

A smile played on his lips. He might have fun looking for a new mother for Luka.

***

Sharon peered through the pane on the kitchen door. Except for the light above the stove, the house was dark.

With her pistol ready and her heart nearing her throat, she eased back the screen door and twisted the inside door's handle. Damn. Locked.

Quietly, she closed the screen door and stepped back off the porch. Nicole had shown her where an extra key was kept. Using the pen light on her own key ring, she found the extra the rock in the flower bed and the key under it. She tiptoed up the steps again and this time unlocked the door and stole inside. Immediately, Max barked.

She refused to think of her family as she swept the dining and living room, listening for any movement upstairs. Hearing nothing, she headed toward the laundry room to where apparently Max was locked up. Hugging the door's frame, she swung the door wide, ready for an attack by the dog, but none came. Max's barking pitched. She heard his cage rattle and flashed her light in his direction and gasped at the sight of blood seeping across the floor. "Nicole."

A moan.

Sharon hit the lights.

"Oh my, God." She raced to the cage, slipping on the blood and grabbed the wire top and steadied herself. Nicole had already lost a lot of blood and was barely conscious. She had to get the woman out and stop the flood of blood before it was too late, but the son-of bitch had locked the cage with an industrial strength plastic tie. She dropped to her knee and spoke through the rods, "Don't worry, Nicole. I'm here. I'm going to get you out and call for help."

She punched 911 into her cell and raced to the kitchen to find a knife to cut the tie.

***

The moment Will's cell had latched onto a tower signal, his phone blared. While maneuvering the town's sleepy streets, Gary filled him in on Sharon's suspicions and that she was checking out the safe house. His CUFF team had also been alerted and were already on the move to the area where the GPS showed Nicole's Junker headed north toward the New York border.

Will's gut rolled. There was no doubt in his mind this case was going to end tonight. He just hoped it didn't end badly for anyone other than Gorgon.

He turned off his car's lights, rounded the corner and rolled to a stop behind Sharon's empty SUV. With his gun drawn, Will hopped from the car before the engine did its whine down. Most of the houses on the block still showed signs of activity within them, but not Nicole's. The bungalow was dark.

He raced through the shadows toward the front door, watching for any sign of his best friend's wife. As he crept along the house to the back, Max barked like a mad dog. The lights inside came on. A shadow crossed over the pulled kitchen drape and he froze. He heard kitchen drawers being yanked opened.

Adrenalin overload had his heart pumping faster than his veins could handle. Keeping low under the porch's rail, he rushed to the back steps. With his Glock trained on the doorway, he climbed a step at a time.

The dog's insane bark and deep throated growl scared the shit out of him as he reached for the door handle. Knowing whoever was inside, now knew he was there, he flung the door open and jumped inside along Max, ready to fire.

Empty.

The laundry room door stood open. Max loped

around his legs and dashed off into the washroom. A bloody trail of footprints leading into the room caused Will's stomach to roll.

"Get out," Sharon yelled. "Hang on, hon. I've called for an ambulance."

"Sharon." Will skidded to a stop as his heart dropped to the floor. Nicole lay half inside Max's cage. "Is she..." He couldn't say the words.

Sharon looked up over her shoulder. "Will, thank God you're here." She sliced the rope holding Nicole's hands together. Free, she wrapped a cloth around Nicole's wrist and held her arm up in the air. "No, but..."

Blood marked Nicole's face and arms, her shirt, and her jeans. Sharon knelt in a puddle. Her hands now coated red.

Nicole's blue lips called to him.

"I called 911. They should be here any second. She's in shock. Get a blanket. Over there." Sharon nodded toward the shelf above the washer and dryer.

Will's heart broke as he grabbed the blanket he and Nicole had lay upon that starry night in the back yard. She needed him to be strong. He pushed his horror away and dropped to his knees beside Sharon. Quickly, he covered the woman who had stolen his heart, tucking the blanket under her chin.

"Here hold her arm up." Sharon instructed. "I'll open the front door and put Max in the bedroom upstairs so he's out of the way."

Will changed places with Sharon and gingerly laced his fingers around the blood soaked cloth. "Luka? Is he here?"

Sharon shook her head while wiping her hands on another towel she grabbed from stack atop the washer. "Unless he's hiding. Stay here. I'll double check every nook."

Will swallowed, staring at Nicole's ashen face. Luka was only a child. Had he witnessed his mother's attack?

He brushed his fingers across her cheek. Her skin was cold as the floor. Damn. He was supposed to protect her and he'd failed.

He leaned over and placed his forehead against hers. His tears marked the blood smearing her beautiful face. "I'm so sorry. I should've--" the words failed to pass by the emotions clogging his throat. "Please don't leave me. There is so much I need to tell you."

Eyelashes brushed against his cheek and he pulled back.

Nicole struggled to open her eyes. Her tongue peeked out between her thin lips. "Will."

He couldn't stop the burst of relief that escaped him. "I'm here. Did Gorgon do this?"

"Yes," she spoke so soft he'd barely heard her. "Luka. He has Luka. Stop him. Promise me." Her eyes drifted closed.

Will felt her pulse weaken.

Chapter Forty

Will had pushed his car's speed to the limit navigating the dark, winding, rolling Appalachian Mountains. He'd almost lost traction and careened off the side twice because the road was slick with wet leaves. He checked the digital clock as he rolled to a stop and jammed the car into park. It had taken him a little over thirty minutes to catch up with his men, and Gorgon.

Nicole's blood stained his jeans. He checked his cell which hung silent on his hip. He had signal. Sharon said she'd text him the moment she had any news. Nicole had to be okay. He couldn't imagine his life without her and Luka.

Will sprinted toward the gas station. A quick scan told him at least a dozen state police officers crouched in the shadows beyond the luminous circle lighting up the building located a half-mile south of the interstate. Beyond them, a deep forest with dangerous terrain filled with sink holes, sharp shale pits and murky quarries stretched for miles. The Pennsylvania State Troopers had barricades up, stopping traffic from both directions from coming into the area. Everything was quiet except for the occasional slap of a moth against the gas station's overhead lights. There was nowhere for Gorgon to escape, except hell.

"Does everyone have their headsets on?" Will whispered into his mic.

"Roger that," Chase's voice crackled into his ear piece. "Including the state police."

"Good."

"Where are you?"

He could see Chase and Aden hunched behind the agency's unmarked van parked next to the air pump station. Aden stared through a set of field glasses, peeking through the windows of the van. Chase had his weapon drawn and was also keeping guard on the building. "Coming up behind you now."

Chase glanced over his shoulder and signaled for him to stay low as he approached.

"What's the status?" Will cut the corner and rushed through the dry reeds to approach the van at a protected angle and took the position on Chase's right, between him and Aden. He pulled his Glock and checked the clip.

Chase twisted his wrist and glanced at his watch. "Gorgon took the kid inside going on five minutes ago."

Damn. Five minutes was too long. "He's not going to stay in there forever. Once he's out, we're not going to stop him from getting in that car and driving off without blowing this place to hell."

"According to the station's diagrams, we've got two twenty-thousand gasoline tanks in ground," Aden added, dropping his field glasses and locking onto his gaze. "One stray bullet and poof. We'll have one big ass hole."

"Fuck." Will swallowed. They had their work cut out for them if everyone was going to go home in one piece. "How many civilians inside?"

"I spied seven. Cashier, a donut shop worker, a cleaning person and four customers."

"With Luka that's eight." Will drew in a calming breath and stared toward the building, hoping to get a glimpse of the boy who had stolen part of his heart over the past four months. He had to keep a level head, if everyone was going to live.

"If we let him leave, we take the civilians out of the equation," Aden whispered.

Will shook his head. "Everyone except Luka. Gorgon gets Luka in that car and my gut tells me he wouldn't get out. No. We need to take him out here. Before he exits the building."

"How?" Chase shifted in place. The kid's adrenalin already cascaded through his veins.

"We're going in." Will started to step around his man, only to be stopped.

"Not without a vest. Here." Chase reached under the van and grabbed a protective vest marked with the U.S. Marshal logo.

"I taught you well."

"Yes, sir." Chase winked.

Will donned and secured the vest in record time. "Can you see Luka anywhere, Aden?"

"Negative. They might be in the john."

"Good. Gorgon isn't suspecting anything. We're going to walk in the front door, rush the civilians out and when he and Luka come out of the bathroom, we'll take him out. Sound like a plan."

"As good as any. Copy that, SP1. Hold fire." Aden pressed his mike to this throat. "Safety net the civilians."

"Roger that, CUFF."

Will held Aden and Chase's stares and nodded. "On three. One. Two. Three." With weapons aimed, they moved out, rounding the van and heading toward the store's entrance at different angles. There was no reason to lay out the game plan once they were inside. They'd worked as a team long enough to know exactly where each would take up position.

Will entered first, swinging the door wide and immediately put his finger to his mouth, quieting the cashier whose eyes rounded in surprise. "U.S. Marshals," he said softly, signaling for the woman to move out from behind the counter while his men entered behind him and swung to the right and left and disappeared down the aisles.

"What's going on?" The cashier asked in a hushed tone.

"A man with a young boy came in here. Where are they?"

"He asked to use the bathroom." The woman's hand trembled as she pointed to the rear of the store.

"Is there another way out of here?"

Gasps of surprise rose above the radio music floating from the ceiling speakers. His men were encountering civilians. In a few seconds, they'd rush toward the exit, hopefully quiet as not to alarm Gorgon of their presence.

"The back door," the cashier's wide eyes darted anxiously toward the back of the building. "It's off the office. But it's locked."

The direction of the office was opposite the bathrooms. Gorgon was trapped. Will squeezed her hand firmly. "Good job. Now, I need you to lead these people off to that side of the building." He pointed away from the bathroom side of the building in case Gorgon came out. He didn't want to tip him off that something was amiss seeing people race away. Everything had to appear normal. "The state police are waiting to take to you to safety. Go."

The woman nodded. She signaled for the customers to follow her and with a minimal amount of noise they cleared the building.

Biting down on the worry still bubbling up in him, Will swung around and noted that his men had turned the rounded mirrors reflecting the back aisles to the sides. Gorgon didn't need any help locating them in such a small area.

"Let's give him room to hang himself," Will said into his mic as he made his way to the center of the store.

"I don't want him backing into the corner with the kid. Chase, you've got the back corner. Aden, cover the front. If the kid sees me, he might move away from Gorgon enough that we can take him out."

"Roger that," both men responded.

Before Will could blink again, he heard Luka's voice.

"I want my mom."

"Forget her," Gorgon growled. "She doesn't want to be with us."

They were right on the other side of the aisle moving toward the break in the shelving. Hunched down, Will could only see the top of Gorgon's head. His fingers tightened around his gun's stock. After what Gorgon did to Nicole, he would love to stand up and put a cold bullet through the man's temple, but he couldn't with Luka right there. He'd take this piece of filth out legally.

"That's not true," Luka cried. "She doesn't want to be with you. You hurt her. I saw her. You're mean. I want my mom. I want to go home."

"You're going to live with me. Now, stop whining before—"

"No. I hate you."

"Owww. Son of a bitch. I'll teach you to bite me. Come back here."

Will heard Luka's scurry and rushed forward and came face to face with the boy as he rounded the aisle's corner.

"Uncle Will." Luka's expression brightened.

Warmth encased Will's heart. He grabbed Luka and pulled the boy behind him just as Gorgon rushed around the corner. Will leveled his gun at the Russian's chest. "Don't move, Gorgon. U.S. Marshals."

Gorgon's gaze bounced from him to Luka who clung to Will's leg. The Russian's black brows pulled together.

"Uncle? Who are you?" His fingers inched up toward his belt buckle.

"Don't do it, Gorgon." Will's finger tightened on the trigger. "It's over. You're surrounded."

Gorgon's dark glare flickered past him and Will knew Chase had his back.

"Get the kid out of here, Will," Aden said, standing with a gun aimed at the man's back a good fifteen feet behind Gorgon.

Gorgon smiled, bearing his teeth. His hand stayed in place. "So you're the man who Katrina whored herself to."

"He hurt mom, Uncle Will." Luka clutched his leg. "She was crying and bleeding."

He patted Luka's back. "I know, kid. She's okay. She's waiting to see you."

Hearing his words, Gorgon's smile faded and between gritted teeth, he asked, "She lives?"

A smile threatened to lift the corners of Will's mouth. He pressed his hand against Luka's ear. "Yes. She lives, you bastard. She plans to put your ass in a dark cell for life."

Watching Gorgon's jaw clenched and his face turned a fire red, Will knew he had poked the guy's ego too hard. His muscles tensed and he pushed Luka back.

"You will not have my family." Gorgon's hand darted inside his coat.

Will fired off a few quick rounds before turning and shoving Luka to the floor, landing on top of him.

Above, ammo whizzed through the air. Through a slit of eye he saw his men's assault slamming into the son of a bitch, rocking him forward and backward. Blood pelted the goods on the shelves and splattered against the tan vinyl flooring.

Chase howled, "Mother Fucker."

Then silence.

The glassy eyed Russian with his curses still lingering on his open lips crashed against the shelf, knocking can goods on top of Will's legs. Then Gorgon face-panned the concrete floor with a thud.

The refrigeration unit's whirl overtook the silence.

Sulfur filled the air and their lungs.

Aden kicked Gorgon's gun aside and checked for life. He gave Will a thumbs up before heading to Chase, who held his chest.

"The fucker knocked the wind out of me."

"He did more than that. Your arm is bleeding," Aden said, kneeing next to his friend. "Lie still. Let me get a something to stop the blood flow." Aden looked around, spied bandages and gauze, grabbed a box, tore one open and treated Chase's wound.

Luka coughed and squirmed under Will. He pushed up on his elbows and met the boy's wide eyes. "Are you okay?"

The kid swallowed. His dark eyes glistened with fright and remained latched onto his. Luka knew what had just happened.

Not wanting the boy in therapy for the rest of his life, Will said in a calm tone, "Okay. I want you to close your eyes and keep them closed. Promise me."

Luka did as he was told while Will stood and scooped him off the floor.

"You two okay?"

"Yeah," Chase said, presenting a thumb. "Get the boy out of here.

Will nodded, feeling gratitude for the men who had his back. Quickly, he carried the boy away from the sight of his father dead and left his team to clean up the scene.

What both he and Luka needed now was to see Nicole.

But damn, he hadn't heard from Sharon.

***

There was a strong presence guarding her. Nicole's eyelashes brushed against her cheeks as she fought to open her eyes.

"Nicole." She heard the gentle voice calling to her.

"Will." His face was the most beautiful sight she'd ever witnessed. She reached up and ran her fingers across the rough stubs covering his chin. "You look like hell."

A throaty chuckle escaped him. His blue eyes twinkled as they traced her face, caressing her with warmth. "Well, you look beautiful."

"I feel like shit. Where am I?"

"In the hospital?"

The memory of Gorgon's hand on her and the fear in Luka's eyes as Gorgon carried him away rushed back at her. Her wrist and her arm were bandaged with thick padding. An IV drip hung from the side of the bed and clear liquid ran through the tubing and into her left hand through a needle that pinched like hell. Using her elbows, she shifted up on the mattress. "Luka. Where's Luka? Gorgon took him."

Will eased her back onto the bed. "He's okay. He's waiting outside."

She looked at the closed door and then back to him. "I want to see him."

He smiled. "Don't you trust me?"

"Of course I do. I just need to see him for myself." She kicked her foot out from under the sheet intending to get out of bed, put Will stopped her and covered her again.

"Oh, no. You stay put. I'll bring Luka in in a minute, sweetheart, but first I need to talk to you."

Will's gaze fell to the bed between them.

"What's wrong?" She stroked the back of his hand.

"Nothing is wrong." He shook his head. "Gorgon is dead."

He stared at her. She knew he was searching for any sorrow on her part. After all, she had been Gorgon's woman for seven years. But she only felt hatred for the man, nothing more, and she showed her relief. She relaxed against the mattress. "Are you sure?"

"I was there."

"Luka. Did he..." She couldn't imagine the sense of loss her little boy must feel.

"He was there, but he's okay. He was trying to get away from Gorgon. He saw what Gorgon did to you and he didn't want to go with him. He wanted you. He fought to get away and when he did, I was there." He took her hand between his warm ones. "Gorgon knew about us."

She nodded. "He overheard me talking to Sharon earlier."

"Seeing me and having Luka choosing me over him, put Gorgon over the edge. He pulled a gun, but before he got off a shot, my team took him out."

Her nightmare was over. A tear of joy escaped out of the corner of Nicole's eye. Her thoughts turned to her son. "Did Luka see what happened?"

"No. I wouldn't let him see his father afterwards. He didn't ask to either. Luka knows what happened and he knows his father was a bad man. I'm sure it's going to take time and counseling, but I think the kid is going to be all right. He's got a strong mom who loves him, and me to help him--if you let me. I love you Nicole and if you'll have me, I'd like to be part your lives."

Tears blurred her vision. A few short hours ago she thought she was going to die and that she'd never see Luka or Will again. Now, she had a life filled with love to look forward to. "I love you too."

Will rose from the chair. His bright eyes stared into hers, promising decades of happiness.

She pulled Will to her and lost herself in his warm kiss.

The door creaked open. Sharon coughed. "Will, I can't hold them off much longer."

Breathless, Will pulled back from her embrace.

"Them?" She searched his face. "What is she talking about?"

"I have a surprise for you. Let them in, Sharon."

"What? Who?"

Grinning, Will stood and took her hand, giving it a gentle squeeze.

The hospital door swung open and in the threshold stood her parents. Tears of happiness flooded down her cheeks. Luka was cradled on her father's hip and clinging to his neck, just as she had done.

About The Author

Autumn Jordon is a quiet nut with a reputation for finding trouble. She is a Romance Writer's of America National Golden Heart finalist and a Golden Leaf Winner. She lives along the Appalachian Trail in northeast Pennsylvania with her husband and Irish Setter, Mac. Gardening, horseback riding, hiking the trails of the Pocono Mountains and golfing with her husband are just a few of her interests.

No matter what Autumn is doing, she's busy dreaming up ideas to put the characters of her romantic suspense novels in grave danger. For more info on AJ, please visit www.autumnjordon.com.

13793648R00196

Made in the USA
Charleston, SC
01 August 2012